Books by Jules Barnard

The Blue Series
DEEP BLUE (BOOK 1)

BLUE CRUSH (BOOK 2)

TRUE BLUE (BOOK 3)

BLUE STREAK: A BLUE SERIES NOVELLA (BOOK 4)

NEW BLUE (BOOK 5)

The Halven Rising Series
FATES ALTERED: A HALVEN RISING PREQUEL (BOOK 0.5)

FATES DIVIDED (BOOK 1)

FATES ENTWINED (BOOK 2)

FATES FULFILLED (BOOK 3)

To receive email alerts when new Jules Barnard books go live, and to gain access to FREE Subscriber Extras, including an extra scene that takes place after *Deep Blue*, sign up here:

www.julesbarnard.com/newsletter

*Email information is kept confidential and never shared.

Deep Blue

JULES BARNARD

For Robin, an amazing sister and human being.

You will be missed.

Chapter One

It is one of the blessings of old friends that you can
afford to be stupid with them.

—Ralph Waldo Emerson

M Y LEGS QUIVER like Jell-O as I clamber over the last
boulder on the east side of Eagle Lake. Eric reaches for
me, his sandy blond hair slicked back at the roots with sweat.
This should gross me out, but for some reason he looks really
hot, all sweaty and disheveled. He's not wearing his shirt, and
the close proximity to his muscled chest and golden skin ignites
dirty thoughts of sneaking off behind a boulder and having my
way with him.

My gaze rakes his ripped abs. Long cargo shorts hang low on
his hips, providing a perfect view of the vee of muscles between
his hipbones.

He squeezes my hand and I glance up. His mouth twists.
"Naughty."

"What?" My expression is all innocence, but he knows me.
Later, I plan to investigate those muscles with my tongue.

Speaking of later, where the heck is Genevieve? We'll be up
here all day if she doesn't hurry it up.

It's our first hike in Lake Tahoe since our arrival a few days
ago, but Gen should be in better shape than this. She's a runner
and athletic, whereas I avoid the gym like I'm allergic to span-

dex. I should probably cut her some slack. The altitude in Lake Tahoe is higher than what she's used to, the air thinner. And she's wearing track shoes, while I have on the requisite sturdy hiking boots owned by every kid who grew up in Lake Tahoe. I won't give her a break, though, because her reactions are too hilarious when I don't.

I peek around the boulder. She's just now cresting the stones before the lake. "Light a fire under it, Gen!"

She glances up and swipes her forehead, her chest rising and falling with each deep gulp of air. Her lips pinch and I think her nostrils flare. She crosses her arms and glares.

I smile back.

Instead of moving toward me, though, Gen drops her arms to her sides and takes an unsteady step in the direction of the water. She crouches among the large rocks and I can't see her anymore. A stone flies from her direction into the lake, sending out tiny waves.

I might razz my best friend, but she can hold her own. Taking a break when she knows I want her to hurry her ass up, a case in point. This could be a while.

I turn and meander toward Eric, who's now several feet ahead, the idyllic, small alpine lake providing a perfect backdrop for his masculine beauty. I stop for a moment, taking in the sexy picture, and consider my plan for the summer.

My goal in returning to my hometown is to immerse Gen in Lake Tahoe and lift her spirits, hopefully in the form of a cute summer fling. Gen just discovered—brutally, embarrassingly— that the guy she dated during our last year of college had a girlfriend back home. The bastard showed up with the other girl at the local bar during our last week of school. Douche bag.

Gen didn't cry or drunk-dial him like any self-respecting

twenty-one-year-old would; she went quiet, which is worse. He totally broke her heart, and I worry he broke her trust in men along with it.

The only positive is that she never has to see the A-hole again. We're done with college, and thanks to my badassery, I've secured us jobs at a casino for the summer before we head to grad school.

Grad school. I squeeze my middle and take a deep breath. For some reason, lately, every time I think about the future, my gut wrenches to the side. Tahoe is the perfect place to get Gen's mind off the A-hole and for us to spend quality time together before we go our separate ways in the fall. And maybe it's the perfect place for me to get my head on straight, because I need to be excited for what's coming up in a few months. Right now, the idea of going to law school makes me itchy. That can't be good.

Eric stops at a swath of gravel ahead and yanks off his backpack. He lays out towels and I make my way over. I sit and pull up my knees below my chin, arms wrapped around my shins. I stare at the lake without seeing it, my mind trapped in the future.

Several minutes pass and there's still no sign of Gen. Is she really that tired from the hike?

I glance over my shoulder. I can't see her, and the water where she crouched is like glass. My pulse flutters. It's been too long.

Rocking forward, I push to my feet. "Gen!"

She stands several yards away and raises her hand, ambling toward me like she's on a Sunday drive.

I slump back to my spot and Eric steps beside me, his tall figure casting a shadow. "Serves you right for teasing her." The sound of crunching comes from above and crumbs rain down into my lap.

I flick off a few with my thumb and forefinger. "Tarzan, you want to take your chow somewhere else?"

"Oh, sorry," he mumbles, granola sticking to his lips.

I shake my head and smile. "So, I forgot to mention, my work schedule at the casino will be Tuesday through Saturday."

We've only been here a few days, but Gen and I start work next week and Eric has driven up for a short visit. I have to say, I'm mildly nervous about the counting element of my job as a dealer, which makes me sound mentally challenged. I'm not—I just seriously suck at math. I can write a ten-page essay on the women's movement post industrialization in under an hour, dissect a frog, or explain Keynesian economics, but ask me to add numbers together and my brain blows a fuse. I tend to overprocess the simple concepts.

The sound of mastication has ceased, the only sign that Eric heard me. He's moved a few feet away, his back to me, staring out at the water. He hasn't said anything.

"Saturdays will be good tip nights," I add, "but it stinks that my schedule will cut into our weekends together." Weekdays were too busy with classes and Eric's fraternity obligations back at school, but we hung out every weekend.

He turns, unloads drinks from his backpack, and takes off his shoes. He stretches his arms above his head with a lazy yawn.

"That won't be a problem, will it?" I persist. "You don't have classes Friday through Monday. You can still visit on the weekends if you want."

Though we're the same age, Eric has been a bit of a slacker. He's taking summer classes so he can officially graduate.

He shrugs, eyeing the small rocks below us. He picks up a

smooth, flat one and flicks it with his wrist out at the water. The stone skips across the surface for several beats before sinking. "Work as much as you like. You want to save money for your fancy grad school. I'll be busy with classes."

Okay-y-y. Kind of a noncommittal response, and a bit snarky. This is the first rancor I've detected from him regarding my post-college plans. Eric's never been enthusiastic about my plan to attend law school, but he's also never put me down for it. We haven't discussed the future, but I figured we'd do the long-distance thing while I'm away.

Suddenly, the rift between us these last couple of weeks—and the sexual dry spell I'd attributed to end-of-school-year stress—takes on new meaning. Was he pushing me away?

I don't do passive, so I ask, "You think you'll be able to make it up next weekend?"

Eric rummages around in his backpack. "Probably not." He raises his head and waves to Gen, who finally nears. He seems relieved to see her. "I've been assigned my first project. I'm meeting with study partners next weekend. Then there's a party with the guys I'm going to."

We've been together for two years and have never been attached at the hip, but the way Eric's avoiding my eyes and the tension I sense from him has me on high alert, like there's something he's not telling me. But he'd say so if something were wrong, wouldn't he?

Gen drops her backpack on my towel with a thud, her face red, her mouth turned down.

I mentally pause from overanalyzing Eric to consider my BF. Why does she look upset? I razzed her earlier, sure, but she's used to that, and she dishes it back in equal doses. Was she thinking about the A-hole? Is that what took her so long and why she looks like someone stole her puppy? I lift my chin, brows drawn together, questioning. She shakes her head, but the troubled look on her face remains.

Eric sits beside me and rubs my shoulders a little too roughly. My muscles tense. "Going for a quick dip—anyone want to join me?" He looks from me to Gen.

"Too cold," I blurt absently.

"Didn't bring my bathing suit," Gen says without looking up. She scoops a handful of gravel and pours it slowly onto the ground.

Eric leans over my shoulder and grins lewdly. "Feel free to go in the buff, Gen. I don't mind."

Gen flinches beside me, and I elbow Eric in the ribs. *Ass.* Can't he see something's bothering her?

He laughs and strides to the water's edge.

His stupid comment has one positive effect. It's wiped the depressed look from Gen's face. She shakes her head at his retreating back, her expression angrier than I think Eric's behavior warrants. "Do your hormones ever cease firing?"

"Never," he shouts over his shoulder. He jogs the last few feet to the water, his form tight and athletic, before he dives in. The water is cold enough to shrivel his balls into tiny grapes, but he seems unfazed, skimming the lake in smooth strokes toward a giant boulder in the center.

Gen and I sit in silence as Eric climbs atop the rock like he's Columbus discovering the new world.

She drops the gravel and brushes off her hand on her shorts. "How are things with him?" Leaning forward, she balances her arms on her knees in a pose similar to mine, and stares at her feet.

First, the thing she's not mentioning that's upsetting her,

and now the random question about Eric?

She fumbles with the edge of my towel. "You ever worry about him? With—I don't know—other girls?" She holds up a hand, her gaze flashing to me. "He was joking earlier—about the naked swimming thing. But…"

Seriously, where is this coming from? I don't like the look on her face. Worried. She must be projecting. She's had a shitty time of it, and now she thinks all guys are like the A-hole.

"We're good, Gen."

She lets out a slow breath. "Cool." She smiles her warm smile and my stomach sinks.

Shit. Are Eric and I fine?

Things didn't feel fine a moment ago. I've never worried about him, but I've been busy. Now that school has ended, have things changed?

No, they're still great. I'm overreacting. Eric and I will spend time together at the lake and get back on track.

I notice a crease between Gen's brows. I can't take that look. "What about you? Ready to start dating again?"

She digs her heels into the gravel. "Sure. If a good guy comes along."

Gen has said this before, but she seems uncertain. It's been a month since she got her heart crushed. Not long enough to heal, but we've talked about this. Sometimes getting back out there is the only way to pull out of a slump.

Eric splashes toward us from the water, droplets running down his toned shoulders and chest. I will never tire of the sight. I smile at him, and he grins back.

Eric and I are good. Of course we're good. Gen will be good too. As soon as I find her a nice guy.

Gen is smart, beautiful, and funny as hell, though she

doesn't try to be, which makes her even more hilarious. I'm lucky to have a solid boyfriend, and I want that for her.

With the extra seasonal help at the casino this summer, there should be at least a few decent prospects. If not, we'll scout the local hotspots and see who's around. Most of my friends from home are either still in college or have found jobs in the city, but the populace of a vacation town is ever-changing. Lots of dating possibilities. I'll find someone for her, or at least distract her from the slump she's in and show her a good time.

Lake Tahoe is all about the high. How can I fail?

Chapter Two

GEN AND I approach the seamstress counter in the Blue Casino basement, the hub of lower employee relations. The managers' offices are located above the casino floor, where bosses peer at everyone through stealthy security cameras. Blue stockpiles its uniforms in the basement and allocates them to the minions at the beginning of every work shift. To remove a uniform from the premises is considered stealing. I don't get management's proprietary clamp on polyester, but I'm happy to let them do my laundry for me.

I hand the attendant my claim check and she passes me a pair of black slacks and a white button-down shirt. Boring, but I'll make it work with a few buttons open at the top. Gen hands in her claim check next, and I step away, searching for our lockers. After a long moment, I glance back. She's still in front of the counter, staring at what I'm guessing is her uniform. Her back's to me, so I walk up and look over her shoulder.

"Don't say anything. *Anything*, Cali!"

Oh, God. This is perfect. I couldn't have set things up better.

Now I remember why I chose the dealer position. I'm an absolute wuss when it comes to the cold—I used to dress like an Eskimo during Tahoe winters. Having grown up around the casinos, I know a thing or two about the air conditioning and the cocktail uniforms. I didn't want to freeze my nipples off every day.

I cover my smile with my hand. "It's pretty," I mumble through my fingers.

The look she gives me… appalled, peeved. She's seriously pissed. I don't know why, but seeing her like this always makes me laugh. Gen's pretty mellow, and it's so out of character for her to get angry—like watching an angry kitten or a furious fluffy bunny.

I squeeze my lips together and bend over, holding in a giggle.

Gen leans down, her mouth to my ear. "You. Suck. You did this on purpose!"

I straighten. "How could I do it on purpose? You picked the position."

Aside from the freeze-your-nipples-off factor, I wouldn't have minded the cocktail uniform. I hadn't warned Gen, because I didn't think it was a big deal. She needs to loosen up, and I couldn't have arranged for a more perfect outfit to attract guys to my reserved best friend.

Gen's hands shake as she crushes the small piece of black, shiny fabric in the shape of hot pants and the blue-and-black-sequined bustier to her chest. She stomps away.

"Good luck tonight," I call out, a smile in my voice.

Without looking back, she holds her hand above her head and flips me off.

WE'VE WORKED ALL week and tonight is my first actual night on the casino floor at one of the blackjack tables. I've been trapped in conference rooms, learning how to deal cards. So far, I haven't botched my addition skills, and my riffle shuffle rocks.

The customer in front of me swigs his diluted complimentary drink. He's in a red floral Hawaiian shirt that stretches over a massive beer belly. I'm ignoring the coarse black hair poking through the gaps between his buttons so I won't be forced to gouge my eyes out later. He picks up all but one chip—my tip, bless him—and walks away, and as he does, Gen signals to me from her elevated perch in the Blue open lounge.

I'm not supposed to chat with anyone but my customers. I glance at the pit boss. He's handing out complimentary drink tokens and what appears to be a coupon for a free night's stay to a woman with a blond bob haircut and a designer bag slung over her shoulder. The pyramid of chips in front of her is worth about twenty grand, and while my pit boss distracts her with a room comp, a new dealer replaces the old.

Pit bosses switch dealers when a customer gets too lucky. I have no idea why, but somehow that can break a winning streak. *Sneaky casino bastards.*

The pit boss is busy orchestrating the woman's downfall, and I have no customers for the moment. I wave Gen over. Her job is more social and fluid. As long as she slings drinks, she can talk to anyone, though she does have to be careful about approaching tables outside of her section, even if it's just to gossip with a friend. Higher-stakes gaming goes to the veteran waitresses who've been around five years or more, and those bitches are territorial as hell. And catty. As far as I can tell, they've hazed Gen for no other reason than that she's young and beautiful.

Gen skips the three steps down from the lounge and crosses the wide lane separating us. Every guy she passes rakes his gaze over her, or does a sly double take. Her nearly black hair, hazel eyes, and pale skin are a striking combination. With my strawberry-blond mop, we're like a giant checkerboard walking down the street.

Poor Gen. The universe put a reserved female in the body of a knockout. Her pretty oval face and slender five-foot-ten figure in the skimpy cocktail uniform make her the focus of attention at the casino and she hates it. Even now, she's avoiding eye contact and speed-walking to my table.

We'll have to work on that. Guys tend to think you're not interested if you don't look at them.

She plops her round serving tray on the armrest of my blackjack table, eyes flittering to the side as if she's nervous.

The casino floor is obnoxiously loud, with whistles chiming and bells blaring. I've gotten used to elevating my voice just enough to hold a conversation without announcing myself to the room. "What's up?"

"Don't look now," she says through stiff lips, "but the bartender at the East Bar invited us to drinks with him and his friends tonight."

I stretch my neck like a flamingo and search him out.

"I said, don't look!"

"Why not?"

"Because he might think I like him."

"Do you?" I glance at the guy again and waggle my brows. Medium brown hair, a dimple that flashes whenever he smiles at his female customers—I couldn't have picked a better prospect. "He's cute, Gen."

She fumbles with her cash caddy. "I don't know Mason that well, but he seems nice." Her mouth twists and then softens. "It'd be good to make new friends."

I nod soberly. "I support this endeavor." Project Gen Hookup moving ahead of schedule!

A few hours later, Gen and I pass through the sliding doors at Harrah's and the air conditioning suctions me inside, my ears popping from the pressure.

"Wow," Gen says, eyeing a nearby cocktail waitress serving a slots customer. "It's a good thing you had a contact at Blue and not one at Harrah's, or my ass cheeks would be on full display beneath Cherokee nylons."

"You're welcome," I say. She's been bitching all week about her uniform.

She responds with a meek smile.

We walk to the center of the casino and Gen points out Bartender Mason in the lounge. He's swapped the white and black casino uniform for a pair of jeans and a dark button-down. Broad shoulders fill out the shirt to hot-guy perfection. I nudge her in the ribs a couple of times, signaling my approval.

She swats my elbow and glares. If we weren't close to her new friend, she'd tell me I'm behaving like a teenager, which is why I do it now, when I can get away with it.

Mason stands, a wide smile spreading across his face as he glances at me and takes a leisurely look at Gen in her short denim skirt, T-shirt, and sandals. Neither of us anticipated going out after work when we dressed this morning, so we're both on the casual side, only I'm in skinny jeans and a tank top. A couple of guys sit at Mason's table, along with a girl.

"This is Adam—" He gestures to a dark-haired pretty boy with pressed dress sleeves evenly rolled to his elbows.

Adam smiles and does a not-so-sly perusal of our bodies, lingering on my chest. I'd like to say it's because I have a large rack, but really, it's because I displayed my boobs nicely.

"—and Jaeger."

Jaeger? Like Mick Jagger, except with a long *a*? That name sounds familiar, but I don't recognize the guy.

Jaeger is a head taller than Adam, wearing a casual T-shirt and worn blue jeans, and his arms are as long as a basketball player's. His light brown hair is cut close to his head, and though there's something familiar about his face, I can't place him. He's cute, though, with a strong jaw line and symmetrical features that are too classically handsome to lump him in with the meatheads; his brows don't protrude enough. He's more genetically big than steroid-inflated.

Jaeger gives Gen a cursory glance, then looks at me. His gaze falters, remains a second too long, eyes gleaming down my body and back to my face. He half nods in acknowledgement and returns his attention to his friends.

He hesitated when he looked at me. A sign I'm right about us knowing each other? I can't tell for sure, nor can I ask him about it, because Adam is talking to him now.

I study Jaeger some more and my gaze catches on full lips, trailing down to a very broad chest, muscled shoulders and arms, and—large hands. The guy has strong, well-formed hands. A shiver racks my body. I have a weakness for men's hands... and I've veered off course. I'm checking out men for *Gen,* not me. But the only thing I'd complain about on Eric's body is his long, thin hands. The rest of the package is so good, however, that I happily overlook it.

This is beyond annoying. I swear I know this guy. Did we go to high school together?

I wonder if Gen has noticed Jaeger. If Mason doesn't work out, Jaeger should be put at the top of Gen's list of prospects.

"—we worked at Heavenly together," Mason says, and I tune back in to the conversation. He's just told Gen how he knows these guys.

I take a seat beside Adam and Jaeger, leaving Gen the chair between Jaeger and Mason.

Gen and Mason strike up a conversation about one of the supervising waitresses from work, and I listen in as Adam continues what must have been the conversation Gen and I interrupted when we arrived.

"I don't know what he was thinking." Adam shakes his head in disbelief. "Why would he cheat with prostitutes? Groupies, maybe—but prostitutes? Germs, man. Disease." He mocks a shiver. "Just not right, even for a celebrity."

Gen and I are entertainment news junkies. I run through my mental Rolodex to ascertain which trashy celeb Adam's referring to. The pop star? Or the athlete whose prior reputation was as a virgin former choirboy? It's a tough call. I lean closer to catch the details.

Jaeger eases back in his chair, his shoulder inches away. His body heat crosses the space between us, a pleasant whiff of shaving cream filling my senses, making my heart beat faster. He runs his knuckles down firm thighs, and a ripple of attraction shoots through my belly.

What the hell? I sit up, eyes trained on Adam. I haven't noticed another guy since before Eric and I got together, and here I am, checking out and feeling *things* for one of Gen's prospects, like he's for me.

My gaze darts to Jaeger's face and I wonder again how I know this guy. The more I look, the more familiar he appears.

Jaeger nods as if he's listening to Adam, but he doesn't contribute to the conversation. Almost as though he knows Adam will continue without input from others. Adam's overly chatty. That's annoying. It's a good thing Mason introduced the girl beside Adam as his girlfriend, and I already struck him from the list.

Gen and Mason's conversation dies down and Mason looks up. He pushes a spear of olives from one side of his martini glass to the other. "Why bother getting married? He should have stayed single." He lifts the glass and takes a swallow. Mason has obviously been paying attention to his friends' conversation while chatting up Gen.

Gotta be the athlete. The pop star isn't married. "You're talking about that basketball player, right?" I say.

Mason nods.

"He's a bastard."

A low rumble escapes from Jaeger. I glance up and catch a faint smile.

"His wife and kids will make out, no matter what he did." With his thumb and forefinger, Adam picks a loose thread from the back of his girlfriend Breanna's blouse and flicks it to the floor.

She doesn't seem to notice his anal-retentive grooming of her. "*Adam,* money isn't everything."

"I agree. I wouldn't consider that a good lot in life," Gen says, gripping the glass the waitress placed before her. "The wife has a husband she can't trust and small children to raise—probably by herself."

Ugh-h-h. Don't go there, Gen. You're wearing your heartache on your sleeve!

Mason shoots her a sweet smile. Good. He doesn't seem put off.

The conversation slowly turns to the lighter topics of skiing and snowboarding.

Mason's head notches up, his attention on Adam. "Remember when you thought you saw Gisele on the slopes a few years ago?"

Adam raises his hands for emphasis. "Man, it was her, I swear!"

Jaeger's shoulder dips closer to me. "How have you been, Cali?" His deep voice turns my spine limp and spongy. I could melt from the sound of it and happily live as a sticky puddle on the lounge floor.

We *do* know each other. "I'm sorry—you're familiar, but I can't remember how."

He leans forward, elbows on his knees, head angled toward me without directly looking. "Tyler."

Tyler's my older brother.

It all makes sense now.

Images cross my mind of a tall, slender guy with blond, shaggy hair who used to hang out with Tyler during my freshman year in high school. My gaze rakes Jaeger's hard, well-defined, and heavily muscled body. Is it possible for a guy to add sixty pounds of muscle and a couple extra inches of height between the ages of eighteen and—? I mentally calculate. He's gotta be my brother's age, about twenty-three—no, Tyler skipped a grade—Jaeger must be twenty-four.

His hair is darker, but it was longer and probably sun-bleached when we were in high school. The guy I remember also had an unusual name, though I couldn't say for sure that it was Jaeger. His family was originally from another country. He was quiet, like this guy, and now that I look closer, the face is similar. This must be the same person, and if it is, he's filled out. A lot.

He was also a skiing champion and had a long-term girl-friend.

I never thought he noticed me.

"—you ran over a family of four and almost killed yourself on a low-hanging branch to chase her." The corners of Mason's mouth turn up as if merrily reliving the memory of Adam pursuing Gisele like a jackass.

I glance at Jaeger. He's looking at Mason, a small smile curving his lips. It's the cutest guy smile I think I've ever seen, and it transforms him from large, enigmatic male into something more approachable and appealing. He's definitely going on Gen's list. Not *my* list, because I don't need a list, but *Gen's* list, I remind myself.

"It would have been worth it," Adam mumbles. "If I could have talked to Gisele, I know I could have gotten her digits."

Mason laughs and Jaeger shifts in his seat. His mouth morphs into a full grin, and his gaze strays to mine, hovering. His smile reduces to something sultry and curious and my stomach tightens. For a second, I lose the ability to breathe.

Holy shit. That smile is lethal.

Jaeger hasn't looked at me dead-on since we arrived, and the impact sends my brain tumbling. His eyes are dark green along the edges of the iris, like the center of a pine needle, growing lighter toward the middle. Abruptly, he looks down at his hands, before observing his friends again.

I slump in my seat. This might be Tyler's high school friend, but he's changed.

I'm reeling. I mean, really freaking out right now. I've never felt instant sizzle before, and with *Jaeger*—my brother's friend? That's a no-go zone. I have a boyfriend!

I lift my hand and signal to the waitress. She sees me and walks over. "Shot of Cuervo, please."

Startled faces peer at me from around the table. *What?* "Anyone else want one?"

Jaeger and Adam order a shot.

Breanna purses her lips and glares. "Excuse me!" She pokes her chest and flips her hand out at Adam. "Girlfriend sitting here. Why are you talking about pursuing another woman?"

Oh right, the Gisele conversation. God, that seems trivial compared to the mini-crisis going on in my head.

"Bree, that was way before we met." Adam squeezes Breanna's shoulder.

"Right, 'cause if you saw Gisele now, you would totally ignore her and have zero interest out of your love and respect for me. Is that what you meant to say?"

"Uhhh, yeah. Absolutely." Adam smiles mischievously at his friends while he pats Breanna on the back.

"I saw that!" Breanna snaps.

Mason coughs into his hand, the corners of his mouth upturned.

"Hey, what about you, *bro?*" Adam glares at Mason, who Adam seems to think is the cause of the strife between him and his girlfriend.

"What about me? If I ran into Gisele, the *real* Gisele, and not some pseudo-lookalike, I would have been a hell of a lot smoother than you."

"I'm talking about when you challenged Shaun White. I seem to recall you getting your ass kicked all over the mountain."

Gen absently passes me the green olives from her martini. She must not be too worried about Mason getting razzed by his friend if she's thinking about my stomach. Grinning, I pop one of the olives into my mouth and glance up.

I choke before the olive passes my tonsils.

Jaeger is staring at my throat.

His gaze lifts to my eyes and heat rushes my face. I'd like to say the look he's giving me is one of observation, as though he's watching an exotic bird eat an unusual food. Gen's informed me on more than one occasion that my love of green olives is unnatural. But Jaeger looks sexy, and hot, and his gaze is sending fiery signals to my girl parts.

"I remember you now," I say without breaking eye contact. "You had a girlfriend."

The heat in his eyes disappears. He looks away. "That was a long time ago."

An enigmatic response from an enigmatic person. This is the Jaeger I remember. Quiet. Reserved.

Jaeger glances at Gen and his expression softens. There's no reason to strike him from the list, not when I remember him as a good guy.

"He's an *Olympic champion,*" Mason says, overriding my wayward thoughts. "He had a few more skills than me, but I carved it up pretty good—got in some decent tricks."

Adam frowns and rolls his shoulders. "I'll believe it when I see it."

"Guess you had to be there." Mason shrugs and finishes off his martini. He has a fresh one in front of him that he must have ordered with the tequila shots.

I flag the waitress again and request another shot, chasing it with a second martini to dull the hormones riding me. It's been almost a week since I saw Eric… and a lot longer since we had sex. My libido's been neglected. Any hot guy could incite the reaction Jaeger does.

I listen to the others talk and lose track of the conversation. After a while, I grab Gen's chair. Or maybe her arm. Am I leaning on her?

She glances at me wearily. "Mason, we're gonna get going. Thanks for inviting us tonight."

Crap, those shots that dulled my senses also made me forget to keep tabs on the chemistry between Gen and Mason. Did they hit it off?

Mason smiles politely. "Great to meet you, Cali. I look forward to seeing you around at Blue."

What a sweet guy. He's a keeper, and I'm going to tell Gen so, just as soon as my tongue thins out. "Definitely!" I practically yell. It's the only word I can get past my numb lips.

Gen's eyes widen. "I think we'll take a taxi."

I wave goodbye to the rest of them, and they return the gesture, except for Jaeger, who observes my every uncoordinated move, his mouth tense, brows drawn. I'm drunk, but not so drunk I don't know what a loud, clumsy drunkass I am. Good thing I'm already in a relationship, or there'd be embarrassment on the menu for tomorrow.

We leave Harrah's and I tell the cabbie to take us to the Last Stop. They're open long after the casinos slow, with two a.m. breakfasts that have just the right amount of grease.

Gen slides into a booth. I bump my hip on the table as I slither in across from her.

"You're hammered, Cali."

"Yup." I hiccup, the foul flavor of vomitus and alcohol singeing my tongue. "Need water."

Four glasses of water and a late-night breakfast large enough to feed a two-hundred-pound man later, my mouth regains its dexterity. "Mason's hot," I say casually.

Here's where I unearth the truth about Gen's feelings for Mason. "I'm definitely going to keep my eye out for him at the casino. I need something pretty to look at while I slave away shuffling cards."

I shift my gaze to catch her response. If one wishes to elicit a reaction from the elusive species known as *reservus quietgirlius,* one must poke.

Gen snorts indelicately. "Oh, it's rough for you, isn't it? Try carrying around a fifteen-pound tray all night—in heels."

My brows pinch and I quickly smooth them out. I expected annoyance at my checking out Mason, and she gives me nil. Not cool. Point one to Gen, but I have more in my arsenal.

"Did you see his shoulders and arms? Those snowboarders are in good shape."

"Okay—*girl with a boyfriend.*"

Ouch. That one hit the soft spot. I already feel guilty about my hormonal response to Jaeger. "I'm not actually interested. I just appreciate a nice-looking guy when I see one. I think Mason likes *you.*"

Gen swishes the ice in her clear plastic cup. "He doesn't like me. He's a friend."

Okay, now I'm annoyed. She's not 'fessing up to anything. "He likes you, Gen, and he's cute and sweet. What's wrong with him?"

"There's nothing wrong with him. I'm just wondering if maybe it's too soon for me to date other guys." She thunks her cup on the table, avoiding my eyes. "I haven't gotten over the last one that hurt me."

A perfectly valid point. So why do I feel like the A-hole isn't the real reason she's suddenly shying away from dating? She needs to date other guys in order to get out of her slump.

"I thought you were open to going out? Dating isn't a rela-tionship, it's just… hanging. No strings, just fun."

Gen straightens. "I think maybe friendships are more my

speed right now." She shoves a forkful of hash browns into her mouth, shredded bits dangling from one corner of her lips as she chews.

She doesn't fool me by shoveling in food like a toddler so she can't talk. Gen's the consummate lady. I recognize avoidance tactics when I see them.

"Enough about my dating woes," she finally says. "Let's get in a game of table shuffleboard before we leave." She eyes the back wall where it's located—changing the subject, dammit!

"Fine, but be prepared for an ass-kicking. You know how good I am."

Gen chokes on her last bite. "That's absolutely *not* how I remember your skills at shuffleboard, or ping-pong, or any other game or sport requiring hand-eye coordination. Why do you think I want to play you? I need an ego boost after being called Snow all night by the cougars."

The nickname Snow White is a part of Gen's hazing by the veteran waitresses. "Cougars—are they hooking up with younger guys?"

"One of them stared at Mason the entire time he and I shared our dinner break. She wants to take a bite out of him badly. I don't think those cougars are too happy we're friends. Mason's gotta be at least ten years younger than most of them, but they don't seem deterred."

Gen and Mason had dinner together? Nice. Maybe she'll change her mind about this friends-only business.

"If I were their age and single, I'd be a cougar. So yes, I believe it." I flex my fingers like I'm doing digit stretches. "I wouldn't be so cocky about table shuffleboard if I were you. My dexterity and speed have improved dramatically after long hours of dealing cards."

Gen rolls her eyes. "Uh-huh."

I shouldn't have goaded her. She gives me a Gen Shuffle-board Smackdown of five-zip in under an hour.

By the time we return home, I'm not sure who's more nervous about Gen's future dating adventures—her, or me as her wingwoman, thrust in front of tempting, attractive men.

Or just one attractive man.

Chapter Three

AM OFFICIALLY the card-dealing samurai. I've gotten so good these last two weeks that I can multitask while I work and scope out the action inside the casino. It's like watching Casino Real World. Right now, the sweet brunette swing-shift waitress is flirting with the tall, dark-haired cashier behind the cage, while two other waitresses—who I'm pretty sure have a thing for each other—chat by a row of slots. Over in Gen's lounge, two youngish executives with loosened ties troll for women. Their game is that they are there for an end-of-the-day drink, but I can tell they're looking for a hookup. One of them has been tracking Gen's every move. It's making me nervous, because I don't get a good vibe from these guys.

I deal my next hand and glance into the East Bar, where Gen's safely ensconced, chatting up Mason.

My heart warms at the sight. I'm like a proud mama duck watching her duckling venture into the world. Gen and Mason have been casually flirting for a couple of weeks. Well, okay, I can't tell if the banter is friendly or flirty, but at this point I don't care. Gen's laughing and smiling more, and that's all that matters. This is the happiest I've seen her in months.

Jaeger swaggers up to Mason's bar and my heart pumps an extra beat. He's in a black T-shirt and dark jeans, and my mouth goes dry just looking at him—

"Hit."

Crap, I missed a customer signal. Too much casino-watching.

The woman glares and I quickly deal a card, shoving my head back in the game. But when I can no longer stand the suspense, I glance at Mason's bar.

Jaeger is smiling at Gen, his forearm on the counter, body angled toward her. I can't look away. Corded muscles in his arm flex under his weight, his hand casually curled.

Damn those hot hands. Visions of them grasping my flesh and skimming over my body hijack my mind.

Eric hasn't called, and Jaeger's effect on me is inconvenient. I was hoping Eric would visit and remind me why we're together, because I'm not feeling the love.

I shift my feet, gaze shooting now and then to the trio at the bar. Gen laughs at something Jaeger says and jealousy spears my chest.

This is ridiculous. I *want* Gen to have male attention. Why does this particular guy's attention have me so upset? He was my brother's friend, and for all I know, he's still in touch with Tyler. I should call Tyler and get the scoop.

Two of my customers rise, gathering their chips. They've lost the last three rounds.

I can predict with ninety-nine percent accuracy when a customer will leave. Three rounds of losses have a fifty percent probability, while five or six rounds guarantee they'll be moving along. Tonight I'm hot. No one stays at my table for more than a few hands.

My last two customers—middle-aged mother types—have managed to break even for a half-hour. The longest stretch so far.

Dealer shows a ten. *Not looking good, ladies.*

The woman with frosted blond bangs scrunches her nose. She whispers to her pal, her fake bright pink nails shining in the overhead lights as she cups her mouth. With a nod from her friend, she swipes the table, indicating a hit.

I deal her an eight of hearts and her lips press together in a subdued smile, but her eyes dart warily to my ten.

Her friend hits as well, then holds.

I flip my hidden card. *Ace.*

House takes all.

Again.

I'm even winning when it comes to getting Gen hookedup, so what the hell is wrong with me? Why is it about Jaeger that has me on edge? I need to talk to Eric. He hasn't called since before his visit, and that was three weeks ago. He's texted a couple of times, so I know he's alive.

My tight ponytail is giving me a headache. Holding my hands over the table, I clap them together, and show my palms to the ceiling—and the creepy people watching from the surveillance system—before tugging the strands loose near my temple.

The pressure on my scalp eases, but the sledgehammer inside my head persists. Flashing my hands again, I show I haven't pulled any cards from behind my ears and deal another hand. A new customer sits at my table while I'm looking down, and the fine hairs on the back of my neck tingle.

Jaeger is seated in front of me, his shoulders practically taking up two seat widths.

My heart ricochets inside my chest like a pinball. I can't control the smile that tugs at the corners of my mouth. *Stop smiling!* I compress my lips in a straight line.

Jaeger doesn't say anything at first, but when it's his turn to hit, he swipes his hand and says, "What are you doing after work tonight?"

The first thing that comes to mind is that he's hitting on me. Well, he's hitting—for me to deal him a card—just not hitting on *me*. I need to stop thinking about him like a guy I might be interested in. I'm not interested in any guys. I have Eric.

I pass him his card. "Not much. Why, what's up?"

Peering at the cards on the table, he says, "You feel like joining me and Mason for a Tahoe sunrise tradition?"

Sounds promising. Jaeger, or it could be Mason, probably wants to see Gen tonight and Jaeger's checking in with me because she and I are a package deal. I'm thinking champagne on the beach… he has skills, if this is how he's going to play it with her.

"I'm game. What did Gen say?" I flip my hidden card and add a six to my seven. I deal myself another card.

A king. Dealer busts.

And just like that, my winning streak breaks.

The frosted sisters lost as well, and have already abandoned the table. Jaeger's eighteen is the winning hand.

"She says she'll go if you do." He scrapes up his winnings.

See, I tell myself, *he's just checking in with me. He asked Gen out first.*

But I search his expression anyway, only he's not looking at me. All I see are the tips of his lashes, a full bottom lip, and a square jaw line framed by broad shoulders. I can't tell if he's making sure I'm going so Gen feels comfortable, or if he wants me there. Which is stupid. It doesn't matter whether he wants me there or not. Gen's the available one.

Why the hell am I thinking about this at all? I need to talk to Eric. "We get off at three. What time do you want to meet?"

Jaeger shoves his chips into his pocket—and I'm staring at the corded muscles along his forearms again. Dammit! Can't the guy wear something other than flesh-baring T-shirts? What is this, a strip club?

"I'll pick you up at the front entrance at three thirty."

I force my gaze up.

"Wear something comfortable." His eyes dip, only for a moment—a glance that takes in my polyester uniform as if *it* were revealing. My uniform is the same one every dealer wears—unsexed—and it's not attractive. But that glance was proprietary. And hot.

Jaeger merges with the crowd and my pit boss hands me a new stack of cards. I focus on my kickass riffle shuffle and not the beautiful man striding away from my table.

Chapter Four

"FISHING? YOU'RE TAKING us *fishing*?"

In the time it took us to grab food before the "sunrise tradition," the sky turned from black to dark blue, shedding light on the back of Jaeger's truck. Four fishing poles glint like spears from his truck bed.

I scratch my head, trying to figure out what the hell these guys are thinking. This is not my idea of a good time. Was this Mason's idea, or Jaeger's? I'm adjusting my assessment of their seduction skills by the second.

It's getting close to five in the morning and we're on a beach north of Stateline that I've never been to. Small rowboats are moored at a narrow dock.

Hello? Anyone ever hear of boats with engines? What are we, in the sixteenth century?

My mood is pissy, but I'm freaking tired. And it's cold out here.

Jaeger lifts a box I assume contains tackle and grabs the fishing poles. I've seen people fish. I understand the requisite accoutrements. I just never thought I'd be using them in this lifetime. There's a time and place to acquire fish—laid out on ice in the meat section of the grocery store is my preference.

"Scared?" Mason raises a brow, his dimple in effect. He's goading me?

I cross my arms. "How hard can it be?"

Jaeger is wholly focused on putting together the fishing gear. He's not saying anything, but I think he's aware I'm not excited about this. Could be the extreme animosity I'm giving off.

Jaeger was vague when he invited me, and the two of them have kept the details of our adventure a secret until now. *Very cunning of them.*

They walk to the water's edge and untie the twin drowning contraptions from the dock, then drag the boats to shore. I glance at Gen, who's watching intently. She shrugs and heads for the boats.

Great. How am I going to find her a good guy if she doesn't have the natural instincts to know when she's being properly wooed? The Last Stop for a quick bite and a fishing trip are not what I consider wining and dining.

"Have you done this before?" Gen asks after I reluctantly join her, her face alight with excitement.

Am I the only one who doesn't find the idea of fishing at five in the morning the least bit entertaining? "No. You?"

She peers out longingly at the water. "I used to go with my grandfather when I was a kid, but I haven't been in a long time. This is going to be fun." She wraps her arm around my shoulders and squeezes the blood from my limbs.

Oh God. My headache is returning. I glance at the truck. Is it too late to back out? There's something about luring innocent fish and then manhandling their slimy bodies until they die that makes me want to hide beneath a rock.

Mason turns around. "Gen, you and I are together. Hop in from here. It's easier than from the dock."

Wait, what? I'm going with Jaeger? *Alone?*

"Shouldn't Gen and I go together?" I say. "She's fished before. She can help me out."

Mason shakes his head. "She told me a couple of days ago that she doesn't have a fishing license."

Gen nods in agreement.

Wait, is this the reason we're out here at five in the morning? Gen and Mason talked about fishing and now Mason's taking her? Not exactly my idea of romantic, but if he was listening to something she wanted to do, I can't argue.

"Technically, neither of you should fish without a license," Mason adds. "But we can probably get away with it if we split up. These boats are too small to accommodate both me and Jaeger, anyway, and I don't want to leave you girls alone."

I could admire Mason's protective nature if I wasn't so panicked about being marooned with Jaeger. My stomach is so taut it's threatening to eject the large meal I just ate.

Eric would do this—be a friend's wingman and hang with a girl's best friend so his buddy could get to know someone. That's all this is. That's all Jaeger's doing too. He doesn't care if he's alone with me. Why should I care?

Releasing the involuntary clamp I have on my airways, I breathe deeply and approach Jaeger's boat. The fishing poles are loaded inside, along with a tackle box and a small cooler.

Jaeger reaches out and I take his hand. It's padded with muscle, warm and firm, and it engulfs mine. A shock of heat rushes through my chest, previous dreams of that hand on my body dive-bombing any hope of rational thought. I stagger into the boat, my butt landing with a jarring thud.

Jaeger steps inside and passes me a paddle. I brace myself against the side of the boat, digging my fingers into the metal. Fantasies aren't cheating. Still, this has got to stop.

"Head for the outcrop." Jaeger points to the dark rock wall a quarter of a mile away.

I dip my oar in the water and we attempt a rhythm as we paddle out on to the lake. I'd like to say it's a smooth ride, but I'm chopping and splashing, maneuvering my paddle like a hacksaw. My coordination leaves something to be desired.

"Why over there?" I ask as we near the place he pointed to. "Shouldn't we go deeper?"

"This is deep, and the fish like coves. It's also closer to shore—less labor on our part." He sets his oar down, his gaze intent on my face. For a moment, he doesn't move, he simply stares, his jaw working as if he's trying to decide whether or not to say something.

Gen and Mason are closer to shore than we are. Hushed conversation floats over from their direction, but nothing I can decipher. Jaeger and I might as well be alone. I glance away and focus on the obsidian water.

Jaeger's warm leg brushes my calf as he reaches for a pole. "You've never done this before?"

For a moment, I wonder what he's talking about. The heat from his leg and the proximity of his body has me thinking of make-out sessions and cheating on boyfriends. Multiple yeses to the former, no to the latter.

Then I remember we're supposed to be fishing. "No."

"I'll bait your hook."

"Excuse me?" Why does everything he says sound like a pickup line?

He raises an eyebrow and pulls a wiggling worm from a Styrofoam container. He spears the worm on the end of a hook the size of my pinky.

I throw up a little in my mouth. Why am I here again?

Gen and Mason's boat has drifted farther away and I can't hear anything from them now.

"Here." Jaeger holds out the fishing rod with the worm still wiggling on the end. "Press the button on the reel and drop the line in to the water."

I'm trying to concentrate on his words, but I can't stop staring at the impaled worm. I gingerly take the reel, holding it so Mr. Worm doesn't touch me, or get knocked against the side of the boat, adding insult to injury. Lowering the tip of the pole, I let him float on the lake's surface. Maybe the little guy will get lucky and escape his torture device while Jaeger finishes his instructions.

"When I tell you to, lock the line in place."

Bossy, are we? Who am I kidding; I absolutely need point-by-point instructions.

I press the button and the line sinks, whistling as it descends. Now the worm is drowning. Fishing cannot be humane.

Jaeger gives the signal and I press the button to stop the reel. I grip the rod as if it were an ax and stare at the end, no clue what I'm supposed to be waiting for.

Jaeger pulls another worm from the Styrofoam container and I look away. I know what's about to happen. I can't watch this one's fate at the end of Jaeger's hook.

Why does that bring to mind my own destiny?

At the sound of his line going in the water, I peer over. Jaeger locks his reel and reaches for the small cooler, pulling out a can of Budweiser. He pops the top and passes it to me.

Cheap beer at five thirty in the morning? I will gladly take said beer and drink it like it is mother's milk. The carbonation might settle my stomach. At the very least, a light buzz could dim the sexual tension and sense of doom in the air—or make it worse. Jesus, that's all I need.

If I'm the only one with dirty thoughts, I can deal, but if

Jaeger is attracted to me, too... we have a problem.

"How will I know when I've caught a fish?"

He shushes me and glances over like I've been naughty, which I have—in my mind. "You won't catch a fish if you scare them away by talking too loud," he whispers.

I lower my voice. "Are you going to tell me how this is done, or what?"

His mouth twitches. Without looking at me, he says, "They nibble."

A tingle shoots down my belly and past my thighs. I squeeze my legs together. Again with the dirty fishing talk!

"It will feel like a vibration, maybe a few quick tugs. Don't react right away. Let the fish take a nice bite, then jerk your hook. If you feel more movement, you've caught something."

He pops open a can for himself and we sit in silence, me chugging my beer and waiting to be nibbled, him as still as a stone two feet away.

After a few minutes, I hold out my hand for another beer and my line vibrates. I don't react right away, but my rod has all my attention. Taking the second beer he hands me, I wait, sipping carefully and white-knuckling my pole.

Another small jerk and rattle occurs.

With his gaze on his own line, Jaeger doesn't seem to notice.

The next tug from the mysterious creature below the surface has my rod slipping a fraction from my fingers. I lurch the pole up and wind the reel a couple of times to take up the slack. The end jerks like crazy. I've caught something for sure.

Spinning the reel with quick, uncontrolled strokes, I fight to bring in the wild animal at the end of my line, my adrenaline kicking up a notch. I'm getting this fishing business now. Woman versus beast!

What exactly is down there? Are there freshwater sharks? Because I think I caught one. This fish is a wily bugger. I'm straining and not making much progress.

Jaeger scoots closer and our arms brush. I sense when he sets his pole down. "Need help?"

Before I can answer, the boat dips and my grip loosens on the pole as I correct my balance. Jaeger sinks behind me on the bench I'm straddling, his front to my back.

"What are you doing?" I ask.

"Figured you wanted to know how to reel it in." His deep voice, the light cologne he's wearing, and the feel of his body against mine have me frozen in place.

I choke. "I think I know how that's done."

His hands cover mine, and I instantly release the pole, dropping my hands in my lap. He draws in the line with quick, efficient strokes, and the fish breaches the surface of the water.

It's the size of a minnow.

What the hell? I had a *dolphin* on the end of that line.

I scoot to Jaeger's previous position as he makes a grab for Mr. Slimy and gently unhooks my fish's lip. He tosses the minnow overboard, and the little guy arcs and swims away.

"Why'd you throw him back?" I worked hard for that fish, and Mr. Worm sacrificed his life.

"Catch and release. We're not keeping them, even if you had caught one big enough to eat." His mouth curves.

Sounds like a guy's dating motto. "Hey, now. I don't see a fish on the end of your hook. I guess it takes a delicate touch."

His eyes dart to my fingers curled in my lap. A tingly sensation runs down my spine. He looks me in the eye. "Feel free to exhibit your delicate touch anytime you like."

It's official. Jaeger's brain is in the gutter too.

Now I'm in trouble.

He re-baits my hook and hands me the line.

Time to nip this attraction in the bud. Most hot guys drop about ten notches after I get to know them. I'll ask Jaeger a few pointed questions. That should douse the ardor.

"So whatever happened to you? I thought you were a star athlete. Skiing, wasn't it?"

A beat passes. He stares at the water. "Downhill."

I wait for him to continue. He seems relaxed, but still, like I've hit on something important.

"I don't ski anymore." He adjusts his feet into a wider stance on the boat's metal bottom, elbows braced on his knees. "A bad injury took me out of competitive sports."

Definitely a sore spot, though he appears calm enough. According to my brother, Jaeger was an amazing athlete. He was on track for the Olympics, from what I recall. That's a big deal in a small town. It's also one reason I never thought he noticed me. I was Tyler's skinny little sister. Jaeger had a serious girl-friend and barely glanced my way when he visited.

"What do you do now?"

He takes a swig of the beer he's been nursing since we rowed out. "I carve wood."

An image of the logs with bear heads etched into them and wooden totem poles on the side of Highway 89 flashes through my mind. Wow, this poor guy's life has seriously declined since high school.

"What about you?" He looks over, studying my face. "You just graduated. What's your next step? I'm assuming the casino gig is short-term."

God, if it wasn't, my mom would kill me. She busted her ass at the casinos for twenty-two years to keep us afloat. I have one of those deadbeat dads who calls a couple of times a year and, despite his brilliant brain, can barely hold down a job long enough to cover his expenses, let alone pay child support. Dad's never had his shit together, which meant my mom had to be the adult and raise Tyler and me. She gave up asking Dad for help long before they separated when I was two.

"Yeah, short-term."

Jaeger continues to stare, and I realize I haven't exactly answered the question. I clear my throat. "I've been accepted into law school."

He nods, but the gesture is stiff. "Where?"

"Harvard."

A long pause follows, and I can't tell if the silence is all me, and the worries I have over school, or something else.

Law school is what I've worked for, but somehow, it doesn't feel real, or… right. My visit to the campus last semester solidified those concerns. I've never seen so many preppy kids in one spot. Talk about not fitting in. I grew up around the casinos with a single mom. I'm smart and scrappy, not privileged. The adjustment to campus life at Harvard is going to be huge, the loans crippling. If I work my ass off this summer, I'll have enough for half of my room and board—for the first year. That doesn't include tuition, which costs five times as much. That's where my high-paying legal position will come in after I graduate. I'll essentially be working to pay for my education.

"So, you'll be leaving soon?" His tone is flat.

I don't answer right away. I can't say anything, because even though I pursued this path, I'm not excited about it. No one *wants* to invest a fortune in school, but it's more than that. There are programs that cost less. I'm just not excited about law, period.

There, I've allowed the thought nagging at the back of my mind to rise to the surface. This is what I've worked for and what I should want, but I don't. I've changed, or my needs have changed. All I do know is nothing feels right anymore.

My mom wanted her kids to be doctors and lawyers—important people. I think that's why she went after my dad all those years ago. He'd graduated from Berkeley with honors. Mom discovered too late that sometimes a hardworking man is more successful than a brilliant one.

She couldn't afford full tuition and board for college, but Mom paid half of Tyler's and my college educations by working two full-time jobs at the casinos. She wanted better for us. We did well in school and her efforts weren't a waste. Which is why I can't tell her I don't want the brilliant future laid out for me.

Jaeger asked if I was leaving soon and I still haven't answered. "I guess," is what I finally say, unable to give him anything concrete when the earth feels unsteady beneath me.

Jaeger's gaze drills into me. "You—"

"Jaeger," Mason calls out in a loud whisper. "We'd better go."

Jaeger swivels his head, and I see a motorboat approaching behind him. It's a little ways away, but heading straight for us.

Jaeger reels in his line and drops his pole in the bottom of the boat. He grabs both oars. "Hold on."

I set my pole down and Jaeger's first thrust of the oars jerks me back. We're gliding across the surface fast enough to make hair sweep from my face in the breeze. His arms are like machines, cutting through the water, shoulder muscles bunched and rippling beneath the long-sleeved shirt he threw on over his T-shirt earlier. I can't stop staring. He may have given up the Olympics and professional sports, but he's fit. Must be all that whittling.

Jaeger gets us back to shore in a tenth of the time it took us to get out. He hops from the boat onto the sand and pulls me and the boat up the beach until only half the vessel lies in the water.

He hands me his keys and reaches out. "Hurry. You girls wait in my truck."

I pocket the keys and grab hold of his fingers, eyeing the ground to determine the best way to jump to shore without dunking or injuring myself. Jaeger made it look easy, but he's twice my size.

I brace my foot on the tip of the bow, but my sandal slips on the metal surface. I overcorrect and fall backward.

Jaeger whisks his arm around my back and lifts me from the boat, my chest pressed to him. For a second, my feet are suspended, my face level with his. He's holding me up with one arm like an embrace, palm flat beneath the side of my breast. His chest is solid and warm against mine, but it's his mouth inches away that has my complete attention.

My breaths come in short gasps. Everything else escapes my attention. It's just him and me—the last two people on Earth.

Jaeger loosens his grip and I slide to the ground, my legs wobbling as they hit the sand. The world rushes back, and I look around. I catch sight of Gen and stumble over, but I glance back, wondering if that moment where time suspended itself was a dream. Jaeger is pushing the boat toward the dock, and I still can't decide if I imagined it.

I link arms with her. "What's going on?" My voice sounds breathless.

"Mason says the boat on its way over is the ranger checking for licenses. Nothing serious if we get caught, but the fines are steep."

We climb inside Jaeger's truck and I maneuver into the back seat of the cab. It's light out and I can see his vehicle more clearly. Silver exterior and clean. The truck is brand new. Not bad for a totem pole salesman.

"You catch anything?" Gen asks, her eyes glowing from our adventure.

"Yeah, but we threw it back. Catch and release." I don't mention the size of my fish. "How about you?"

"Nothing. Mason says he'll get me a license and we can go another time."

An hour ago, I would have considered that the worst form of torture, but now the idea has merit. There's something to be said for sitting on a calm lake drinking beer as the sun rises. Or maybe it's the company that makes the difference.

Even after he mentioned his carving career, I'm drawn to Jaeger. He created a new life for himself after he was forced to give up his dream. I can't help but respect him for it.

My attempt to get to know him and be able take him down a few notches in my esteem totally backfired.

"What about you? Did you have fun with Mason?" I quirk my brows.

Gen nods with a bemused smile and looks out the window. "He's a good buddy."

A good *buddy*? Jaeger's seducing my panties off with his dirty fishing talk, and Gen and Mason are forming a friendship?

No, no, no. Either Mason steps up his game, or Gen and Jaeger are getting paired next time. Let her panties drop for the guy. I have a boyfriend.

"What about you? How was Jaeger?"

"He's a good guy, Gen. You should consider him if things

don't work out with Mason."

Gen tilts her head and eyes me. Her lips part, like she's about to say something, but the passenger door opens.

"All good!" Mason announces.

Jaeger slides into the driver's seat and our gazes collide in the rearview mirror. I look away.

"Ranger checked our licenses and let us go," Mason continues. "We'll plan ahead next time and get you one-day passes."

I don't say anything, because I like the idea of doing this again.

Only next time, Gen goes with Jaeger.

Chapter Five

I AMBLE INTO the kitchen at close to two in the afternoon later the same day. We don't usually arrive home from work at six thirty a.m., but the fishing expedition made our wake-up especially late. Gen's by the sink, her eyes half-lidded, slowly scrubbing coffee stains in a trancelike state from the Adult Sippy Cup mug. She yawns. "Eloww."

Translation: *Hello.* She hasn't had her coffee yet, so she's technically not awake. I pour mine into the Sexy Bitch mug. There are about fifty mugs to choose from. Our summer rental sports more mugs than it does dishes.

I open the fridge and scan the door. *There you are, my beauties.* I pop the lid off my favorite deli jar, spear a green olive with a fork, and jam it in my mouth.

Gen gags. "That's revolting. Why are you doing this to me before I've had coffee?"

Innocently, I offer her some.

"Bitch," she says without much power behind it. If ever there was a time to tease Gen, it's in the morning, when she's at her weakest.

I hold up my coffee. "That's Sexy Bitch to you."

Thirty minutes later, Gen's eyelids are fully operational and she's flipping through a *People* magazine propped on her lap in one of the lounge chairs out back. I'm in the chair next to her in a bikini top I threw on above my pajama bottoms, my sketchpad on the table beside me. I started doodling in elementary school. It's turned into an obsession.

My eyes are closed, body angled toward the sun. I like the feel of the sun on me, but I have on SPF one thousand so my skin doesn't crisp and fall off. I'm a pretend sunbather.

The scrape of a page turning rustles beside me. "A waitress from work invited us to dinner tonight."

I pop open an eyelid. "One of the cougars?"

Gen pulls in her chin and shakes her head. "No, not one of them. Nessa's our age and really nice."

"Sounds fun, but I've got a Skype date with Eric."

Finally, *finally*, I managed to pin down my boyfriend via text. I glance at the exchange on my phone from earlier and smile.

> **Cali:** *Thinking of our tubing trip down the American River with all this glacial water nearby. Totally your fault we tipped. Saving that beer was not worth it!*
> **Eric:** *Worth it.*
> **Cali:** *Miss you. Skype tonight? 8 p.m.?*
> **Eric:** *Sure.*

Gen shivers, elbows pressed to her sides. "In that case, I'm glad I won't be around."

I set my phone back in my lap. Eric and I have been known to discuss sex around Gen. It could be because we have no shame, or it could be because it drives her crazy—okay, it's both.

Somehow, though, I don't think our conversation tonight will cover Sex-Skyping. We haven't spoken over the phone in weeks. I'm more interested in getting reassurance that everything is okay. My instincts were right that day on the hike.

Something is up with him, but I've been so busy with my new job, I haven't had time to do much about it.

No point in drawing conclusions until I talk to Eric. I smile, just to irritate Gen. "Probably so."

Mostly I'm nervous. Once I know everything is fine with Eric, I'm sure my head will clear over this thing with Jaeger.

IT'S MIDNIGHT, AND I've officially been stood up.

I've never been stood up—and by my own boyfriend? Friggin' hell!

As I'm digging into my second pint of butter pecan ice cream, the sound of the bolt scraping comes from the front door. Gen walks in. Well, *stomps* is a better description.

I kick up my fuzzy slippers onto our rental's retro wood coffee table (it's actually old as shit, but I'm trying to think positive), and wait for her to set down her stuff and tell me what's up. Because something's definitely up. Her gaze is cagey and she slammed the door closed after she entered.

She eyes my carton of ice cream and huffs out a sigh. "Out of every Ben & Jerry's flavor in existence you picked *butter pecan*? What about cookies 'n cream, Super Fudge Chunk, or, I don't know, vanilla?" She tosses her purse on the floor and plops next to me on the couch, staring straight ahead.

I glance at her, the discarded purse, and then the tub of ice cream resting on my belly, the spoon sticking out like a flag. "Ouch. What's wrong with butter pecan?"

Another long exhale, this time through her nose. "Let me have a bite of your disgusting ice cream."

"*Disgusting ice cream* is an oxymoron. Get a spoon, and I *may* allow your grubby fingers to grace the lip of my carton."

Gen hoists herself from the couch and shuffles into the kitchen. The sound of drawers opening and closing and dishes clanking in the sink comes from behind. There are no clean spoons. I know this because I took the last one. If she succeeds in finding a clean spoon, I will happily donate my firstborn child to—

Gen enters the living room holding up a spoon like it's a trophy. It's bent at a sixty-degree angle with divots on the sides from the garbage disposal, but it's legit.

Damn. Bye-bye firstborn.

She plops next to me, digs a massive scoop from my carton, and jams it in her mouth. Easing the spoon out, she considers her warped utensil. "I met someone."

Ahhh, so that's what this is about. Sounds promising. I can almost forget my Eric misery with this news.

"He didn't talk to me."

Okay, maybe not so promising. "And why is he of interest? Steer clear of the A-holes, Gen. We're looking for good guys."

"I know—believe me, I know."

"But?"

"He kept looking at me, like he couldn't help himself, and then I realized one of the girls at the party is his girlfriend."

I choke on a drizzle of butter pecan running down my throat. "Oh God, no. Please tell me you are not interested in this guy. I thought the last one was an anomaly. Are you attracted to two-timing bastards, or something?"

Gen angles her head, her expression exasperated. "Let me finish. Once I realized he had a girlfriend I wrote him off, okay. But—"

Oh, no. *Nooo.* She's rubbing the sharp divots in her spoon as if to smooth them out, her train of thought lost. I'm afraid to think where this is going, and refrained from exploding all over her ass by a hair. The last thing she needs is the situation she escaped.

"—we sort of ran into each other in the hallway, like literally, we bumped into each other." She turns to me, her eyes searching my face. "Cali, I've never felt that before. When he touched me... God, I don't know how to explain it."

Oh, I think I know. I grind my teeth, vividly remembering when Jaeger caught me from falling out of the fishing boat and time stopped. Hormones—pheromones—whatever. Lots of them wreaking havoc.

This is not good. It's all wrong. Neither of us should be feeling this way. Not with these two people. It's my stupid advice coming back to bite me in the ass. I pushed Gen to get out there, and look what's happened. If she hooks up with A-hole number two, it'll be all my fault.

She shakes her head. "I've never felt that kind of attraction. Not with anyone, especially not my ex. I can't stop thinking about this guy." Her petite nose scrunches. "It's annoying."

I hear you, sister.

I shift until I'm square with her. "Listen to me. Forget that guy. He's no good or he wouldn't be staring at you with his girlfriend in the room, and rubbing on you—"

"He didn't—"

"Whatever. Point is, you have the power to choose. You don't have to fall in love with someone who will break your heart. That's not love."

She sniffs in a deep breath and nods.

"Don't forget Mason and Jaeger. They're both hot *and* single. Very important detail right there."

Gen looks at me as if she's miffed. "It's not like I *wanted* a cheating boyfriend." Her voice catches, and now I feel bad.

I put my hand on hers. "No, but not all guys are trustworthy and you need to be careful. Stay away from the ones who give you"—I shake my head and look around—"I don't know, a gut feeling that they're hiding something. There's a good chance they are."

A vision of Eric flashes in my mind. I should take my own advice.

"You're right."

I watch her, trying to detect what's going on inside her pretty head as she chews the corner of her lip. "Eat more ice cream—it'll make you feel better."

Gen digs her warped spoon into my carton, and I do too. Sugar-shock therapy after the evening we've both had is in full effect.

"The good thing is, you never have to see this guy again."

She glances at me guiltily.

"*What?* You didn't make plans with him…"

"No! But I sort of made plans to meet Nessa tomorrow. They're friends. He may be there."

"So, don't go."

"Awesome." She glares. "I'll just become a hermit. You're the one who pushed me to get out."

Dammit, she's totally right. Foiled by my own advice.

"Look, come with me," she says. "They're going to that place you talked about, Zephyr Cove. It'll be fun and you'll be there to intervene if I need it, which I won't. The guy… he doesn't seem the aggressive type. This is probably all one-sided anyway. There's nothing to worry about."

Chapter Six

ELEVEN IN THE morning is pretty early given our swing shifts. Even on our days off, we stay up late and sleep in late. But some of Lake Tahoe's best experiences occur in the a.m., which is why I'm on the sand at eleven in the friggin' morning, waiting for Gen's friends to arrive.

I'm facedown on my towel and Gen's sitting next to me, fidgeting with her purse and her trashy book, and anything else her hands graze. I so have a bad feeling about this outing. It's her life, but it's hard to watch someone you care for make the same mistake twice.

Nothing actually happened between her and the guy she met last night, so I say nothing and attempt to simmer down. Matter of fact, I'll take a catnap while we wait.

I'm just getting into pre-sleep body twitch mode when a shower of sand splashes the side of my face, shattering the beginnings of a dream involving me buck naked, sitting on the rock in the center of Eagle Lake, completely alone. I'm not disappointed that one ended. It was one of those anxiety dreams, but still. What the hell?

I sit up slowly, rubbing the sleep from my face, along with a bucket of sand granules. Long, muscular golden legs with a dusting of blond hair obstruct my vision. I gaze up, shading the sun with my hand.

Mason. Thank God. This is who I need to get Gen's mind

off bad influences.

"Cali! Sorry about that. You okay?" He squats in front of me and grabs the football that wedged in my armpit. He smiles at Gen.

Gen's leaning on her arms, grinning back. She looks comfortable and relaxed. Which I can only assume means that the fidgets earlier were because of the other guy, not Mason. It's not like she knew Mason would be here today.

"I'm okay," I say, a sinking feeling settling in my belly as I consider just how much this other A-hole has affected my best friend, and what that could mean. "No harm done." I try to look around Mason, but his snowboarding behemoth shoulders block my view. "Who are you with?"

"Jaeger." Mason plants the football in the sand beside him and drops to a seated position. *Guess he's staying a while.* "Too beautiful to go to the gym this morning. We came here instead."

I lean all the way to the side, and that's when I see Jaeger— talking to a petite brunette. She's wearing a tiny red bikini and smiling at him. The dread from a moment ago vanishes, and my stomach tightens, chest burning. *Who's that?*

Jaeger looks over and our gazes connect. My breath catches, and suddenly my heart's humming like he wasn't just talking to another girl, igniting jealousy.

He says something to the brunette and walks away toward us, his long strides eating up the sand. The girl stares after him, her face a bit forlorn, and then I don't know what she's doing, because my mind goes blank.

Jaeger is shirtless, his broad, muscled chest and shoulders lightly tanned, narrowing to an eight-pack above low-slung swim trunks. His legs aren't skinny like most tall guys, they're proportional and well muscled, just like the rest of him. Even the vertical scar down the middle of his knee appeals in a rugged way.

My heart hammers. Suddenly, it's hot as hell out here, though my hands are ice cold. I smooth out my towel and dust off the sand the football splattered on me.

Jaeger walks up and sits next to Mason, one arm on his knee. "Hey."

I smile. It's all I can manage. He smells like sunscreen and something so yummy... I'm trying not to let it show, but I'm literally sniffing out his scent. I have issues.

He grins playfully. "Been fishing lately?"

There are several ways to interpret that comment. Immediately, my dirty mind goes to innuendo. "No, you?"

He shakes his head and grabs the football Mason propped between his hand and the sand. Mason doesn't seem to mind, since all his attention is on Gen, who's telling him about the friends we're meeting here.

Jaeger looks over my shoulder to the barbecue section, and I do too. It's still early and no one's there yet. "Come on." He stands with the football under his arm, hand outstretched.

I reach for it and he pulls me up. "Where are we going?"

"To toss the football around."

Oh shit. *Shit, shit.* "Uhh, probably not the best idea. I'm not good at catch."

Or sports, but no need to give him the dirty details.

He glances over his shoulder, increasing the distance between us along an empty patch of beach. "I'll be gentle."

Why do I translate everything out of his mouth into something sexual? I need to stay away from this guy. He's messing with my head.

Jaeger throws me the ball and I lunge for it, though, of course, I miss. I pick it up and dust it off, then gamely throw it back the way I always throw a ball—like I'm launching a grenade. I can't help it. Gen has tried to show me how it's done, but I can't seem to get the hang of it.

My toss lands a dozen feet from Jaeger even though he ran for it. He picks it up and stares at it, then turns and walks toward Gen and Mason.

"Where are you going?" I call.

He doesn't answer. He keeps walking until he reaches Mason and firmly sets the ball beside him. Mason absently puts a hand on the football while he continues chatting with Gen.

Jaeger turns and stalks toward me.

Oh shit. "What?"

He nears me like a lion preparing to pounce. "You're not allowed to play catch. *Ever.*"

My heart thrums in my ears. "I just need a little practice," I say nervously, a combination of excitement and uncertainty bubbling inside.

He shakes his head. He's only a few feet from me now. "You need to be punished for that toss. It was pitiful."

My jaw drops, but instead of fearing the overgrown male stalking me, I'm turned on, and too curious to see what's he's going to do to care that it might not be right. I shutter my expression. "You are mean, you know that? *Umff—*"

Jaeger picks me up and throws me over his shoulder.

"*Hey!* What are you doing?" I quickly adjust my navy bikini top to keep my boobs contained.

"Dunking you. That's your punishment."

I scream like a little girl. "Stop! The lake's freaking cold! Please don't." But I'm giggling, and he's hot beneath my bare belly, and his arm is wrapped around the back of my thighs, making my skin tingle. My ass is bent in an unflattering position over his shoulder, flat and wide, and I don't even care because I'm laughing so hard. "Jaeger, I'm serious. I hate the cold."

"You grew up here—you can't hate the cold." The sand disappears below us, replaced by clear blue water.

Shit, he's deep enough now that my toes graze the freezing surface. "I do—I do—please stop," I say, but I'm smiling and I can hear it in my voice, so he must too.

He glides me down the front of his chest, my breasts pushing up between us. We're eye level, my legs submerged in ice-cold water to my knees, but I'm hot as hell. He's warm, and we're warm, and my breath hitches.

The corners of his mouth turn up. "What will you do to get out of your punishment?"

My gaze flickers from his forest-green eyes, downturned slightly at the edges, to his full lips. I want to kiss him. If I were single, I'd lean in and gently kiss the corner of his mouth, teasingly.

I glance back to his sensual eyes. They're darker and his smile has slipped, his chest rising and falling quicker.

I swallow. *Shit.* I have to stop this. "Please don't put me in the water."

He must read something on my face, because his brows pull together. He stares for a long moment, then bends over. For a split second, I think he's going to dunk me, but instead, he curls his arm beneath my knees and cradles me to his chest.

His mouth curves and he leans down and dips my feet in the water. I gasp, but he doesn't drop me—he carries me to shore.

Jaeger sets me on the sand. "You're safe. For now."

I don't know what just happened, but I think he sensed my hesitation and backed off. I'm glad of that, but at the same time, I'm not. I should tell him I have a boyfriend—if I still have a boyfriend; that's still up for debate—but he hasn't asked, or made an overt pass that would force the conversation. To say something now would be presumptuous.

We walk back to our friends. Gen's folding her towel, and I look past her to find that the barbecue pit is occupied. The people we're meeting must have shown up.

Jaeger's quiet as I grab my towel and start folding it up. He's got to know I'm attracted to him, but I can't tell if his flirting is merely a wingman maneuver to keep me occupied while Mason talks to Gen, or if he's seriously interested.

Mason looks over. "Cali, I was just telling Gen about the party we're having next weekend. You guys should come."

Gen glances up while putting away her things, and smiles. It's not a tight smile, flagging me to come up with some excuse. It's friendly and warm. Happy.

This could be a good opportunity for her and Mason to get to know each other. "Sure. I'd love to go," I say.

Gen grabs her beach bag and swings it over her shoulder. We say goodbye to the guys and make our way to the barbecue pits.

Halfway there, I glance back. Jaeger and Mason are jogging down the beach, passing the pretty brunette Jaeger was flirting with earlier. She's off to the side, smiling his way.

I don't know why I care. It's like some sick torture I'm putting myself through. I shouldn't be attracted to him, but I am—and I can't help feeling jealous over another girl who's able to flirt freely with him. Which makes me feel terrible, because no matter what's going on with Eric right now, I don't want to be that kind of girlfriend.

THE BARBECUE IS in full force, and I discover through conversations that a handful of Nessa's friends are from the local Washoe tribe. One of the guys, Zach, is even a dealer I recognize from work. I continue to chat with Gen's new friends, all the while keeping an eye on her over by the barbecue.

Why?

Because Lewis—the guy she had the spark with last night—is freaking hot as hell. And his girlfriend, Mira, is here with him. She's a bombshell with shiny, long dark brown hair, and she's been sending eyeball darts Gen's way for the past hour.

No joke, there could be a catfight. Gen's at the barbecue talking to my dealer buddy, and Lewis, who's six and a half feet of deliciousness—he might actually tower over Jaeger—walks up.

This is so much worse than Gen indicated. Lewis wants her and she has no idea.

Lewis has been playing it cool for the past hour, but he's been watching Gen when she's not looking. Not good.

I glance at Lewis's girlfriend. Oh yeah, Mira has her eye on them. Nothing gets by that chick. She's sipping her beer and standing very still, glancing at Lewis in between fake smiles with Nessa, who's chattering on about who knows what.

Tossing more chips on my plate at the picnic table, I mentally prepare to intervene if necessary.

Zach steps away and Lewis hands Gen a hot dog. He leans down and says something in her ear, touching her shoulder. Gen's chest rises, her body leaning toward him. I'm convinced I can see actual sparks.

Casino Real World has infiltrated the beach.

I glance at Mira. She's not even pretending to listen to Nessa anymore. Nessa's eyebrows pull together and she follows Mira's glare. Shit is about to go down.

Gen's frozen in place, her chest rising and falling too quickly. She glances up, her expression serious as she meets Lewis's eyes. They stand like that for a few seconds. Mira looks ready to wrestle Gen to the ground, and I'm a breath away from breaking up the eyeball sex Gen and Lewis are having, when Lewis's mouth kicks up at the side and he walks away.

Damn, and I thought *my* situation sucked.

Eyes wide and unblinking, Gen scans the area and sees me. She says something to Zach, who reappeared a second ago, and hightails it to my side.

"I have to leave. *Now.*"

"On it," I tell her.

We thank Nessa while Lewis sips his beer to the side, subtly watching Gen.

Oh, yeah. Gen definitely needs to stay away from this guy. She's no match for him. With high cheekbones, a straight nose, masculine full lips, and a smooth tan complexion, he's tall, dark, and delicious, and he wants her. No woman could fight that kind of attention.

Gen squeezes my hand and I glance over. Lewis has her in a staredown.

Damn, I wouldn't be able to look away either.

I haul her toward the car. When we're far enough away, I ask, "You okay?"

She nods, but she's staring straight ahead and not speaking.

"Gen, what the hell was that?"

"Something that has to stop." She takes a deep breath. "I won't make plans with Nessa next time unless I know he's not coming."

Chapter Seven

G EN AND I lie low over the next week. I run into Jaeger once at the casino while I'm working, and he reminds me about the party this weekend. I told him I thought we'd be there, but my first priority is to talk to Eric. I can't stand not knowing what's going on. Eric has avoided me for a month and I've had enough. I'm driving to my old college tonight, where he still lives, to talk to him.

It's Friday and I manage to get off early. Gen is letting me borrow her car overnight and I'm crashing at my friend Reese's place near Dawson University.

The drive down goes faster than I expected. That's what happens when you spend the entire time trying to figure out how to ask your boyfriend why he's avoiding you without sounding completely pathetic. I've decided it's impossible.

It's dark out, but all the lights are on at Reese's when I pull up.

Reese has a serious boyfriend, so I don't see her as often as I used to when we were freshmen, but we've remained close. Conveniently, she found a job on campus after graduation and still lives in town, while most of my friends have moved on to greener pastures.

I knock on the door to Reese's apartment, and she answers in black skinny jeans, heels, and a designer sequined top.

"Bow-chica-bow-wow," I singsong. "Going out?"

She drags me inside. "Yes, and you are too."

"Actually—" I stop her, standing in the middle of her simple living room, which consists of a plain, muted brown couch and armchair, and a television. It always amazes me that someone as fashionable as Reese lives in a home without flair, but her roommate is down to earth and Reese's aesthetic obsessions tend toward clothing and accessories. "—I was planning on finding Eric, then crashing early."

Reese's roommate Elena waves to me from the kitchen, her dark, wavy hair pulled into a messy bun on the top of her head. She's in flannel pajama bottoms and a ribbed tank top, stirring something that smells like beef stew in a large pot. My mouth waters. I wouldn't mind throwing on flannel PJs, forgetting this whole confronting Eric business, and joining her.

Reese studies my face. "What's going on? I figured when you asked to stay here instead of with Eric, something was up."

"To be honest, I don't know what's going on." Which means there's a strong possibility I'll be making a butter pecan run in the near future. After two years together, I'm pretty sure things are over between Eric and me. What other explanation could he have for four weeks of avoidance?

"Okay." Her eyes narrow. "So what's your plan?"

"Find him and figure it out?" *Then eat my weight in butter pecan?*

I'm pretty sure I know what Eric's going to say, but I still need to hear it. When your boyfriend doesn't call for a month, doesn't return your calls, and doesn't appear to care whether you breathe—what was that ingenious book title?—oh yeah, *He's Just Not That Into You*. There's no sense in pretending everything's okay, because it's not.

Reese drums her multicolored nails against her lips—*are*

those rhinestones on the tips? "What do you think about going to a bar?"

My upper lip curls. "Umm—"

"I only suggest it because I've seen Eric out a few times. Some of my coworkers have run into him at the bars too."

Okay, that's weird. I have no flippin' clue where Reese works on campus. She's vague about it. "Your coworkers know him?"

She waves her hand absently. "Never mind that. The point is, you might have better luck running him to ground at a bar."

And doesn't that just sound depressing? I have to hunt my boyfriend down to get him to dump me. "I guess that's as good a plan as any."

A sad smile crosses her face. "Let's try Big Billy's. It's the new hotspot on Friday nights." She scans my outfit. "Don't take this the wrong way, but… did you bring anything else to wear?"

I glance at the baggy jeans and T-shirt I threw on for the drive. "Are you trying to tell me I look like crap?"

"If things are as bad as I think they are between you and Eric, you should look hot. Make him see what he's missing."

Hot. Jaeger makes me feel hot, and desirable, but my boyfriend doesn't. Something's wrong with that picture. "Okay." My voice comes out shaky. When did I become this broken, pitiful thing?

"So, what did you pack?"

I pick at my T-shirt.

She shakes her head and grabs my wrist. "Come on, we'll raid my closet. My mom just sent a batch of new clothes from Rodeo Drive."

I forgot how rich Reese's Hollywood parents are. This should be interesting.

An hour later, I'm dressed in a black mini, a butterfly-style top, and five-inch heels, entering Big Billy's. My old college town is small, but you'd be surprised how dressed up people get. The clothes I'm wearing are mild compared to the short, sequined ensembles blinding me.

Reese and I squeeze through to the packed bar. We order Purple Hooters and beers, and Reese lifts her shot glass. "Cheers!"

I gulp down the grape-flavored concoction, and chase it with beer that tastes like piss. There's a special on tap and I'm trying to conserve money for graduate school.

It isn't long before Eric walks in. He's dressed in faded jeans and his favorite vintage 2006 World Cup T-shirt with an open short-sleeved button-down. He's surrounded by a group of friends.

I don't feel the urge to run and hug him, which is what I would normally do. Yes, he's been shitty and inattentive, to say the least. I'm not happy about that. I don't like the limbo our relationship has been in, but I've been telling myself that my attraction to Jaeger is because I haven't seen Eric. Well, I'm sitting here, staring at my boyfriend, and I don't feel anything stronger than fondness.

What the hell?

Without the bond of school connecting Eric and me, it's like there's no anchor and nothing is left. Was our relationship really that shallow?

Reese stares at me from across the booth. She glances from me to Eric, but doesn't say anything when I don't go to him. In the meantime, Eric approaches the bar with his friends and immediately turns to a leggy blonde in dressy shorts that ride up her crotch, while his friends wait for their orders.

Eric leans in and touches the girl's thigh. A sharp burn sears my gut. Eric's not here to help a friend hook up, he's flirting to score. He could have broken up with me at any point and moved on, if that was what he wanted. Instead, he dragged things out.

Suddenly, I'm not sure what we shared. I thought trust, at the very least, but this is bad. Is it worse than me flirting with Jaeger, though? I don't know. I question everything—my actions, Eric's actions—but after the effort I made to have this confrontation, the idea of walking up to Eric right now makes me want to hurl. I'd rather leave.

I don't.

Eric and his friends take a booth a few tables over. He's smiling at something one of his friends says as I approach. The friend sees me and elbows Eric in the arm. Eric lifts his head, the smile dying on his face.

My heart squeezes. Despite everything, I thought Eric cared for me. He seems shocked to see me, yes, but also annoyed. Like my presence has ruined his night, and that feels like shit.

This is not love or caring. I don't deserve whatever this is.

Eric slides out of the booth and grabs my wrist. "Let's talk outside."

He's walking too fast for me to keep up as we cross the bar. I yank my wrist from his hold and he glares at me as though I'm being a defiant child. The bouncer at the door stamps our hands and we exit Big Billy's.

Eric strides to a park bench at the far end of the block, as if he's afraid someone will see us. He sits and waits for me to do the same. "What's up?" The tone of his voice is curt.

"Seriously, Eric? I should ask you that question."

He lets out a tense sigh, leans on his knees, and drops his

head in his hands. "I'm sorry. I know I've been a jerk, not calling and all. It's just—I meant to say something when I visited you in Tahoe... Fuck, Cali." He looks up. "I chickened out."

Does he think our relationship will fade into the ether like some fog, as long as he avoids me? Son of a bitch. I'm not leaving until he says it. "Well, I'm here. Spit it out, Eric."

"I—I want to break up."

"No shit?" I go heavy on the sarcasm, because what the fuck? Any sort of confession the weekend he spent in Lake Tahoe would have been better than dragging things out for as long as he did. "And you thought avoiding me would be better than just saying so? A word of advice, Eric. Give the girl you're dating a little respect and break up with her *before* you move on."

"I haven't," he says quickly. "Moved on. Not really. I want to, though." He looks down and sighs heavily. "Look, Cali, you're leaving, and I'll find a job and all, but you're going to Harvard to become a lawyer. We're just... different. I can't see us together."

All of a sudden, memories like missiles blast through my gray matter. Eric getting trashed and leaving me at a bar to find my way home. Eric, more times than I can count, putting his friends ahead of spending time with me. Eric never introducing me to his family. Why didn't he introduce me to his family? There were always reasons to excuse his behavior—my friend would give me a ride home, or I had to study and couldn't hang out anyway—but I was so focused and confident I never saw the truth.

Eric was a shitty boyfriend.

He and I shared good times, and he had his sweet moments,

but this is some serious stuff I blocked, because of what? Arrogance? I was so confident I could make it work that I settled for a relationship, which, in actuality, kind of sucked. And it only took distance and an attractive ghost from my past to realize it.

Holy shit. What have I been doing? "Goodbye, Eric." I start to walk away.

"Wait. I—we can still be friends."

I don't know how to read the expression on his face. It's not hopeful—more like resigned, as though he doesn't want to be labeled the bad guy.

"I don't think so." A part of me hurts at the idea of never seeing or talking to Eric again, but I can't be his friend. First of all, he's a crappy friend, considering how he broke up with me, and thinking back to some of the things he's done. Second, I need distance from him and what I realize now was not a good relationship.

Eric's jaw drops slightly, but he makes no move to stop me as I head for the bar. Reese is waiting with another Purple Hooter. I don't feel like drinking, but I down the shot, because she got it to cheer me up. She doesn't ask me what happened, but the look in her eyes says she already knows.

Eric and his friends leave promptly after he returns to the bar. I stay as long as I can without making it obvious I don't want to be there, which lasts about twenty minutes.

Reese's blond Viking boyfriend gives us a ride home, and after watching trashy TV for a couple of hours with Reese and her roommate, the snot and tears and choking hiccups come after they go to bed. I silently cry myself to sleep alone on their couch, because regardless of how well I've done in school, I feel like I've been living the rest of my life with blinders on.

Chapter Eight

THE RETURN TRIP to Tahoe is therapeutic. I cry until I'm dehydrated. I haven't decided if I'm weeping over how humiliating last night was, or the end of a relationship. A bit of both, I think.

With a stop at a small sandwich shop in Placerville, I splash water on my face. My turkey club is soggy and tastes like cardboard, my drink like sugar water, but I chew and swallow and get back into the car. Before turning on the ignition, I call Gen.

"There you are," she says. "How did it go?"

"He dumped me." My voice comes out strong, but there's a slight quiver.

Eric and I needed to break up, but I still care about him. Now that it's over, I know I'll miss him. Not in an *I'm in love* kind of way, but in a *this is the guy I spent the last two years with* way.

A moment of silence passes. "Cali—I—wow. I'm sorry. I know that's what people say to make other people feel better— I've heard it enough times these past few months—but in this case it's the truth. He didn't deserve you."

"I know. Now."

She lets out a soft sigh. "Where are you? I could find someone to take me—"

"I'm fine. Just leaving Placerville."

"Okay." Her voice sounds hesitant, and then, "Oh, no."

"What?"

"We told Jaeger and Mason we'd go to the party tonight. But don't worry. I'll text Mason and tell him we can't make it."

The part of me that hurts from rejection—which makes no sense, I wanted things over in the end as much as Eric did, but there it is—wants to crawl into bed and wallow. The other part, the part of me that has encouraged Gen to get back out there after her breakup, insists we go to this party. "No, we'll go."

"Really? Are you sure?"

"It'll be good for us."

"Don't do this for me. I'm fine."

"I want to. I need to get out." Out of my head—away from the self-pity.

THE STEPS UP to Mason's townhouse are located just down from the Heavenly Ski Resort. Dark, abandoned lift chairs glint in the moonlight, voices and music from the party carrying in the evening air.

Gen knocks on the front door and steps back, waiting. She's wearing jeans and platform sandals. I'm in non-ass-cheek-baring dressy shorts, flats, and a light, fitted sweater.

A minute passes and no one answers, but we can hear the people inside. I shrug. "Try opening it."

She twists the knob and the door swings wide on oiled hinges. The sound of music and talking elevates to ear-blasting proportions. Bodies are everywhere.

I scan until I see Jaeger's head above all the rest. He's in the middle of the room, talking animatedly.

That's weird. He's usually pretty subdued.

Warmth spreads along my limbs at the sight of him, and this time, I don't need to feel guilty about it. Arms linked, heads slightly bowed, Gen and I merge with the crowd, charging through like a pair of mini-linebackers.

Jaeger glances up. A broad smile sweeps his face, sending my heart into hyperdrive. Within seconds, he's by my side, dragging me to his solid chest and draping an arm over Gen's shoulders. "Ladies! You made it."

This is where I want to be. Attraction aside, there's something about Jaeger that's so comforting and natural, it's like I should have been here all along.

Jaeger settles us under each of his muscled arms and guides us toward the kitchen, illuminated like a beacon within the mood-darkened apartment. He heads to the keg and pours out two beers, then nods to a corner in the dining area where his friends are located. The crowd parts for him as he walks over, Gen and I tucked close behind.

Mason's hair and clothes are rumpled, as if it's been a rough night. Adam stands beside Breanna, but she doesn't look happy. It could have something to do with the fact that Adam is chatting up the girl next to him.

God, I'm sick of shitty boyfriends.

Mason spots Gen and his slightly glassy eyes light up. "You made it!" He grabs her waist and gives her a tight hug, taking a deliberate step back to run his gaze down her body. "And you look really pretty."

A flush spreads over Gen's cheeks.

Nothing like Gen flustered over male attention to put a smile on my face.

Mason steps closer and drapes an arm over her shoulders. Oh, yeah, he wants her. Not that I doubted it, but with Mason in what I presume to be a drunken state, it's obvious.

Gen subtly leans away, which is baffling. Mason's a little tipsy, but he's hot and sweet. She should be all over that.

I nudge her closer, just to be annoying.

She reaches back and pinches the thin skin on my forearm. It hurts like a bitch. I should never underestimate Gen in a test of physical prowess. The girl may be all that is elegance and poise, but she has her scrappy moments.

Point taken. Cali's matchmaking operation is shut down. I've proven I'm a poor judge of mates.

I glance at Jaeger, who is still inexplicably animated this evening. He's actually doing the talking in a conversation with Adam. No matter what mistakes I made in choosing Eric, there's no question that Jaeger is a good guy. And to confuse the situation even more, I don't think Eric is a bad guy either. He just wasn't a good guy with me. Which means good guys can be bad guys with the wrong girl…

My brain hurts. I'll take a partial differential equation any day over this shit.

Maybe I should give up the whole dating thing for a while. Take a vacation from it. Focus on the future. Law school…

Okay, maybe just the immediate future, not the post-immediate future I'm not ready for.

A sharp heel punctures my musings and my ballet flats, breaking the skin on the top of my foot. My gag reflexes activate. *Mothereffer!*

Before I can even hop on one leg and attempt recovery, I'm knocked to the side by a bony hip as the wielder of the heel, wearing a cellophaned-on dress, latches on to Jaeger.

"We're taking shots. Join us," says the girl with… crap, I'm not even sure what color her hair is. It's sort of striped—brown?

68

blond?—it's nearly impossible to tell. She yanks Jaeger away.

Jaeger hesitantly follows, glancing back without making eye contact.

I sip my beer, fighting the urge to throw my cup at the girl's head. She's all over him, and I hate it.

I hate it that I hate it.

Breanna and I talk for at least an hour, and I'm so proud of myself. I don't look for Jaeger once. This is a massive accomplishment, because I'm obsessively glancing every few minutes at my iPhone to keep my subconscious occupied. However, in my colossal effort to keep from looking for Jaeger, I've lost Gen.

I remove my visual blinders in order to make sure my best friend hasn't been roofied. I spot her a few feet away in a corner, loomed over by a medium-sized guy with a black jacket and too much hair product. Gen in platforms is over six feet tall, so she must seriously be leaning away from this guy to be nearly hidden.

The place is crowded and I'm trying to determine the most efficient way to reach her when I spot Mason. He's facing me and I wave for his attention. Amazingly, in all this chaos, he sees me and smiles. I gesture to Gen with a distressed look on my face.

Mason glances over and frowns. He immediately navigates his way through the crowd, slapping a large palm on the guy's back. He pulls Gen out of the corner to his side. Casual words are exchanged between Mason and the unnamed male, then Gen and Mason walk off.

I catch Mason's eye and give him a thumbs-up. He nods in recognition, but instead of bringing her over, he walks Gen across the room and up a flight of stairs. Gen doesn't seem distressed. She's grinning, and not a fake grin. This one's genuine. I assume she's okay and return to my conversation.

Several more minutes pass as I listen to Breanna complain about Adam's flirting with other women before I decide it's time to check on Gen. "Breanna, watch my cup?" I hand her the beer I've barely touched. "I want to find out where Gen went."

"Yeah, no problem." She looks around, confused. "I didn't see her leave."

"I think she's with Mason, but I want to make sure."

Breanna's mouth twists. "And interrupt? If she's with Mason, they might be…"

Gen is the last person to have casual sex with a guy at a party. I'm a hundred percent certain I won't interrupt anything like that, but there's a wide range in between. I hate to ruin Mason's moves, but I'm not in the mood to trust anyone right now.

"I'll cover my eyes before I walk through any doors."

Breanna laughs. As we part, she turns to say something to Adam a couple of feet away, but he's talking to a different girl this time. Breanna spins in the opposite direction and slams back her drink.

I do not see that relationship lasting. And I wouldn't blame Breanna if she were the one to end it.

I round a corner at the top of the stairs and a hand reaches out, pulling me inside one of the bedrooms. "*Gahhh!*"

"It's me." Jaeger chuckles in my ear.

Nice. He thinks this is funny? He almost stopped my heart with that maneuver.

"What are you doing?" I punch him in the stomach, which only bruises my knuckles.

He looks down and shrugs it off, as if I patted him on the belly like a good boy. He guides me into the room by the shoulders. It's small—a second bedroom that seems to serve as an office, with a couch against the wall.

Before I know what's happening, Jaeger plasters me to his chest and falls backward onto the couch.

I'm sprawled on top of him, legs sliding off his waist in an inelegant partial straddle. He lies there with a goofy grin on his face, his arms loosely draped over my back.

I could get up if I wanted to, but I don't. "Well, this is"—I glance pointedly at my position atop him—"interesting."

He squeezes me lightly.

Jaeger is enormous compared to most guys, but I've never felt afraid with him. In fact, lying on top of his warm, utterly masculine body is amazing, and oddly comforting.

I study the unguarded look in his eyes. He's not as rumpled as Mason, but, by my estimate, he's three sheets to the wind. "How many beers does it take to topple a giant?"

Jaeger squints and raises one hand. His fingers flick as if he's counting. After an absurdly long time, in which I yawn and examine my nails while lying on my hot man-chaise, he finally says, "Twelve? No, fourteen—we downed two this morning."

"Fourteen! How are you even conscious?" I press my fingers to his neck, pretending to check for a pulse.

His baseball-glove-sized paw captures my hand and flattens it against his chest, his eyes closing contentedly. After a second of hesitation, I lay my head below his chin and consider how strange this moment is. I'm on Jaeger, in a loverlike pose, only he's *my friend*. And yet this is the only place I want to be. I won't analyze that thought too closely.

After a minute, Jaeger's breathing changes.

What the... He did not just fall asleep. We may be friends, but I'm still *a woman*, and, I like to think, fairly attractive.

I squirm a little to test my theory.

He doesn't move. A light purr emanates from his throat, growing deep and steady.

Goddammit, he fell asleep!

Great. Just great. What does it say when a guy passes out with a girl plastered on top of him? The hits to my ego just keep on coming.

I press one ear to his wide chest, listening to him breathe. After a while, it grows creepy—on my part, not his—so I roll off my man-chaise and stand, collecting the remains of my dignity. I wouldn't mind cuddling longer, but in Jaeger's unconscious state, that would make it weird.

After exiting the room quietly on a frustrated sigh, I close the door behind me. This party was just getting fun, hanging out alone with Jaeger.

Down the hall another door opens. Gen walks out, followed by Mason. She sees me and relief washes over her face.

What did Mason do? I spear him with a glare. He nods with barely a glance at me, and continues down the hall and around the corner.

"Are you okay?" I ask Gen.

"Yeah." Her face is calm, so I relax a little. She glances after Mason. "I'll explain in the car."

And she does. It turns out the party was a bust all around.

Mason tried to kiss Gen in his bedroom and she dodged it. I tried to cuddle with Jaeger and he passed out. No one got lucky tonight. Not my goal, but still.

My brilliant plan to help Gen is in a shambles and my own relationship drama battles hers for biggest disaster.

Chapter Nine

"YO, SIS, WHAT'S up? I was just thinking about you."

My slightly overprotective brother, Tyler, is a slob, but he's a good brother and I could really use his company. I rang him up, hoping he'd be up for a stay while he isn't working.

"What do you think about coming out to Tahoe?" I say over the phone.

Tyler is a community college teacher with summers off, so he's available. As long as I don't tell him about Eric—he hates my ex—having Tyler around will help take my mind off things. There's a small voice in the back of my head that wants to pump Tyler for information about his old high school buddy Jaeger, but I'm ignoring it.

He chuckles into the line. "Funny you should ask, because I'm here."

"What? Where?"

"With Mom. Came out to see her new digs."

My mom just bought her first house, in Carson City. She's rented her entire life, so this is huge.

"You should check it out," he says. "It's not much, but she's proud. It would mean a lot if you came."

Jesus, as hard as my mom worked at the casinos to put Tyler and me through college, *I'm* proud. She only recently relocated to Carson. She's got a stable job with benefits there. It pays less than what she made in Tahoe, but Carson City has lower living costs. "I will, I promise. I've been getting settled with my job and all, but I'll come out as soon as I can."

"Well, don't take too long, or you'll be leaving again."

For grad school. How could I forget?

"So, what do you think?" he asks.

"About what?" Tyler doesn't know about my reservations over school. I'm avoiding thinking about them, but they're fixed in my subconscious.

"Dude, what's up with you? About me driving out."

Oh right. "Tyler, I called you, remember? I already said I want you to visit."

"Cool. I'll be there in a couple of hours. Everything okay?"

I wouldn't call my brother the most perceptive male, but he can be at inopportune times. "Yeah, fine."

And it will be. Now that things are officially over with Eric, I'll eventually move on. It's everything else that has me screwed up. The reason I couldn't see how bad my relationship with Eric was. My reservations over grad school. At some point I'll have to address these issues. Just not now.

Two hours later, Tyler walks in the door and drops his duffel on the dark brown wall-to-wall carpet of our rental house. We picked this place for its proximity to the lake, but it's the size of a dog kennel and the furnishings look like something from a seventies sitcom.

Tyler lifts his brows warily. "Where do you want me?" He peeks inside the single bedroom. "I don't mind spooning with Gen, but you snore."

"I do not snore!" I punch him in the arm and he grins. "You can sleep in the loft," I tell him.

We both tip our heads back to view the alcove above the

kitchen.

Gen and I have a single bedroom, but there's a small loft above the kitchen with a sketchy pull-down ladder. Neither Gen nor I wanted to risk our lives to go to the bathroom in the middle of the night, so we share the queen downstairs.

"Leave your stuff here; there's not much space up there."

His gaze is dubious. "Is there a bed?"

"There's a full mattress on the floor. You'll be fine."

Tyler digs into his duffel, already spilling shit across our living room floor.

"Tyler, our place is small. Rein in the clutter."

He bites into the PowerBar he unearthed from his crusty bag and scratches his flat belly. "Can't. Not my nature."

This argument's a losing battle. He's totally right and sometimes I wonder how he manages to attract as many women as he does. Physically, I suppose he's good-looking. His hair is wavy and a little longish and hipster, especially when paired with his dark reading glasses. I'm not going to call the color *red*, because he'd kill me and it's not totally accurate. Let's call it *chestnut*—a medium brown with red highlights. Lots of red highlights. Neither of us are carrot tops like our mother. I am forever grateful for our father's plain brown hair.

Tyler and I both have pale blue eyes, and that's probably our most redeeming physical quality. I often get complimented for mine by the opposite sex. I assume he does too. Add to that a six-foot-two athletic build, and I suppose some women might find him attractive, if you look past his slovenly ways, flash temper, and myriad other annoying habits I've had to live with all my life.

As a brother, though, he's protective, funny, and loyal, and I'm really happy he's here.

OVER THE NEXT couple of days, Tyler and I hit our favorite food spots and he visits me at the casino. He brought his mountain bike, so when I'm sleeping in the a.m. after working late, he entertains himself on the trails with a buddy who still lives in town.

Having Tyler around has been good for my morale. He keeps me distracted, and he has no patience for mopers. He's highly vocal about it too, usually in the form of an insult that pisses me off and snaps me from my depression.

The weekend's almost here and I'm working tonight, but Tyler has dropped in for a visit. He's gambling at my table and I'm kicking his ass, which is sweet music because he always beat me at cards growing up.

"Damn, Cali, when did you become a shark?"

I'm trying to act professional, but I can't help shooting Tyler a smug look when my customers aren't looking. I have three decks in my dispenser, which reduces a player's ability to make predictions. Tyler counted cards when we were kids, but three decks is a lot, even for him.

Despite my best intentions not to, I've obsessed over asking Tyler about Jaeger. I don't want to give my brother the wrong impression. Knowing him, he'd assume I had a thing for his buddy and get all overprotective. But it's been long enough since Tyler arrived that I think it's safe to venture onto the subject.

My last customer saunters off and I deal Tyler another hand, ever-so-casually saying, "So, I think I ran into one of your friends from high school. Do you remember that athlete, Jaeger?"

"Who? You mean Jaeg?"

Jaeg. That's why his name was familiar, but not. He went by a nickname in high school. "Yeah, isn't he the one you said was going to the Olympics?"

"For skiing. Of course I remember him—he was one of my best friends. But he's not going to the Olympics—or he didn't go." Tyler swipes his hand for a hit, and then hits again after I deal the card. He busts with a king, a three, and a nine. "Shattered his knee. Dropped off after that."

So that's how Jaeger's sports career ended. I saw the scar on his knee at the beach, but was too busy appreciating his body in swim trunks to think anything except that the scar looked rugged and manly. Athletes are intense about their sports. Olympic athletes border on obsessive. It had to have been difficult for Jaeger to start over. My brother is by no means a champion athlete, but even he gets aggro when it comes to training on his bike.

Jaeger's new wood-whittling profession should reduce his appeal, but for some reason it doesn't. I'm not sure if it's the effort it must have taken to reinvent himself that appeals, or if it's just him, in whatever form, that I'm attracted to. And that scares me. It's too soon for me to pursue someone else.

"What's Jaeg up to?" my brother asks. "I've lost touch with him over the years."

"His friend works here." I point to Mason at the East Bar. "Gen and I have hung out with them a couple of times."

Tyler pockets his remaining chips and stands, glancing at Mason's bar. Only a couple of customers hover in front of Mason and the other bartender at the moment. "I'll go talk to your friend and ask about Jaeg. Maybe we can get together before I go home."

The idea of me, Tyler, and Jaeger in the same room is unnerving. I'm hoping Tyler's plans with Jaeger do not include me. The last thing I want is for Tyler to pick up on my attraction to his friend and give me a hard time about it.

Tyler sidles up to my table a little while later, but I'm busy and can't talk. It's not until the next day that he brings up his conversation with Mason.

He pulls milk out of the fridge and drinks from the carton like the animal he is, while I paint my toes on the kitchen floor a couple of feet away. "What's on the docket for tonight?"

He shoves the milk back on the shelf—mental note: *Throw out carton with Tyler germs*—and drums his fingers on the counter. The high energy he's exuding leads me to believe he has something in mind.

I carefully rub a pink splotch off the tip of my big toe with a paper towel. "Nothing. Why?"

"Your friend Mason gave me Jaeger's number. I got a hold of him and he invited us to his parents' place for dinner tonight."

I mentally gasp. I'm not ready to see Jaeger. My newfound freedom might propel me to do something stupid, like attack him for hot rebound sex. "Umm—"

It's possible that the attraction I've felt for him stems from my frustration with Eric. That I was grasping for attention and Jaeger was the closest good-looking guy available. There's also the possibility that Jaeger paid me attention to give Mason time to chat up Gen. He and I were paired together in the fishing boat so Gen and Mason could be alone. And later, Jaeger hauled me off at the party, I presume, so that Mason could make his move.

Or there's the possibility that this thing between Jaeger and me is real. And that's what really scares me. I don't want to get hurt again, and crappy relationship or not, Eric's betrayal hurt me.

"What's wrong? I thought you became friends with Jaeger this summer?"

"I did," I say, hesitantly.

Tyler rubs his forehead and looks around. "We don't have to go. I'd like to see him, but I'm here to visit you."

Tyler leaves tomorrow. Today's the only day he has left to visit Jaeger. They were tight growing up. I can't in good conscience say no. "You should go, Tyler. You don't need me there."

"He invited everyone, and his mom's cooking her best dish. Just come, Cali. And bring Gen. It'll be fun. His parents and sister are great."

There's no logical excuse I can give not to go after that declaration. Maybe this will work out. "Okay. I've been trying to set Gen up with Jaeger anyway," I say absently.

My stomach goes sour at the thought of Jaeger and Gen together. Now that Mason is a no-go after Gen refused his kiss, Jaeger is the only person left on the list of prospects. I never should have starting that stupid list. Why did I think she and Jaeger would be good for each other?

I don't want to rebound with Jaeger. I like him too much. Which is also why I'm not eager to set Gen up with him.

Tyler squints. "You're setting those two up? Really?"

I glare. "What's wrong with my best friend?"

"Nothing. She's fucking hot."

Sometimes it's difficult to believe my brother is a role model to undergrads. He's a hundred percent adult when it comes to his students. I'm not even sure he notices the pretty girls who plant themselves in the front rows of his lectures. It's like he shuts off his guy brain while at work. But get him home, and he's as immature and horny as any twenty-three-year-old.

Tyler's mouth twists as if he's attempting to reach some deep philosophical conclusion, which, for his analytical mind, is probably a challenge. "It's just… well, I guess I can't see them together. They're both reserved, you know? Aren't opposites supposed to attract?"

His assertion pleases me, and now I'm a terrible friend. But it makes me physically sick to consider Jaeger and Gen in a relationship. I've gotta scrap that idea.

I had everything figured out—life, love. It turns out I suck at relationships and my plans for grad school might be my worst decision yet.

"You might be right. Just don't discourage her from dating. Gen's had a rough few months and she's only now coming out of it."

He holds up his hands. "I want nothing to do with this." He points at me. "And you should mind your own business. Let Jaeger find his own woman. He doesn't need you meddling."

But what if he chooses the wrong girl? And what if she gives in because she's messed up in the head and on the rebound?

Chapter Ten

YEARS AGO, I visited Jaeger's parents' house when my mom asked me to run up and grab Tyler for a soccer game. I waited in the entry while Tyler changed into his uniform. As I recall, his parents were warm and friendly, with awesome Austrian accents. Jaeger and his sister have American accents, but they were born in the U.S., or moved here shortly after—I'm not entirely clear on the details.

Tyler does the honors and knocks on the large, elaborately carved wooden door while Gen and I wait patiently beside him. I lean closer, taking in the subtle design in front of us. A landscape of mountains juts toward the sky, with streams, and birds, and all manner of wildlife. The door flies open and I flinch, my nose too close to the surface.

Mrs. Lang ushers us inside and doesn't appear surprised at the fact that I nearly fell into her home. She must be used to strangers gaping at her front door.

She grabs my brother in a bear hug. "Tyler, so good to see you!" This actually comes out, *Tylar-r, zo goot to see yu!* with her Austrian accent. "And Cali, such a beautiful, grown-up woman." She hugs me too.

I introduce Jaeger's mother to Gen and we enter the cavernous living room with its massive windows overlooking a breathtaking view of the lake. I vaguely remember the floor plan of the first level, but the furniture has been updated with plush leather couches, cream woven throw pillows, and blankets in Native American zigzag patterns.

A beautiful girl with long blond hair rises from a barstool at the island separating the living room from the kitchen. "Tyler, Cali, you remember Jaeger's sister, Kerstin?" Mrs. Lang asks.

I don't, but my brother does. He's grinning like a boy with a bag of candy. Beautiful blondes, beautiful brunettes—he's pretty equal opportunity. *Beautiful* being the main criterion.

Behind Kerstin, on the other side of the island, Jaeger opens a sliding door, entering the room in front of a tall, handsome older man with light, wavy brown hair peppered with white.

Deep in conversation, neither man notices us. Words like *crushed granite, compaction*, and *interlocking pavers* fly from their lips as they dust off their feet on a mat. Jaeger glances up, catches his sister standing, and scans the room. His gaze lands on me, and his mouth twitches.

He walks over to my brother and they greet each other with a manly, backslapping hug, the force of which would have knocked me over. Introductions are made for Gen, and all of a sudden I get shy. Which isn't like me. But this is the first time I've seen Jaeger since my breakup with Eric. The party doesn't count, because he was so drunk I'm not even sure he remembers pulling me into the bedroom and falling asleep with me on top of him—a humiliation from which my ego shall never recover.

The group of us chats for a bit and it's not long before Jaeger's mom announces dinner. She made beef stroganoff and we eat it family style around a large trestle table made of what looks like reclaimed wood planks. The food is delicious, and Jaeger's parents and Gen, of all people, keep the conversation going.

Gen and I have flip-flopped. Tonight she's the talkative one, while I'm quiet. Or maybe she can tell I'm uncomfortable and she is doing her best to make up for my conversational ineptitude.

"What made you decide to move to the States?" Gen asks Mr. Lang.

He dabs the corner of his mouth with a cloth napkin. "We own a family business that specializes in soft plastics. Two of our factories are located in California. I work from home, but travel often to the factories. We liked California and decided to move here when Jaeger was a baby so that I'd have more time with the family."

A plastics empire. Explains the enormous home on the lake. The timetable accounts for why neither Jaeger nor his sister has an Austrian accent.

"Lake Tahoe provided an excellent training location for Jaeger when he was competing," Mr. Lang continues. "My wife and I were very happy with our decision to move."

The dishes are soon whisked away and Jaeger's parents disappear downstairs, while Gen, Tyler, Jaeger, Kerstin, and I sit around the table with a bottle of expensive wine. Mrs. Lang also left a batch of apple strudel, which Tyler and Jaeger are inhaling.

With his parents gone and Jaeger sitting across from me, I can't help glancing over. He looks up at the same time I do and smiles. I return the smile, but his brows crease together, eyes scanning my face.

He stretches his arm across the table and tugs the sleeve at my wrist. "What's wrong?"

I plaster another smile on my face more fake than the last. I shake my head. I may be loud and outspoken, but it comes from genuine conviction. I'm no good at lying, even when my best interests are at stake.

From the moment Jaeger walked into the room with his dad, electric zingers have been shooting through every cell in my body at strategic moments. During chance eye contact—Jaeger tugging my sleeve—it doesn't take much. It's like he's the plug and my body is the electrical receptacle. And isn't that a raunchy yet accurate analogy.

I don't want this. The timing is off. I'm not ready for anything serious. And for some reason, I get the sense that a casual hookup with Jaeger would destroy me in a way the breakup with Eric didn't come close to doing.

Jaeger continues to stare, the puzzled expression shifting to mild worry. I look down at the table, avoiding his eyes.

"Remember when you tried to grow sideburns, Tyler?" Kerstin says. "All you managed were patchy blotches." She beams and my brother frowns.

I like this girl. Kerstin must have spent time with Jaeger and my brother in high school if she remembers Tyler's facial hair misadventures.

"He was so determined, he let them grow to his jaw line," Kerstin continues to Gen, "convinced that the added surface area would thicken his burns." Kerstin snickers and I do too.

That shit was funny as hell. Tyler looked like a patchy Chewbacca for a month. The best part is, Tyler's facial hair grows bright red. But even that didn't deter him.

As funny as this conversation is, I can't sit while I sense Jaeger's knowing eyes on me. I rise and walk a few feet to the large windows overlooking the lake.

Nothing interrupts the electric vibe between us tonight—not other relationships, not alcohol. What I'm feeling is pure and real. He's even in tune with my conflicted emotions, and that can't be good. The invitation to see if something could happen between us beckons, but I can't give in to it. Jaeger is a temptation I'm not ready for.

"What's wrong with her?" my brother mumbles to Gen.

Bugger, no! I swing around, but before I can send Gen the evil eye and warn her to keep her mouth shut, the new, more outgoing Gen speaks.

"Her boyfriend broke up with her," she says under her breath, though everyone hears. I can hear and I'm a few feet away. "How do you expect her to act?"

"*What?*" Tyler says loudly, eyes flashing to me. "Is that true?"

Kerstin sits straighter and glances hesitantly at me. Gen has her mouth open, frozen in place, as if realizing her mistake.

I instinctively glance at Jaeger, praying he wasn't paying attention, but he's holding a forkful of apple strudel near his mouth and staring at the table. His gaze slowly moves to mine and his eyes darken. He sets down the fork, jaw flexing.

"Tyler," I say quietly. "We'll talk about it later."

Tyler balls his hand into a fist on the table, his eyes narrowed. "I hate that dipshit."

Excellent. Perfect time to hash this out. Thank you, Tyler. I will kill you when we get home, along with Gen.

"You're not getting back together with him, Cali," Tyler declares.

I let out a long-suffering sigh and look to the ceiling. "Genevieve, whatever happened to best friend confidentiality?"

Gen covers her mouth, grimacing. "I'm so sorry, Cali," she mumbles through her fingers. She drops her hands helplessly. "I thought he knew."

Jaeger looks off into the distance, his mouth tense. I never told him I had a boyfriend. Why didn't I tell him? A million logical reasons kept me from mentioning it before, but nothing comes to mind now. I feel like I've betrayed him, and that's the last thing I want to do. I know firsthand how it feels.

Jesus. I'm no better than Eric. If Jaeger and I are friends, which we are, my relationship status should have come up. Now it's too late.

Jaeger stands and busses the last dishes from the table. He offers more wine to everyone, his gaze barely touching me.

Tyler, Gen, and I leave shortly after the last drop of wine disappears, and I want to throw myself into the lake. Getting dumped by Eric was humiliating, sad, and enlightening in a painful, growing-up sort of way. Our relationship was shallow. I realize that now.

But tonight—the betrayal on Jaeger's face? I'm devastated.

What have I done?

Chapter Eleven

THE CASINO IS packed tonight. So packed, I'm having a hard time keeping track of *employee relations*. And dammit, I need the distraction of Casino Real World to keep my mind off my personal drama.

The waitress and her cashier lover have called it quits, considering the glacial looks she's casting him, but the two cocktail waitresses, who caress each other at every opportunity when they think no one's looking, are going strong.

Personally, I don't understand it. Not the gay part—who cares about that? But why the heck would you feel up your lover in front of the black surveillance half-moons covering nearly every inch of the casino ceiling? At least the cashier and the waitress were discreet about their relationship. The other two tongued each other in front of the lounge bartender tonight. I could have done without that visual.

The casino's primary focus is money, and making certain it doesn't flow out faster than it flows in, but you've gotta be stupid to think the execs aren't watching the employees. And call me prudish, but I sort of think foreplay on the job is inappropriate.

It's almost the end of my shift and the casino has slowed to a smooth wave of customers. A group of college-aged guys slips past my table. They look familiar. One of them stops in the middle of the aisle that separates my pit from the lounge where

Gen works. His friends follow his gaze and slap him on the back. They walk off to the roulette table, while he saunters up the steps.

No. No, no, no. *Not the A-hole.* I glance around frantically, searching for someone, anyone to help. I just took a break and can't leave my table for another hour, unless I feign illness, which I'm strongly considering.

Gen and Mason haven't been as friendly since the party, but I don't sense animosity from him. At least, I hope his pride isn't too bruised he wouldn't help Gen out. But he's slammed with customers, and flipping liquor bottles like a circus performer. My gaze catches on one of his customers, because the guy literally stands out from the rest. I can't see his face, but I'd know him from any angle. That's how aware I am of Jaeger.

Jaeger glances up as if he senses me and nods, the gesture stiff. Before he turns away, I wave him over. His brow quirks sardonically, an uncharacteristically brassy response, but he grabs his drink and saunters toward my table.

I shuffle three new decks and one of my customers leaves. Sometimes they do that, as if the new cards will break their streak.

Jaeger's standing to my left. Even if I couldn't see him from the corner of my eye, I'd know he was there. The air shifts when he's around.

"I need a favor," I say. I glance at the lounge. Gen's ex has her cornered and she doesn't look happy. "Will you go up to Gen and pretend you're her boyfriend? Be obvious about it so she knows you're there to help."

"You want me to be Gen's boyfriend." Jaeger's tone is low, laced with warning.

I glance up, startled. *What?* No, I don't want him to be her boyfriend!

"Look, I can't explain it right now, but that guy she's with is a creep. I'd rescue her if I could, but as you can see"—I sweep my hand in front of my customers—"I'm a little busy."

Jaeger stares at me, his masculine fingers dwarfing the cup in his hand, the tips white as if he's a second away from breaking the glass. "What do you suggest?"

I deal out a new hand. "I don't know... just... ah—" It's not easy to multitask with my best friend's traumatic encounter unfolding.

"Grab her ass," my balding customer in dark sunglasses says. He sniggers. "He'll get the message." His skin is shiny with sweat, the ice-cold air conditioning no match for his girth.

I glare at him and glance back at Jaeger. "I don't think *that's* necessary. Just treat her like you would a girl you're dating."

"Give her a sweet kiss," chimes the elderly woman in high-waisted grandma jeans and a bright orange cardigan.

Holy hell, these people are killing me!

Jaeger slams back his drink and thumps it so hard on the felt I wince. Mouth compressed, he spins and strides toward Gen.

Heat rushes up my neck. *Shit.* He won't... he wouldn't...

Jaeger closes in on Gen and her ex-boyfriend. Relief flashes across her eyes, swiftly replaced by uncertainty. Without breaking stride, Jaeger wraps his arms around her waist from behind, leans down, and tucks his face against her neck.

I inhale sharply, feeling a stab of jealousy so intense I can't breathe. My eyes burn and my palms tingle where they're clenched. He's doing this because I asked him to—and it hurts like nothing before.

I was right. Losing Eric was nothing compared to what it would be like to lose Jaeger. This is fire and rage and sheer misery, and I want it to stop.

Gen's ex steps back, gaping. He shifts his feet and seems to be saying something to Gen, but she's not paying attention. Her head's tilted back with a smile as Jaeger nuzzles her neck, whispering something into her ear. She nods.

Son of a bitch!

"Oh, that'll convince the boy she's taken," says the woman with the orange cardi. "Good for him!" She smacks the table, rattling the chips.

"Hey—" I snap my fingers at both my customers. "Pay attention, people!" I glare at Mr. Sweaty Sunglasses. "Hit or stay?"

What is wrong with me? I just asked the guy I'm infatuated with, who's still mad I didn't tell him I had a boyfriend, to feel up my best friend? It wouldn't be Gen's fault if she fell in love with him. Given the right timing, I would.

I'm a blind dumbass.

The A-hole flings his hand in the air as if he's done with Gen and stomps out of the lounge, his face contorted and flushed. I'm seconds from clawing my way over the blackjack table to break up Gen and Jaeger—players, pit boss be damned—when Jaeger looks directly over. His mouth curves into a subtle smirk.

He knows what this is doing to me, damn him.

Jaeger loosens his hold on Gen and takes a step back.

She looks stunned and happily flustered.

Please don't let her want him, or my life is about to be miserable.

HOURS LATER—AFTER the A-hole incident—I'm in the employee basement, waiting at a cafeteria table for Gen to meet me for dinner break. I have another ten minutes before I have to return for my last hour on the floor, and I'm desperate to find out what happened between her and Jaeger. I got the disturbing gist from my vantage at the blackjack table, but I want—no, *need*—to know the details, and how Gen feels about him after he rushed in to rescue her.

Gen enters the cafeteria and crosses the room with a smile on her face. At least the encounter with the A-hole doesn't seem to have had any lasting ill effects. That's something.

She points to the doodle I've been absently working on while I wait. It vaguely resembles the mountain landscape etched into the front door of Jaeger's parents' house, only my doodle is made of shapes rather than lines.

"That's really good." She looks closer. "Is that entire tree made up of"—she cocks her head—"*triangles?*"

"And squares and trapezoids. So what happened with the A-hole? I saw him swoop in, but I couldn't get away."

"Oh, God! How does he know I work here? We stopped dating before I decided to come to Tahoe. Weird." She shakes her head. "Can you believe he wanted to see what I was doing after work? As if I'd meet up with him. Is he on something?"

"What did you say?"

"I told him I was busy, which isn't true. Jaeger walked up before he could pester me about it." Neither of us are very good liars, so I understand her worry. Gen smiles. "Jaeger was so sweet, Cali."

I clear my throat. "So what did Jaeger do?"

A devious edge morphs her dreamy expression. "Put the A-hole in his place. Nothing says *I'm not interested* more than *I've moved on with a smoking hot guy.*" She leans back in her chair, satisfied. "It was a beautiful moment."

I'm sensing bloodlust from my gentle best friend, and I'm not sure whether to be proud or fearful. "Yeah, I caught the tail end of that. The A-hole looked pretty pissed."

She huffs out a breath. "You know what's funny? I don't even care, as long as he stays away."

"I think it's a safe bet he will." I fill in the mountains on my napkin with quadrilaterals, determining how best to go about asking my next question. "What exactly did Jaeger say? I saw him whisper in your ear."

Her eyes squint and then soften. "Nothing, he just asked me to help him with something tomorrow." She reaches across the table and steals a fry.

I stop breathing and my hand stills on my sketch. He wants to see her? Like, spend time with her?

I bite the inside of my lip until a coppery, metallic flavor runs over my tongue.

Her eyes flicker to my napkin and she lifts her chin. "Hey, if you're going to throw that one away like you do your other drawings when I'm not looking, I want it."

Gen always asks for my doodles. I've never understood why.

I draw in the last shapes on my mountain—every square inch of the napkin is covered in geometric shapes depicting the lake—but all I think is *it's done*. Gen and Jaeger are going on a date tomorrow. That's the end of any *us*.

It's my own stupid fault. I hesitated, fearful of ruining things with Jaeger if I acted too soon after my breakup. And then, like an idiot, I pushed Jaeger on Gen. I'd only wanted to help my friend out with her ex, but what was I thinking? It was my plan in the beginning to set Gen and Jaeger up, but the more I thought about it, the less I liked the idea. I was finally sure at Jaeger's parents' house that the attraction between us was genuine. Now, what if all Jaeger and I can ever be is friends?

Men think they're exclusive with their man-codes, but women have rules too. Even if Jaeger and Gen don't work out, dating your best friend's ex is forbidden.

My stomach lurches under the fries I just ate. I pass Gen the napkin and stand. "I'd better get back."

"Hey, is everything okay? You don't look well."

I smile reassuringly. I may not be the most altruistic human being on the planet, but I'm devoted to the people I love. My goal was to see Gen happy this summer and set her up with a nice guy. She seems happy, and Jaeger *is* a nice guy.

I got what I asked for.

And isn't that a bitch.

Chapter Twelve

I'M ON THE patio in my bikini top and pajama shorts, doodling. It's all I can do to defuse thoughts of Gen and Jaeger's date today. I woke up early, irritable and out of sorts, and found a plain notepad in a drawer in the kitchen. My drawing this morning is larger and more elaborate than my usual, depicting the casino in all its glory. There's a line of slots and a waitress flagrantly leaning over her customer, sugaring him up with a drink and a smile, and eyeing his pot of coins. A busboy wipes a table behind the waitress, snatching a twenty from her cash caddy. In the background, a man in a suit preys on a pretty waitress while sipping a drink in the lounge.

The scene is my rendition of the casino subculture—what I've been calling Casino Real World. Security guards the house's money, but not the people within. The powerful prey on the weak or clueless, and everyone's out for themselves.

The sound of pipes rumbling from below the house erupts as I finish my sketch. Gen's finally up and in the shower. She said on our way home last night that she and Jaeger were going out around lunchtime, and it's already eleven thirty.

Not two minutes after the pipes begin their noisy caterwauling, the doorbell rings. "Gen! Door!" I yell.

The last thing I want is to see Gen leaving with Jaeger. If they want to date and make babies, fine, but I don't need to be a witness.

The doorbell rings again, followed by a couple of firm knocks. I lean back and pull the screen door open. The water's still whining through the pipes.

Shit. I hobble off my lounge chair and walk to the front. Jaeger's silver truck is visible through the living room window. I take a deep breath and calmly open the door, plastering on a bland expression.

Jaeger's wearing a red baseball cap and a navy T-shirt, his shoulder muscles bulging from the way he hunches to get his hands tucked inside the pockets of his jeans.

I swallow hard. Why does he have to look so good? The aftershave he wears mixed with fabric softener and something unique to him wafts toward me, and I want to tongue his neck. Damn him. I take a step back. Everything about this situation is just cruel.

He leans on the doorjamb, eyes blatantly running the length of me before resting on the pad in my hand.

"Come in." My tone is terse, but whatever. I'm doing my best here. I toss the pad on the couch and walk to the bathroom door. The shower is finally off. "Gen! Jaeger's here."

When I turn around, Jaeger is staring at my sketch. I sweep over and pick it up, tucking it under my arm.

He looks me dead in the eye as if this, too, I've kept from him. "Nice drawing."

"It's nothing. Doodles. So"—I'd better say it before I'm too angry to—"I wanted to thank you for helping out last night. Gen's ex is a jerk. I didn't want him bothering her." I pause for a second, deciding how much of my feelings to reveal. "You were very convincing."

Jaeger's eyes narrow and he scans my face.

I duck my head and tuck my hair behind my ear. I

shouldn't have said that. I slide the pad facedown on the kitchen counter and shift loose papers around while we wait for Gen.

I always answer the door in my bikini top and it's never bothered me before, but it does today. I should have put on a shirt, I think, adjusting the strings along my ribs. When I look up, Jaeger's gaze is following the trail of my fingers. He quickly looks away.

This is awkward. "Want something to drink?"

He shakes his head and sinks onto the couch. Gen walks out of the bathroom in shorts and a T-shirt. She hurries into the bedroom, her wet hair dampening the back of her top. "Be ready in a minute," she says, smiling prettily at Jaeger as she passes.

A few seconds of uncomfortable silence later, Gen pops back into the living room, hopping on one foot and fastening her flats, a small purse dangling across her chest. "Ready. Sorry to make you wait."

Jaeger rises and moves to the door, opening it for her. He follows her out. "See you later, Cali."

This is it. The defining moment when Jaeger goes from being an available guy to off-limits forever.

"Goodbye," I say, but they've already left.

INSTEAD OF STARING at the front door, waiting for Gen to return in order to interrogate her about her date with the guy I have a crush on, I check email. Two messages have arrived from Harvard Law, one with information on orientation, the other on financial aid.

It almost makes me angry how much the program will cost.

I've considered deferring for a year, though that's seems more painful. Like dragging out the inevitable. I never considered the money until this summer, working full-time for the first time in my life. The tuition isn't a problem for the trust fund kids, but it is for me. Maybe I shouldn't have ruled out the less expensive programs. But that doesn't feel right either.

Law school is everything I've worked for, but lately it feels like someone else's dream. The cost to attend would probably seem worth it if the program were something I felt passionate about. My mom used to joke about Tyler and me becoming lawyers and doctors, but really, she didn't care what we became, as long as we made something of our lives. Tyler was the science geek, while I latched on to the idea of arguing for a living. That was a good enough reason ten years ago. Now, with a future in law staring me in the eye, I'm having second—and third—and fourth—thoughts.

I'm so confused and emotionally wrung out I don't know which way is up. I shut off the computer, change my clothes, and grab the keys to Gen's car. It won't help my mood to be here when they return.

I search the fridge and jot down a list of groceries we need. Before I head to the store, I stop by the bank to deposit my tips, which consist of a hell of a lot of singles. Most of my tips come in the form of chips, but there are purists who give cash. According to the bank teller, I'm either working at the casinos or I'm a stripper. I'm keeping her guessing.

A farmers' market is going on in the bank lot, so I park across the street. As I exit my car, a man in crew sandals, beige shorts, and sunglasses exits a motel nearby with a woman I recognize from the casino. She's the sweet waitress who was crushing on the cashier.

Head down, she walks out of the motel room without a backward glance at the man. There's a swagger in the man's step that's missing from the woman's rapid departure.

I stare until they're gone, because the scene bothers me. The waitress looked seriously upset. Obviously, she and this guy are having some sort of liaison. What's disturbing, aside from the fact that the woman didn't look happy, is that I think the guy is one of the executives from the casino who trolls Gen's lounge.

I shake my head. I have too much to worry about without piling on creepy Casino Real World drama.

The errands take less time than I anticipated and I return to the house early—seconds before Gen returns with Jaeger.

My timing sucks.

Jaeger walks around the hood and nods. "Cali," he says, a happy little smile curling his mouth. He walks with Gen toward the front door, but reaches over as he passes me and grabs one of the large grocery bags from my arms. "Let me get that." He relieves me of the second bag as well.

"Okaaay." I should be grateful for the help, but Jaeger looks too pleased after his date with my best friend and I'm trying extremely hard not to be jealous.

It's not working.

I follow them inside the cabin, and Jaeger sets the groceries on the counter.

Gen and Jaeger look at me and then at each other, a secret message passing between them. Gen grins warmly at Jaeger, and that's all I need to see.

"I'll leave you two alone," I say, and cross to the back door. I want to be anywhere but watching the two of them say their lovey goodbyes.

"I'll see you later, Gen," I hear Jaeger say as I open the back door and step out onto the patio.

Gen joins me seconds later. "Hey." There's a quiver in her voice that only comes out when she's nervous. "What have you been up to?"

What have I been up to? I'm fucking dying, trying to keep busy because you're with the guy I want to kiss and make out with and glue myself to!

I wave toward the bags of groceries warming on the kitchen counter. "Errands."

Gen sits in the lounge chair beside me and pulls up her knees, feet flat on the plastic.

"How about you. How was your date?"

She looks over nervously. "Fine. It wasn't a date, though. We were just getting together. He wanted to show me something."

I'm sure he did. She doesn't elaborate, and I'm feeling too stubborn to ask for more information.

"Cali, I was wondering—can I have that sketch you did today?"

What? That's what she's thinking about? We are seriously in two different worlds right now. In fact, there's a deep chasm in our friendship that I'm responsible for. If I hadn't dragged Gen to Lake Tahoe this summer, none of this would have happened. Eric and I probably would have broken up, but at least I wouldn't be in a love triangle with *my best friend.*

"Why?" I ask, because the request seems odd under the circumstances. There's no way Gen can't feel the strain in our friendship. Or maybe, because I'm the one who caused the problem, I'm the only one who knows it exists. I never 'fessed up to my feelings for Jaeger. I've been too busy denying them.

She brushes nonexistent dirt off her shorts. "I don't know. I just liked it."

"Sure, Gen," I say harshly, rising as I do. I'm taking out my anger on her and she doesn't deserve it, but I can't help myself. "Have whatever of mine you want." I walk inside the house, grab the pad, and toss it on her lap.

Her lips part, her expression shocked.

I don't say anything. I don't put away the groceries. I simply walk out the front door and leave.

Chapter Thirteen

AFTER SPENDING THREE hours throwing hand-sized rocks into the lake, I returned home with a sore arm and apologized to Gen for going off on her. I told her I'd had a bad day, and though she inquired as to the cause, she didn't insist I elaborate when I made it obvious through avoidance tactics that I didn't want to discuss it.

Gen said her afternoon with Jaeger wasn't a date, but why would Jaeger ask her out if he wasn't interested? And he seemed so happy afterward. I'm not convinced there isn't something there. Gen could be saying it wasn't a date because they just started hanging out. I can't tell her how I feel about Jaeger until I know nothing is between them. I pushed her to date him; I won't put her in the uncomfortable position of having to choose between us.

Jaeger has come into the casino a couple of times this week to visit Mason since his non-date with Gen. Each time, he's kept to Mason's bar, which gives credence to Gen's assertion that they're not dating, though she is busy at work. And every time he's around, my heart quickens and my body heats. No matter what I tell myself—that it won't work out, I screwed things up and he's not interested—my body's visceral response doesn't care. It's infuriating.

I just got out of a relationship; I should be going all introspective and loner. At the very least, deciding whether or not to follow through with grad school. Instead, I'm conflicted about school and thinking clearly about the kind of guy I want in my life.

Eric was good-looking, but shallow and—I realize now—selfish. Why I think Mr. Totem Pole Carver is any better is beyond me, but there's something about him that's deep and a little scarred. Like he's been through shit and come out on the right side. This, in addition to the fact that puddles of drool form in my mouth whenever I look at him, and I'm drawn—even though he may be dating my best friend.

Gen and Jaeger might not be dating—yet—but she could like him. I never told Gen how I felt about him. Nope, I pushed him right in her path. In my defense, that was before I realized my feelings for him were real and not because of how crappy things were with Eric. This last incident with Gen's ex was just bad timing. Maybe that's all Jaeger and I will ever have—bad timing.

This evening, Jaeger's been in Gen's lounge for the last hour with an attractive, slightly older woman with long, dark hair and a petite figure. At first, I thought she was one of his mom's friends by the way they greeted each other—cordially, but with familiarity. She's dressed in a black sheath dress with diamonds the size of pebbles in her ears. She's younger than his parents, but her expensive attire fits his parents' upper economic bracket. The more I observe, though, the less certain I am that they're only friends.

A man in dress slacks and a polo shirt passes my table and walks up the stairs into the lounge to Jaeger and the woman. The pretty brunette places a proprietary hand on Jaeger's arm and introduces the two men.

I glance at Gen, who laughs at something her customer says.

She's not paying attention to the Jaeger tableau, and I can't understand it. I'd like to detach the roulette table and mow the lady he's sitting with down like a bowling pin, and Gen's all casual, easygoing. What the eff?

Jaeger shakes the man's hand and offers him a card. Jaeger carries business cards? For his totem poles?

Jaeger is dressed in dark slacks and a white collared shirt, the top button undone and revealing the edge of a white undershirt. I've never seen him dressed up and the image disturbs me. His wide shoulders strain the fabric along his chest, highlighting muscles while still looking professional. He makes weathered jeans and T-shirts unbelievably hot, but dressed up, he's like *GQ* photo-spread man candy.

The woman he's with seems too old for him, but I have to admit they look good together, and it's eating me up inside. The only positive I can think of at the moment is that Gen and I get off early tonight and our shift is about to end.

A cluster of new dealers approaches the pit and I finish my round. Before heading to the basement, I walk over to Gen. "You almost off?" I don't glance at Jaeger, seated in the corner.

Gen piles four shots of bright green liquid on her tray. "In a minute—just need to deliver these. You still up for the club?"

In spite of a herculean effort not to, my gaze strays toward Jaeger. The business associate has left and the woman has her fingers on his forearm, using his body for support while she leans in to tell him something. "Yes. I need—something."

Gen's eyes widen in approval. "I'm *so* happy you aren't letting things with Eric get you down." She charges off and passes out the last of her drinks, closing tabs.

Eric? Nope, not thinking about Eric—a testament to the tenuous connection we shared and proof it wasn't meant to last.

Gen returns to the bar and wipes her tray. "You sure you don't mind if Nessa joins us?"

"No," I say absently. "Hey—" I shrug my shoulder in Jaeger's direction. "That doesn't bother you?"

Gen glances over. "What, Jaeger and that woman? Why would it?"

"I thought you guys were, you know, hanging out."

Her gaze flutters to me, and her shoulders tense as though she's uncomfortable. "We're friends."

Gen hands a stack of dollar bills to the bartender. Waitresses give bartenders a percentage of their tips at the end of their shifts. She turns to me. "Ready to go?"

Gen and I generally tell each other everything, but lately, that doesn't seem to be true. Each of us seems to be holding something back. I'm not ready to disclose my secret feelings for Jaeger, and I've sensed for a while that Gen's keeping something from me too.

We change in the Blue basement, where we discover Nessa has invited someone else to our girls' night. Lewis's beautiful girlfriend, Mira, will be joining us.

This should be interesting.

I'm wearing heels, skinny jeans, and a blousy, low-cut tank. Gen's in slim jeans as well, but her top is less revealing. Her boobs are bigger than mine, but she refuses to display them to full advantage.

The only way to get to the Blue nightclub is by passing the lounge. I tell myself I won't peek, but of course I do. Jaeger is still sitting with the pretty woman, his head bowed toward her as she leans on his arm and speaks near his ear.

I clench my fist, nails grinding into my palm. He hasn't once acknowledged Gen or me this evening. I wouldn't have pegged Jaeger for a player, but flirting with me, then taking Gen out, and now hooking up with an older woman? What the hell?

We walk inside the club, the steady pulse of dance music washing over me in a wonderfully distracting way. The only thing that could make the vision of Jaeger and the woman sliming on him less vivid would be a shot of Cuervo, or Patrón if I'm in the mood to pamper myself, which I damn well am.

Fortunately, I'm with three attractive women. It doesn't take long before men start buying us drinks. Mira may be hostile, but she's unbelievably beautiful and luring all kinds of attention to our booth. Before I know it, I've downed five shots. A warm numbness settles over my limbs.

I slide from my seat. "Going dancing. Anyone wanna come?"

Gen shakes her head, posture slumped, eyelids drooping. She's well past *tipsy* and teetering on *hammered*.

It's safe to say I'm not the most conventional female, but Gen is, and seeing her drunk is funny as hell. I pull out my iPhone and snap a picture.

Her mouth parts in slow motion. "Heyyy!"

Before she makes a grab for my phone to purge the awesome photo I caught of her drunk off her ass, I swagger away, swinging my hips to the music.

I don't care that I'm on the dance floor by myself, waving my arms in the air like a lunatic. I could be making a perfect idiot of myself, but all that matters is that I don't feel anything.

Not a damn thing.

No humiliation over the way Eric dumped me, no fear about the future, not even the jumble of emotions Jaeger elicits.

A new song transitions from the last and I shut my eyes, moving to the rhythm. Within seconds my balance wavers and I blink, throwing out my arms. I search for a visual horizon above the moving bodies to stop the spinning. My gaze lands on the wide, overcrowded bar off to the side. A tall blonde in a red dress looks over and our gazes connect. She looks an awful lot like Jaeger's sister.

I slam my eyes shut and twist around. When I open them, the Kerstin lookalike is gone, but so is my balance. I stumble to the side like a child in high heels. A pair of arms brackets me from behind.

I swivel my head up and around. I'm pretty sure the guy supporting me is attractive, but the dance floor is dark, with blue and purple flashing lights. Given the heavy buzz I have going on, I could be totally off base. Then again, what has good-looking ever gotten me?

He smiles and slides his arms down to my waist. I spin around and drape my hands behind his neck. He immediately pulls me close until our hips grind, the scent of heavy cologne and perspiration choking me as we sway to the music. Dampness seeps through his shirt and onto my fingers, and though he doesn't smell bad, he doesn't smell appealing.

Without waiting for the song to end, I slip from his grasp, evading his grabby hands, and push through the crowd to the nearest exit off the dance floor. Where I end up is a different part of the club entirely, filled with lounge-style sofas and small square tables.

Where am I?

I glance around, searching for my friends, and recognize someone else. Seated at the table in front of me is one of the executives who hangs out after work watching Gen in the lounge. One of the trollers.

He and the guy he often hangs with look alike from a distance. I can't tell if this is the guy I saw leaving the motel with the waitress or if it's the other one. They both have businesslike short hair and symmetrical features. The only reason I can distinguish either of them from a million other preppy professionals is because they're young for casino executives, and they each wear Blue insignia rings.

I've only seen a few executives in possession of the Blue rings. Zach, the dealer who's friends with Nessa, filled me in on Blue protocol and how management receives thick gold bands with sapphires for exemplary performance. The two trollers wear them, and it's one reason I recognized one of these guys leaving a motel room the day I ran errands.

I'm buzzed and frustrated, and tired of preying men. And since I've lost all ability to filter my words, I walk over and say, "Hey, you're the guy who's been checking out my friend."

The man makes a slow perusal of me, his attention landing on my chest. "And now I'm looking at you." His mouth kicks up at the side in a charming smile that must hit the mark with the ladies more often than not. "I've seen you around as well. What's your name, pretty girl?"

He's sleazy, but his smile comes across as guileless. And he called me pretty. I must be feeling extremely low, because just that small bit of attention is enough for me to let my guard down.

I'll regret this tomorrow, but for now, I'm as big a sucker for flattery as any other lonely female. Besides, I can handle his type. "Cali."

"Cali, I'm Drake." His eyes narrow as if he's trying to figure me out, or maybe it's because I'm swaying. "Would you like to join me?"

Drake, the lounge-trolling executive, is pretty attractive up close, with dark hair and whiskey-brown eyes. I'd put him in his upper twenties. He's polished and smooth in his tailored shirt and pants. Different from the guys I've dated. More mature. Worldly.

A vision of Jaeger in his *GQ* gear flashes like a strobe in my mind. But Jaeger and I have never dated, so he doesn't count. I clench my fists.

"You look like you could use a drink," he says.

A good point. I don't need a drink, but I could use one.

I sit and Drake flags the waitress. "What would you like?"

I tell him my order and it arrives in record time. Given my level of inebriation, which becomes more apparent with every attempt at normal activity I take, like, say, walking, I ask the waitress for water as well and sip my cocktail. Drinking is all fun and games until there's puking involved. Water helps prevent the casualty.

I'm buzzed and unable to think too deeply. That's enough.

Drake asks me questions about my job at the casino and how I like living in Lake Tahoe. I follow the flow of conversation until the topic of summer excursions comes up and I happen to mention the fishing trip.

Drake's hand squeezes my shoulder from the back of my seat. "Cali, are you all right?"

I look up and blink. Images of Jaeger in the boat, talking dirty fishing talk, leads to the most recent image I can't get out of my head—of him with the older woman clinging to him like a barnacle.

We haven't even dated, yet somehow I must have let Jaeger in. Because seeing him with Gen, or anyone else, shouldn't bother me as much as it does. "Yes—" I swallow the bitter flavor in my mouth. "Fine." My smile falters.

Drake doesn't smile back, though his expression remains kind. "Would you like to leave?"

Escape the casino and Jaeger?

I nod eagerly.

Chapter Fourteen

RATIONAL THOUGHTS MOVE like sludge, while a fast forward of Jaegerathon plays in Technicolor inside my head.

Drake gestures to a back door. "Shall we?"

I follow him numbly from the club. He's been kind. Maybe I misjudged him. He could be as lonely as the rest of us, sitting in Gen's lounge, searching for someone special to come along.

It's not until the door to the club closes and cool air nips my arms that I realize I can't leave without Gen. And that maybe leaving with someone I've just met isn't such a great idea.

"Wait." I stop and look around, my heartbeat quickening. I don't recognize this part of the parking lot. "I came here with friends. We have to go back." I reach for the door handle, but it's locked from the inside.

"They keep these locked. We'll have to go in through the casino."

And see Jaeger with that lady? No, thank you. I wrap my arms around my middle, shivers vibrating my spine.

At my hesitation, Drake slips his jacket over my shoulders. "Do you have a phone?"

I left my purse with Gen, but my phone is in my back pocket. I pull it out.

"You can contact your friends from here and tell them I'm taking you home, or we can walk inside. It's up to you."

The slow cog that is my brain on alcohol filters this information, processing a slight sense of unease in the pit of my belly. Probably not the best idea to go home with a guy I would have been leery of before tonight. But the lights are bright in the parking lot, providing a sense of security. And I have no desire to walk past Jaeger with his woman.

It's a short drive to my place. I could call a taxi, but Drake's right here. Besides, I don't have my purse and money.

Drake works for the casino as an executive—recognized for stellar performance, no less. How dangerous could he be?

I shoot Gen a text.

Cali: *I left the bar. Getting a ride from a coworker. Please bring my purse when you leave. See you back at our place. Get some digits, will you!*

I don't wait for her response. If she worries about me, she'll check her phone.

Drake leads me to a dark sports car. I have no idea of the make—that kind of detail is beyond my cognitive ability at the moment.

He opens the passenger door and I ease onto tan leather seats, slipping off his jacket and draping it over the center console.

"Where do you live?" he asks from the driver's side.

Another twinge of uneasiness hits me, as if beneath the alcohol haze, common sense lies in wait. I don't like the idea of giving a stranger my address, but I really want to go home. Besides, Drake works at the casino. If he wanted my address, he could look it up. I give him the information and he programs it into his GPS.

Within minutes, we're pulling into my driveway. "Thanks

for the ride," I tell him, and open the car door to get out. "You were right, I wasn't feeling well."

"You're welcome." He gets out of the car at the same time I do.

I shouldn't worry. It's dark out and he's probably just walking me to the door, but I do worry. I'm worried I gave him the wrong idea.

I slip behind the fence where we hide the spare key. No way I can get around him seeing me do it. It's either that, or I'm locked out. I make a mental note to change the location of where we put the hide-a-key tomorrow.

When I return, Drake's waiting on the darkened doorstep.

Gen and I forgot to turn on the porch light before we left. This wouldn't be a big deal, except that having the lights off sets a certain romantic mood I'd rather not encourage.

"Thanks again for the ride. I think I'm good from here."

Drake sidles closer, resting his hand lightly on my hip. He flashes his charming smile. "How about a short visit?"

I step back, my shoulders brushing the door. "Not tonight. Another time, maybe?"

He nods slowly. I can't see his eyes clearly in the dark, but I sense calculations going on behind the pregnant pause. "A kiss goodnight, then?"

He leans forward and my hands flash to his chest, urging him back. "I don't—"

Drake dips his head, my arms no barrier when he's half a foot taller. His mouth closes on mine even as I'm pushing him away. He doesn't seem to notice, or care, since he's too busy grabbing my neck and angling his tongue inside my mouth.

Every danger instinct goes off inside me, a fine sweat breaking out along my spine despite the evening chill.

My brain moves in rapid fire, registering each breath, a rough hand grabbing my wrist, pinning it behind me in a gesture meant to be sexy, or an assault—I'm not sure which. Either way, it's unwelcome. Drake's body pushes me flush with the door. The only sounds are the shifting of our feet, and the smacking of Drake's rough mouth amid the struggle for control.

Rapid footsteps penetrate through the panic.

"Off!" a deep, familiar voice shouts a second before Drake is ripped away.

Jaeger stands between us, his back to me. I have no idea how he got here, or why he's here. But the relief is unimaginable.

"Is there a problem?" Drake casually shifts his collar forward. Jaeger must have wrenched it when he grabbed him.

Drake saunters closer, careful to remain clear of Jaeger. "The lady came home with me. I don't see how this is any of your business."

"It's *her* home and she asked you to *leave*," Jaeger says. "Get. The fuck. Out!" He reaches back and drapes a long arm over my shoulders, pulling me close. My heart slows; my breathing calms.

The threat in Jaeger's voice stuns me, but my body instinctively curls into him. Frankly, I'm surprised anyone managed to create this level of anger from Jaeger. He's the gentle giant. But Jesus, is he scary when he's mad.

"Cali—" Drake steps to the side and grabs my wrist, tugging me.

I twist my arm away. Does the man have a death wish? Or is he just so arrogant he thinks a guy twice his size can't touch him? "Please leave," I tell Drake.

His jaw clenches as if he's refusing to give up a toy.

Jaeger lets out an angry sigh, pushes me behind him—*what the hell?*—and punches Drake in the face. *Holy shit!*

Drake lands on the ground, rolling, grasping the front of his face. There's no blood, but that had to have hurt.

Jaeger leans over him. "Do. Not. Touch. Her. That was a warning tap. The next one won't be."

Drake hastily rises and brushes the powdery Tahoe soil off his trousers. He glares at me. "Not what I had in mind for tonight," he says, and stalks away. He fires up his expensive sports car and tears out of the driveway in a spray of pebbles and pine needles.

Jaeger tilts up my chin with his finger, searching my face. "Are you okay?"

I nod, wondering what in the hell just happened. "What are you doing here?" Drake's car rounds the corner at the end of my street, his taillights disappearing. "How did you know…?"

Jaeger rubs a hand down his face and lets out a tense breath. "Kerstin. She told me you left the club drunk with some guy." His face contorts. "What were you thinking, Cali?"

This side of Jaeger, the angry, protective side, is something I've never seen before, and it's totally hot—not that I wish to ignite it unduly.

I wasn't thinking when I left with Drake. In fact, I purposely tried not to think. About Jaeger. But that's not something I'm going to tell him. "I made a mistake."

"You made a mistake? You—" Jaeger steps to the side and runs his fingers through his short hair. "Do you understand what that—that *psychotic asshole* could have done?"

Yeah, I kinda do, and I'm trying not to imagine it. The last half-hour has sobered me up.

I rub my eyes and move to the front door, unlock it, and

walk inside, my fingers and arms trembling. Jaeger lingers on the threshold. "You can come in," I tell him.

He walks inside and shuts the door.

I fill a glass of water in the kitchen and offer it to him, but he shakes his head. I take several gulps from the glass, cleaning the taste of Drake from my mouth.

"I'm sorry for yelling." He lets out another strained breath. "But you can't go home with people you don't know. Matter of fact, don't go home with anyone unless it's a friend."

I spin around. It was stupid to go home with Drake and I learned a painful lesson tonight, but where does Jaeger get off telling me what to do? "What about you? Did you take your lady friend home before you came here? It's okay for you to leave with some random person, but not me?"

"I'm not a hundred-pound female," he growls. "He could have hurt you, Cali."

Before I dated Eric, I'd left parties a time or two with guys I had just met. But in those cases, I knew the guy's fraternity brothers, or we had friends in common. There were dangers in college, sure, but we lived in a bubble where people knew each other. The risks were lower.

Jaeger's right. I ignored my instincts tonight and treated Drake like I would a guy from school. It was foolish and dangerous, but that doesn't give Jaeger the right to treat me like a child. "I said I made a mistake. I don't recall having a second big brother. Why did you follow me, anyway?"

He sits in the center of the couch, taking up two-thirds of it, his legs spread wide the way guys do because they don't wear skirts or feel the need to hide their private parts. He leans his head against the wall behind the cushions and stares at the ceiling. "I thought the guy could be bad news."

I look around searchingly. "And you knew this how?"

He glares at me. "He's a guy, and you'd been drinking. I wasn't taking chances."

My eyebrows pinch together. Jaeger's reaction to Drake was rather heated for someone I'm casually friends with, like he was taking things personally. Why the hell would he leave his date to follow me home on the off chance Drake was a serial killer?

"What about your lady friend?"

"*Client.* She's a client, Cali."

"She's pretty handsy for a client. Do all clients feel you up?"

Jaeger's gaze narrows on my face. He sits forward and grabs my waist, pulling me between his knees until I have no choice but to shift and sit on his leg or fall into his chest. I choose the leg, slowly sliding off onto the couch beside him, my legs dangling over his lap.

His arm braces me from behind. "You scared the shit out of me tonight." His green eyes are intense and worried.

"I'm sorry," I say, surprised.

Jaeger presses my face to his chest, cradling my head. "Promise me you'll never do anything like that again."

I'll promise him anything, as long as he keeps holding me like this. "I won't. Totally stupid," I mumble, nuzzling his shirt and breathing in his clean scent.

Jaeger leans back and our eyes meet for a long moment. The intensity makes my breath quicken. He lowers his head slowly until a puff of air from his nose tickles my skin. His lips graze mine, a delicate touch that is the total opposite of Drake's mauling. Jaeger's gentleness speaks of heat and longing, and something deeper I can't put my finger on. But I want it.

If I thought the attraction between us was powerful, the electricity his lips generate is coiled, sizzling need. My fingers clutch his shirt.

This is what I've craved. All night, all week—since we first met.

Jaeger pulls back, keeping an inch of space between us. His breaths fan my chin, thumb rubbing circles along my hairline. "Is this okay? After—"

I lean up and fasten my mouth to his in answer. Whether I acknowledged it to myself or not, I've been waiting for this kiss for weeks.

His fingers slide into my hair, angling my head for better access, and I'm drowning.

My belly tightens, body arching toward him. I wrap my arms around his broad back and pull him close until we fall backward onto the cushions with him on top.

His weight feels amazing. Not crushing or forced, but just enough to fire more need. I'm a sea of sensation and all we're doing is kissing. My legs squeeze his hips, drawing him closer.

A short, guttural moan escapes his mouth and his hand drifts from my hair, down my throat, to my chest, wrapping around my breast. He pulls his mouth away and runs kisses along my chin and neck. "Cali," he whispers, cupping my breast and rubbing his thumb over my nipple.

It's not until he says my name again that the lust clears enough to register that he's attempting to communicate with something other than body talk. I look into his eyes.

"When is Gen getting back?" he says.

Wha...? Gen? Shit.

Panic spears my gut, and not because I'm worried Gen will walk in on us, though she could. I forgot all about Gen and Jaeger and the possibility that something exists between them. After all the encouragement I've given Gen to get back out there, here I am making out with a guy she may actually like.

What am I doing? I squirm out from beneath him, my anger piqued at myself and the idea that Jaeger could be playing me. Gen is my best friend. Enough of this. I have to find out what's going on between them.

I swallow and attempt to gather the rest of my brain cells that scattered the minute Jaeger loomed over me with his large, heated body. "I don't know, but she was pretty drunk when I left. She'll probably be home soon."

"Maybe I should leave." He stands and adjusts his pants, which I realize now house a very large, impressive bulge. I glance away.

If I ask Jaeger about Gen now, I'm not sure I'll be able to tell truth from lie. The subject needs to be addressed soberly, when I'm not reacting passionately to my protector. "That's probably a good idea."

Chapter Fifteen

THIS MORNING MY head feels like I thrashed it against a sharp boulder a few thousand times, but I've held back the queasies thanks to a few green olives and dry toast. Gen, however, has not fared as well. She's in the bathroom puking her guts out.

"You okay in there?"

She doesn't answer, so I open the door a crack and check on her. She's hugging the bowl, her cheek affixed to the rim. I open the door wide. "You don't look good. Do you want me to take you to Urgent Care?"

"No," she says without moving. "Just need quiet time with the toilet."

I grab two washcloths from the cupboard and soak them in cold water. I drape one across the back of her neck.

Gen moans. "Feels good."

"Here." I hand her the other. Her arm wavers unsteadily in the air. I grab her fingers and direct them to the cloth.

I keep a close eye on Gen for the rest of the day. By evening she's eating but still feeling pretty crappy.

The full force of what could have happened last night with Drake if Jaeger hadn't shown up hits me as the day wears on. I will never do anything like that again. And afterward, with Jaeger? Clearly, I wasn't thinking. I was *feeling*, and allowing it to control my actions. If there's something between Jaeger and

Gen, *I* could be the other woman this time. Gen can barely trust as it is after the last A-hole played her. The level of betrayal in this situation would be so much worse.

I haven't told her about Drake, because to do so would mean explaining why Jaeger showed up. Gen goes to bed early and I decide to talk to her about everything when she's not so sick. I need to get to the bottom of what's really up with her and Jaeger. She says nothing, but I can't shake the feeling she's holding something back.

THE NEXT DAY, Gen is gone when I wake. She left a note, saying she had errands to run. I texted her and told her not to worry. That I'd grab a ride into work from one of the dealers. I don't want to wait to talk to her about Jaeger, but holding off a few more hours until we get off work won't kill me.

I approach the seamstress counter at Blue and hand the lady my ticket to claim my uniform.

"Sorry, honey," the attendant says. "Boss needs you to visit the supervisor. Elevators off the lobby, second floor. They'll direct you from there."

That's weird. I've only interacted with the head dealer and a pit boss who manages new trainees. I've never gone upstairs to the big guns—the people observing Casino Real World through stealthy security cameras.

I nod to the attendant and jog up the stairs to the casino floor and the wall of elevators off the lobby.

Up the elevator, the second floor of the building could not look more different from the rest of the casino. A section of cubicles takes up a good portion of the space, which is so institutional and wrong compared to the high-end décor of the gaming and customer areas, yet an upgrade from the yellowing paint and metal lockers of the basement. Offices line three sides of the floor, with one large double door labeled SECURITY in the center of an entire wall.

"I'm Cali Morgan," I tell the receptionist. "The seamstress asked me to come here."

The receptionist drums bright red nails that disappear briefly as she tucks back shoulder-length reddish-purple hair that under no circumstances came from nature. Those nails flash back out and pluck a sticky note from the desk. "Right this way."

I follow the receptionist down the hall. Her heavy eye makeup and hair are casino glam, but the modest skirt and blouse she wears keep her respectable. I'm going to take a wild guess and say she worked the casino floor at some point.

We pass the security area and come to a different hallway lined with offices spread farther apart. The receptionist knocks on a door with ROBERT MIDDLETON, GAMING on a metal plaque to the side, and we enter.

In the office, a man of middling years with sandy blond hair and a dimple in his chin taps a few last keystrokes on his computer. "Thank you." He nods to the receptionist and she closes the door behind her.

I have a strange feeling about this.

What could I have done wrong or right to land me here? I'm not the fastest dealer, but no one has complained so far. I haven't miscounted, which is more than I can say for other new dealers. If miscounting or botching a riffle shuffle were cause for dismissal, half the summer dealers would have been axed.

Robert Middleton stands halfway and gestures to a chair. "You must be Calista. Have a seat, please." I never go by my full name, but I don't correct him. Something in his voice tells me this is serious.

He sits down in his wide leather chair, a large picture window looking over the mountains and lake in the background. Blood rushes through my veins, pulse pounding at my throat. This guy is big time. Why would he call me up here?

Leaning on his forearms, Robert Middleton steeples his fingers. His jacket is off, but he's wearing a white dress shirt and a striped taupe business tie so tight the skin at his neck folds above the collar. "I'll get right to the point. We're going to have to let you go."

My jaw drops, eyes unblinking. *What?*

I mean, that thought occurred to me, given where I am, but I didn't actually think it possible. I've never in my life received anything less than an A-minus, let alone been fired from an internship or work position.

"I don't understand," I finally say.

"It's very simple. You are here as a summer employee. We have a probationary period of three months for all employees. If at any point during those three months we feel the collaboration isn't a good fit, the casino may terminate without cause. It's been brought to my attention that your conduct does not fit our culture and that you would do better somewhere else."

His poker face is perfect. I get nothing from his expression. "What conduct are you referring to? I'm not trying to be argumentative, I just don't understand what I've done that would warrant this."

"I'd rather not go into specifics, nor am I obligated to. Your termination is effective immediately." He stands and walks around his desk, gesturing to the door, a waft of spicy aftershave making my stomach roll. "Please return to the front desk. The receptionist has a packet of closing forms for you to fill out."

Somehow I manage to rise, my legs shaking like crazy. Robert Middleton holds out his hand. I stare at it for a moment, then snap out of my daze and grasp it. His handshake is firm and decisive. "Best of luck to you, Ms. Morgan."

This cannot be happening. *How* is this happening?

My throat goes dry, and tears burn the backs of my eyes, but I walk to the receptionist desk and the violet-haired woman.

When I finish filling out forms, I step inside the elevator escorted by one of the security guards—as if I were a felon. The receptionist said the security guard is customary, but I've never felt so low in my life.

The guard promenades me across the casino floor, past Gen handing out drinks in the lounge. She doesn't see me, but Mason does. He glances up from his bar in confusion.

I know the feeling. I swallow and keep walking, mortified. They told me not to talk to anyone, and the last thing I want is to announce what's happening.

After the guard leaves me in the parking garage, the tears I held back spill down my cheeks. I shuffle my feet along, shocked and in a daze, toward the rows of cars, searching for Gen's, then I halt.

Shit.

Gen has the keys and the receptionist said I couldn't return before tomorrow, when my employment status would be announced.

I walk to the edge of the garage overlooking the fields of cars below and lean my head on the cold metal bars. What am I going to do? I needed this job for school. My savings from this summer would only cover a fraction of the costs of my first year, but still. I'll have to request more loans, which may take my entire life to pay off. I'll be a well-paid corporate slave.

Opportunities like Harvard Law don't come around every day. I should be grateful. And yet I'm not. It doesn't feel like a dream, it feels like a burden.

Chapter Sixteen

I'M SITTING IN my favorite spot in the backyard on the lounge chair, where I've been for the last half-hour staring at the trees. I didn't bother removing the purse from my arm. It seemed like a lot of work. I can't wrap my head around the fact that I just got fired. It makes no sense.

A vibration zings my ribs where my purse rests. I reach inside and grab it. "Hello?"

"Cali, are you okay?" Gen's voice sounds high-pitched and panicked. "Mason said you left the casino escorted by a *security guard.*"

"Yup," I choke. The rain of tears has dissipated, but my voice hasn't fully recovered.

"What happened? Where are you?"

"Home. I took a taxi." I gulp a deep breath and rub my nose, which is likely bright red from all the crying. "I was fired."

"*What?* Why?"

I'm about to say *I don't know* when a memory of the other night pops into my head. No. He wouldn't... would he? Drake was pissed when he left. Pissed enough to take revenge?

"I—I don't know."

"This is crazy, Cali. You can't get fired. You haven't done anything wrong."

I filter through the events of my last night of work, and the time I spent at the club. Had I done something employees shouldn't? The casino gives drink tokens to employees at the end of every workweek, to be used at Blue bars. Administration has no problem with drinking and gambling at their facility. They'd probably be happy if we blew our entire paycheck on the house.

I drank and danced, which is no big deal. The thing that was a big deal was getting a ride from Drake and Jaeger punching him, *an executive of Blue.*

Would Drake take that out on me? In this way? Male pride makes men do stupid things. I sure as hell don't know Drake well enough to say he wouldn't have had me fired. He proved himself a jerk, possibly worse. Jesus.

And I can't tell Gen any of this yet, because I haven't told her about Drake and Jaeger and what happened that night. It's too much to fill her in on over the phone while she's working, and I want to do it in person anyway. "Supposedly employees are provisional the first three months. The casino doesn't need a reason to release me. The head of Gaming said—"

"You spoke to someone *upstairs*? They never bother with us."

"Yeah, well, this guy did. He said I don't fit the casino culture."

"Are you kidding me? You're a genius, soon-to-be Harvard Law student. Not to mention classy and beautiful. What are they looking for? Dropouts with bedhead and poor manners?"

Hmm, interesting theory. Some employees fit that description. "No, I don't think that's it, but I doubt I'll discover the truth. They're not required to tell me."

"This is so weird... and not right." She lets out a loud sigh. "Forget about Blue, Cali. Who needs them? You have a bright future ahead."

I pinch my lips and breathe through my nose, holding down the ball at the back of my throat. "Right." Having this job while I figured things out with school was my buffer, and now it's gone.

Gen returns to work, but promises to come straight home after her shift. Talking to her had the positive effect of waking me from my catatonic state on the patio.

I only spent thirty minutes in the casino, but my clothes and hair carry the burnt tang of cigarette smoke. I want to purge every reminder of that place. I grab my favorite threadbare sweats and T-shirt, and take a shower.

Wet hair dangling down my back, I flip through television channels, searching for a smutty reality show to make my life appear normal.

My cell phone vibrates. It's a text from Jaeger.

Jaeger: *Have you eaten?*
Cali: *No. How did you get my number?*
Jaeger: *Gen. You like burritos?*

Ah hell. Does Gen know he's texting me? She must if she gave him my number.

He's catching me during a vulnerable moment. I can't say no. I want to see him. Nothing's going to happen with Gen on her way home—though that wasn't much of a deterrent the last time. I shove that thought aside.

Cali: *Chicken, please.*

Twenty minutes later, a knock sounds at the front door and my pulse jumps. It's probably Jaeger, but I peek out the window anyway. I've had too many surprises, and with my suspicions about Drake, anything's possible.

Jaeger's silver truck shimmers in the light from the porch. I open the door and find him standing there in blue jeans and a heathered gray sweatshirt, a brown paper bag in his hands.

"Hey." He glances at my sweats and smirks.

After his text, I rolled the waistband so I wouldn't have a saggy butt and put on a bra, but otherwise, I look like crap. "Come on in."

Jaeger sets the bag on the counter. "Cups?"

"Behind you." I point to the correct cupboard and reach for plates, then set them on the table in the dining nook.

Jaeger walks over with a glass and two bottles of Dos Equis. He pours me one and gulps from his bottle.

I take a large swig, the carbonation burning my oversensitized nose. It's no longer bright red, but it's still stopped up from all the crying. "Ahhh"—even so, Dos Equis tastes like a little bit of sunshine—"I needed that."

Jaeger smiles and pulls out four bundles wrapped in white paper. He sets three on his plate and one on mine. Neither of us wastes time before digging into our food.

"So," I say in between bites, "I'm guessing Gen told you what happened?"

He nods. "Mason saw you escorted out. I talked to Gen."

My face warms. This entire evening has been one huge kick in my ass. I'm certain I did nothing to justify being fired, but it's still embarrassing, like having my credit card refused at the checkout counter because someone stole my card number. The finger points to me.

"Did she ask you to check on me?"

His gaze rises. "No. I sent myself."

"And how did she feel about that?"

He stares at me for a moment, his gaze perplexed. "I didn't

ask."

He doesn't seem guilty, just matter-of-fact. I take another bite of my delicious burrito, stealthily studying his handsome face and broad shoulders. I can tell by the sauce that he picked up the food from my favorite *taqueria*. "Well, thanks. I appreciate you coming."

Jaeger's mouth pauses mid-munch. He stares at me for a moment before lifting his beer and swallowing. "What will you do? Will you look for another casino job?"

"I got the position through one of my mom's contacts. She told us about summer hires and put in a good word. It's late in the season. I doubt there are any left." I set my half-eaten burrito down and wipe my mouth with a napkin. "I'm supposed to leave for school soon. I've saved enough money to get through the summer. I won't make Gen pay our rent by herself. My mom's in Carson City. I could always spend time with her. She's been asking me to come out."

Jaeger polishes off his burrito and bites into a taco, drumming his fingers on the table. "So you'll have time to kill."

I'm not sure why he sounds happy. Nothing about being fired seems positive. "I guess."

Jaeger glances at my half-eaten burrito. "Finished? Ready for dessert?"

"You brought dessert?"

"Of course."

He downs his last taco and we wash the dishes. I'm putting away utensils with my back turned when I hear rustling sounds coming from Jaeger's magical paper bag. I look to see what he's up to.

He sets a jar on the counter.

It's... "You brought me green olives?"

He slides the jar to me, and I'm speechless for a moment.

I look up, and he's smiling. "How did you know?"

"I'm observant." He must see the question on my face. "You gobbled them like grapes at Harrah's."

This is the sweetest thing a guy has ever done for me. I want to wrap him up, throw him on my bed, and have my way with him. I grip the counter and slow my breathing. "Thank you."

Jaeger pops the jar open. He plucks an olive and stretches his hand to my mouth. I part my lips and he slips the olive inside. My tongue grazes his finger on the way out.

He stares at my mouth as I chew. "More?" he asks absently.

I nod. "What about you? You having dessert?" I pull out another green beauty.

He clears his throat. "Watching you eat is dessert." He grins naughtily.

This is trouble. How am I supposed to stay away when he's like this? My panties evaporate just looking at him, and then he's funny and sweet and brings me green olives. I have no defenses.

"But I brought something else for me. You mind if we go out back?"

A change of scenery would be good. Outdoors—away from bedrooms—even better.

WHEN JAEGER ASKED me to carry the paper bag outside while he went to his truck, I wasn't expecting him to return with a mini hibachi grill.

What the hell? "You cannot still be hungry after dinner. You ate half a cow in *carne asada*."

He chuckles and sets the grill on the cement. He pulls a

lighter along with a protracting spear from his back pocket.

The man comes equipped.

He lights coals inside the hibachi and waits for them to heat, then pulls a bag of marshmallows from the paper bag. Now I know where this is going, and I like the way he thinks.

I sit back in my lounge chair and wait for Jaeger to roast a marshmallow. He's one of those "golden brown all over" kind of people, while I typically set mine ablaze and see what happens.

By the time Jaeger deems the marshmallow baked to perfection, my mouth is watering. He slowly eases the golden ball off the spear and places it on a square of chocolate between two graham crackers.

He's been a complete gentleman the entire time I've known him. He won't try to eat that without offering me some…

With deliberate slowness, he brings the s'more to · his mouth—

I whimper, and he looks over, eyebrows raised, as if he knows I'm about to tackle him for his food. "Would you like some, Cali?"

He's teasing me. I've had one of the worst weeks of my life, and he's teasing me.

I pick up a pine cone and chuck it at his chest. He deflects it easily and laughs.

"Give me a bite, dammit!" I say.

He shakes his head. "Bossy."

"Yes, I am. Let that be a lesson to you."

A crooked smile crosses his face. My palms sweat at the mischief behind it. Instead of handing me the s'more, he leans over until he's a foot away and lifts it to my mouth.

I narrow my eyes at him. A smile curls my lips. "You like

feeding me."

He stares at my mouth and nods. "Mm-hmm."

That's dirty. I like it. Two can play this game. I lick the chocolate dripping down his index finger, taking my time. Jaeger's face tenses and he breathes in, his gaze on my tongue running along his long, thick finger. I take a bite of the s'more and lick my lips. "Mmm, good."

His mouth parts slightly. "You've got some—" He indicates the side of my mouth.

I intentionally lick the other side.

He looks in my eyes. "You're teasing me?"

I nod slowly.

Jaeger lets out a slow breath and sets the s'more on top of the paper bag. "I don't like to be teased." His face is devoid of emotion, and for a moment, I think he's serious.

Before I know what's happening, Jaeger drops the head of my lounge chair till I'm flat on my back and climbs on top of me, lightly pinning my arms above my head.

I let out a squeak. He grabs both my hands with one of his, licks the side of my mouth where the chocolate was, and tickles my ribs with his other hand.

"Stop!" I free a hand—he isn't holding tight—and grab his tickling fingers, twining them with mine.

"What? You don't like the punishment for naughty girls who tease?"

I'm grinning, because despite my misery, I'm having fun. I always have fun with him. "This isn't punishment."

He smiles boyishly. "No, I guess not. I'm a lover, not a fighter."

His eyes grow serious and he leans down and kisses me softly. He tastes like chocolate, and something else yummy that I associate with him. The gentle kiss evolves, transferring into something hot and needy. I wrap my arms around his back and he leans more weight on me.

I love the way he holds me, the way his kisses are deliberate, not sloppy and fast in order to get somewhere.

Jaeger shifts his hips between my legs and my breath catches, thighs softening around his waist. He moans in my mouth and presses again—

The lounge collapses—well, the bottom half, anyway—and our legs slam to the ground.

Jaeger laughs. "*Shit*. Are you okay?" He makes no move to get off me, and I'm glad. I like him right where he is.

I look down at the damage. The bottom support posts are bent in half. "Crap, how will I explain this to Gen?" I squeeze him tighter so he knows I'm going to be very upset if he tries to get off me right now.

He kisses the side of my mouth and runs his hand down my ribs to my stomach. "Blame it on me. Tell her I sat on it," he murmurs.

His tongue finds the inside of my mouth and his hands travel up and down the length of my body for the next half-hour on that broken lounge chair—until the telltale sounds beyond the fence reach my ears.

Guilt flushes my chest and I push away lightly. "Gen is home," I whisper. "We should get up."

I did it again. How could I do it again? I have to know without a doubt that there's nothing between Gen and Jaeger. I don't think there is, but I need to be sure.

Jaeger groans and pecks me on the mouth before pushing up.

"What's going on with you and Gen?" I blurt. Gen's answer

didn't fill me with confidence the one time I asked, and Jaeger's here now, no sexy protector pheromones coursing through me to muddle my brain like they were after the Drake mauling. My mind's a little fuzzy after all that kissing, but I can't hold off asking any longer.

He puts away s'more paraphernalia, his head cocked to the side as if confused. "What do you mean?"

"I mean, are you guys—um—well, hooking up?"

Jaeger freezes. "*What?* Why would you think that?"

"You took her out the other day. I wondered... I mean, she said no, but I have to be sure."

He looks away as if thinking, and then slowly shakes his head. "I wanted her opinion about something I'm working on. It's not... No, Cali, I'm not hooking up with Gen. I can't believe you thought that after—" His hand lifts to me and then drops. "I would never do that. I'm not like that."

I believe him, but I can't say I know him well. "What *are* you like?"

He's quiet for a moment, replacing the top of the hibachi. "I'm not going to lie. For a time I hooked up a lot, but that was a while ago. There were things going on—things I was trying to deal with. Obviously, I didn't deal with them well, but I got over it and I'm not like that anymore. It wasn't the real me." He stares into my eyes. "But even then, I would never have hooked up with one girl and then turned around and pursued her best friend." He rubs his jaw. "I also didn't, ahhh—*date*—more than one girl at a time. Too complicated."

So he didn't screw more than one girl on the same day, but there probably wasn't much lag time in between. I can deal with that. He was younger then. It's slutty, but I don't expect less from a twenty-year-old guy who was hot enough to have anyone he wanted. As long as he's not like that anymore.

I'm not a virgin, but I'm loyal, and despite what Jaeger might think of me after I let Drake drive me home, I don't sleep around. Make out, for sure, but not sex. That I reserve for relationships. It's my one prim and proper rule, if you can call it that.

Gen opens the screen door. "There you are. Hey, Jaeger. I didn't know you were coming over." She looks at the lounge chair I'm sitting on and the bent legs. "You eat too much tonight, Cali?"

"Shut up!" I toss a pine cone at her head, but she's farther away than Jaeger and my aim is not exactly accurate. Gen doesn't bother deflecting because the pine cone lands wide. Okay, it lands in the next county.

Jaeger shakes his head and stands, holding the warm hibachi by the handles, the paper bag stuffed under his arm. "We're going to need to work on that."

"I thought you said I'm never to throw anything ever again."

"And did you listen?"

Shit. He has me there.

Jaeger walks to the back gate. "Later, Gen. Cali, I'll see you tomorrow."

Tomorrow?

"Eleven a.m.," he calls from the driveway.

I trust what Jaeger said about him and Gen, so if he isn't hooking up with her, what is going on? There's something Gen isn't telling me.

Chapter Seventeen

T HE NEXT MORNING, Gen growls. "Friggin' hell." She spilled about a thousand Cheerios onto the kitchen floor.

A few roll out of the kitchen and I kick them back inside. "Better clean that up."

She squints across the counter, her eyes half-lidded, a lock of hair sticking straight up on one side. "Why are you up? You're jobless. Shouldn't you be sleeping until two or three, or job-hunting?"

I deserved that. "Touché. Jaeger told me to be ready at eleven, remember?"

She grumbles a response. Something about noisy roommates and waking too early.

Oopsie, I might have made a little noise in my eagerness to get ready for my date.

The coffee maker pours a stream of deliciousness into the pot. It's almost done, but... screw it. Gen's grumpiness is in top form and requires evasive action.

I pull out the carafe—it's one of those auto-stop ones—and pour her a cup. "Here."

She takes a sip, dustpan in hand. "*Ahhh, gracias.*"

My cell phone rings. I grab my purse from the counter and toss everything out until I locate my phone at the very bottom.

"Hey, sis."

"Tyler?" This is weird. He must be back in Boulder, but I

don't usually hear from him for a few weeks after a visit. "What are you up to?"

"Still out and about," he says.

"What does that mean?"

"Well—um—I'm hanging with Mom."

Tyler visits in the summertime, but never for more than a couple of weeks.

"Did you lose your job?" I say in a panicked rush. Great. Friggin' great. Both Morgan kids can't screw up their futures. It'll crush Mom.

"Relax. I didn't lose my job. Just needed a break from Boulder."

Tyler loves Boulder. "Okaaay. What's your plan?"

"Well, I was thinking I could come back out there for a bit. I'm bored in Carson. Mom's new place is nice, but it's too flat here. Nothing to do. My buddy in the Keys wants to show me new bike trails. I could crash with him, but he's got a girlfriend, and... you know."

"Crowded."

"Right, so what do you think? Can I camp in your loft? I'll stay out of your hair. Promise."

"Stay for as long as you like. You don't have to pretend to be invisible. I like having you around—but don't tell anyone I said that."

He laughs. "Your secret is safe with me. But you might change your tune if I see any guys sniffing around your place. I'm still your big brother."

And he's friends with Jaeger. That could get complicated. What would Tyler think of us, and whatever it is we're doing? "I'm twenty-one, Tyler. You can lock the big brother protective crap away. I'm not a virgin."

He lets out a deep breath. "I'm going to pretend I didn't hear that. And you can tell Gen I've got my eye out for her too. Any guys entering the abode will have to pass the Tyler Detector."

"This should be fun," I say flatly.

"I knew you'd agree."

JAEGER PICKS ME up right on time and he cometh bearing gifts.

"How did you know I like lattes?"

He smiles from the driver's seat. "Green olives I deduced. The latte was a lucky guess."

"You have good taste."

This time I get the full effect of his gaze. "Yes, I do."

My face grows warm and I peer out the window, hiding the flush I know is there. Being strawberry blond doesn't exempt me from everything that comes with being a redhead. But at least I narrowly missed freckles.

"So what are we doing?" We've passed Stateline. Wherever we're going it isn't in town.

"I'm taking you to my house. I'd like to show you what I do."

We talked a little about ourselves last night, but showing is always better. I have a good idea of what he does for a living—I've seen the woodcarvings by local artisans littering the side of Highway 89 my entire life—but if he wants to show me, I'm game.

A few minutes later, Jaeger pulls into a long gravel driveway, tall pines towering majestically along the sides. A clearing at the end opens to a house next to a square building with a similar pitched roof and approximate size. Beyond the two structures, the lake peeks through more pines. Most people with this real estate would have clear-cut and widened the view of the lake, but the owner has kept it fairly natural.

It's a nice house. Really nice. I didn't think Jaeger lived with his parents, but I figured he rented an apartment like Mason. How much does a bear and totem pole carver actually make?

Jaeger steps out of the truck and closes my door behind me. "Let's take a look at the house first. I've got lunch ready." He moves ahead to open the front door.

What is happening? Lattes and green olives, the home-delivered meals—that's all A-game material.

Is he *wooing* me?

My memories of early dating rituals are hazy. Eric didn't make much of an effort in that department. Both Gen and Jaeger have denied there's anything between them, so that's no longer a barrier. Jaeger is Tyler's friend, and I will for sure receive shit for that, but I can deal with my brother. Eric and I are history, and I've mostly recovered from being dumped. By all accounts, I should be jumping all over Jaeger with my normal abandon, yet something still holds me back.

I don't want Jaeger to be a rebound, that's true, and I worry about it some, but not as much as before. Jaeger's different. We're different. If I allow it, I think this could be something serious. But life is confusing right now. I don't know what I want to do about school, but I also don't want to mess up what's between me and Jaeger. Because I like it. I like it a lot.

Jaeger walks up the steps to a small covered porch with logs for support beams and a wide stone chimney with a built-in outdoor grill. Picture windows off the porch face the lake. He unlocks the door and we step inside the house.

It's not what I expected.

The exterior was spectacular, but anyone can rent a place that looks good from the outside. The interior and what you do with it is something else entirely, especially when it comes to men.

There isn't a hint of guy-shabby chic anywhere inside Jaeger's place, not even your token crooked wall hanging. A modern, comfortable-looking sable sectional faces the hearth, a massive TV to the side of the fireplace. The art around the room is the real deal, colorful, but masculine to match the decor. There's a dining table like the trestle table inside Jaeger's parents' house, only this one is carved with Mission-style accents.

Jaeger strides past the kitchen island and opens a stainless steel refrigerator. "Can I get you anything to drink?"

My mouth is parched, but not from thirst. Nerves are getting to me. Who is this person with the beautiful home, wooing me like I've never been wooed before? And am I ready for him?

He's everything I never knew I wanted.

I thought I was self-confident to a fault, and that was how I ended up with Eric. We fell into a committed relationship, because *I* persisted and determined we would. I was at the top of my class, destined for a great career. A guy's not sure? You charm him into being sure. I made it easy for Eric to be with me. I didn't complain about him going out with his friends. Didn't ask why he never introduced me to his family. He didn't have to work for us. I made it happen.

But this thing with Jaeger is different. We're on equal ground emotionally and intellectually, and it makes me nervous. What have I to offer? I have no job, an uncertain future... it was all fun and games when I thought I had a leg up professionally, but I'm beginning to wonder about his totem pole business.

"Just water, thanks."

Jaeger hands me a glass and pulls out a blue ceramic bowl from the refrigerator, containing a fluffy green salad with sliced strawberries on top. A plate of raw meat joins the salad on the counter.

He turns on a grill in the cooktop and spreads out slices of meat. "Make yourself comfortable," he says over his shoulder. "This will take about ten minutes. We'll eat, and then I'll show you around."

I glance at his immaculate home. It makes the cottage Gen and I live in look like a shanty. "Do you mind if I go outside? I'd like to take a look at the lake." And gulp in air.

Jaeger gazes at me, his expression approving. "That's why I picked this place. For the view." He smiles and wipes his hands on a dishtowel, his shoulders tense. I wonder if he's nervous too. "I'll come get you when it's ready."

The familiar scent of pines fills my lungs, grounding me as I walk to the edge of the yard. I pass the workshop, curious about it—really curious—but I don't peek inside.

A log swing with plush cushions faces the lake above the stony shore. I take a seat and tuck my legs beneath me, clenching my hands together.

Being with Jaeger is easy. I don't have to strategize to get him to want to spend time with me. He makes it happen. I've never had anything I didn't have to work for. School was easier for me than for most people, but I still put in time and energy. This thing with Jaeger is natural, and it scares the shit out of me.

I'm not sure how much time has passed when the swing moves of its own volition. I glance up, and Jaeger slides in beside me, placing his hand lightly on my ankle. We gaze at the lake together without talking. I've never felt this kind of calm and peace with another person.

He leans close, his chin above my shoulder, nose nuzzling the lobe of my ear. "What do you think?"

I gather he's talking about the view and not his hand on my leg, which is very distracting. "I love it."

He shifts and lifts me onto his lap, his arms a protective enclosure. "I want you to be happy here."

I tense. This is so much. He's so much. I have nothing to offer.

His brow furrows as though he senses my thoughts. He kisses my cheek and then my mouth, his hands running up and down my arms in a soothing manner. I lean into him, my body going slack. Tingles spread from my core as he deepens the kiss. I wrap my arms around his neck, running my fingers through his short, soft hair.

Jaeger breaks the kiss first, but he doesn't pull away, he holds me close. His pulse pounds against my lips at his throat. "We'd better go in or I'll want to stay here for a while. Our lunch will go bad." He lifts my chin and pecks my lips. "To be continued," he says with a knowing look, and leads me into the house, his hand wrapped around mine.

The tri-tip salad is delicious. The guy seriously knows how to cook, while I've been keeping the frozen meal section of the grocery store in business. We finish our food with a glass of red wine, and he gives me the tour of the house.

I've already seen the great room, which includes the dining area, kitchen, and living room. Down the hall, the master bedroom faces the lake, while on the other end of the house sits a second bedroom and a large office that holds a couch, a pinball machine, and another massive TV. In other words, a man-cave.

The man-cave is more in line with what I expected from the home of a twenty-four-year-old. Medals and a few trophies are piled haphazardly in a glass case, along with other odd guy curios, like signed baseballs—and a pair of boxers with a woman's lipstick mark.

"Nice boxers."

"Oh—yeahhh... That's from a while ago."

"Yours, I assume?"

He nods, a sheepish smile crossing his face.

"But someone else's lipstick, I hope?"

Jaeger grabs my hand and pulls me to his chest. "One of the random celebs that came through town."

I frown, imagining the female vacationers looking for hookups, and spotting Jaeger. No one could pass him up.

He kisses my mouth, my lips stiff and unyielding. "I'm not proud of some of the choices I've made in the past, but that's all behind me now," he says.

What choices? And what does that mean? This entire date feels serious, like he's trying to tell me something.

"Come on. I'll show you my woodshop."

Jaeger pulls me out a back door, across stone pavers, and into a huge, open indoor space filled with machinery and some type of ductwork sprouting from a table in the center. There's a comfortable-looking leather couch to the side, and a couple of doors at the back of the building.

He points to the doors. "One of those is a bathroom, the other a drying room with fans."

In the corner of his shop stands an eight-foot carved wind-ing trellis. "That's really pretty." It's bigger than anything I imagined him working on, and far more beautiful.

"Wedding arbor I'm making for a client's daughter." He presses gently on the curve of my lower back and guides me forward. "I've done cabinetry and other extras, but my bread and butter is over here."

Tiered slats built into the lower half of one of the walls are filled with dozens of square and rectangular flat wooden etchings in every size. Next to them, a display shelf with a square black velvet drape hangs from the wall. Jaeger pulls out one of the smaller etchings, about two feet by two feet, and places it on the shelf.

I stare for a long moment without saying anything, because my throat is tight and I'm not sure words will come out. I've seen art in museums and from local artisans—there's a boatload of shops in town. But I've never seen anything like the carving in front of me.

At first glance, three deer graze in various poses, as if the artist pulled them from a photograph. Upon closer inspection, the grain of the wood is worked into the design, though the only actual carving is of the deer and not their surroundings. The etching isn't cheesy or cheap. It's beautiful. Elegant. Nature carved on nature, and I can't stop staring.

"Well? What do you think?"

"I—wow. It's nothing like what I imagined. It's real art." That sounds lame, but it's the truth, I'm sorry to admit.

He chuckles and replaces the piece in its slot. "You thought less?"

"I thought you made totem poles and sold them on the side of the road."

He shakes his head. "Cali, so little faith?"

"Well, how was I supposed to know you did this?" I wave

my arms wildly. "I don't know anyone with this kind of talent."

He picks me up and kisses my lips. "You think I'm talented?"

My toes are a good two feet off the ground. I'd be stupid to argue with him in such a vulnerable position. I twist my mouth. "You know you're talented."

He laughs again and whispers his lips across the sensitive skin at my neck. "I like to hear it coming from you."

His mouth on my neck sends a shiver down my arms. I look into his eyes. "Your work's beautiful, Jaeger."

An hour later, after Jaeger shows me several of his designs, holding my hand and stealing kisses throughout, he drops me off at the cottage with one last hot kiss on the doorstep and the promise of something special tomorrow.

I walk into our outdated, oversized closet of a rental, my head spinning. So this is what the expression *swept off your feet* means. I am floating, and without Jaeger to keep me grounded, I feel like I could drift away. What happened to my substance?

I'm still hovering in the living room when Tyler walks in a few seconds later. He dumps his duffel loudly in the same place as last time—the center of the pathway. He stares out the front window. "What are you doing with Jaeg?"

I sink onto the couch. "We're hanging out."

His mouth parts and his eyes narrow. "What do you mean, hanging out?"

"Dating, seeing each other—you know that ritual men and women do?"

Tyler steps closer. Here it comes, the you-can't-date-my-friend speech. "Cali, I get it that you're going through a rough time. I know the feeling."

He does? He doesn't know I lost my job. He must be referring to the breakup, but what does Tyler know about breakups? He hasn't had a girlfriend since high school.

"Which is why," he adds, "I want you to stay away from Jaeger. He's a good guy. He doesn't deserve to get fucked over on the rebound. He put up with enough shit from women in his past."

I stare, dumbfounded. There it was again, that allusion to Jaeger's past, which Jaeger said was behind him but that I'm getting the impression had left its mark. "Are you warning *Jaeger* away from *me*? What happened to the Tyler Detector and keeping guys away from your innocent sister? And for the record, I *am* a nice girl."

Tyler sits next to me on the couch, the weight of his large body making me bounce on my end of the cushion. "You are, but like I said, you're"—he flaps his hand—"messed up. Unstable right now."

I shake my head in exasperation. "Thanks, Tyler, 'cause I needed my brother to turn on me in my time of need."

He nudges my shoulder. "I'm not turning on you. It's just that I know Jaeg. I know what he's been through. The Olympics were months away when he had his accident. Not years— months, Cali. Training was his life and he lost it all. And then he had to deal with... well—anyway, all of that messed him up."

Tyler rubs his mouth and shakes his head. "I saw the way he watched you at his parents' place. He's a serious guy, and he likes you. If you're not serious about him, don't do this."

The last thing I want is to hurt Jaeger, not that it seems possible. The guy appears pretty self-sufficient, and he doesn't lack for female attention, considering the attractive client I saw hanging all over him. But I get what my brother is saying. I'm a little off-kilter right now, free-falling, as it were. Okay, I have not idea where my life is going and I'm totally screwed up.

The problem with giving up Jaeger is that not being with him would hurt me. I'm happy just hanging around him, not to mention, his kisses turn my limbs the consistency of pudding. I felt terrible when I thought I'd lost him to Gen. I don't want to go through that again. "Why are you really in town, Tyler?"

He stands and rummages in his bag, his movements stiff and jerky. "I had a similar situation with a girl. Nothing I want to talk about."

My big brother had his heart broken? That's a first.

I lay my head on the back of the couch and wince. My stomach is tied in knots. "Well, you're welcome to stay as long as you want." I glance over, and Tyler's staring at me.

"What's wrong? You sick?" he asks.

I rock my head from side to side and gaze at the ceiling. "I'm a loser, Tyler. I haven't told you or Mom yet, but I lost my job." He raises a brow, and I wave off the questions. "Long story."

He sits beside me again. "You're not a loser. You're almost as smart as me, which makes you one of the smartest people on the planet."

Confidence runs in the family.

In comparison to Jaeger and what he accomplished after adversity, I am a loser. At the moment, I have nothing to offer but baggage.

Before I left his place, Jaeger told me he bought his house and workshop with the money he earned. That beautiful place and the property is *his*. He's wealthy—and I thought he was a side-of-the-road salesman. I figured with my college degree, I had the upper hand, but I don't.

I can't stay in Lake Tahoe forever. My mom would have a heart attack, and I'd never amount to anything working one of the myriad unskilled jobs available.

If I obtain my law degree, that would be something. I wouldn't be a loser with no future. I'd have something to contribute to a relationship. Eric booted me when I had things going for me. How would a relationship with someone like Jaeger ever survive?

I am nothing without that law degree.

Chapter Eighteen

T HE NEXT DAY I do laundry and wait for Jaeger to call or text. Yes, that's how lame I've become. I'm sitting around waiting for a guy to call. Gen's having an early lunch with Nessa, and Tyler drove to his friend's place. Not having a car bites now that Gen and I are no longer on the same schedule.

I fold clothes on the bed and glance at the phone every few minutes. It rings, or rather, chimes, and I launch across the bed in a quasi-cartwheel and swipe it off the nightstand.

I take a deep breath and let it out easy. He doesn't need to know I just sprinted to answer the call. "Hello?" I say calmly.

"Hey, Cali."

What the hell? "*Eric?*"

"Surprised?"

"Yeeahh. Kinda."

"I wanted to check in. See how you're doing." He sounds happy, which is pretty annoying. It's not that I don't want him happy, but he doesn't need to rub it in after the way he treated me.

"I'm good, Eric. Everything's good."

"Awesome. Things are going well over here too. I finish school at the end of the month and just accepted a job with a start-up in Silicon Valley. Great benefits package, vacation, the works. Some travel, as well. It's a good opportunity. Lots of room for growth."

My loser ex has a life and he called to brag? "Good for you, Eric," I say, attempting to mean it.

"When do you leave for Harvard?" he asks cheerily.

I rub my forehead with a fist. "Uhh, well, I'm not sure. I guess I'm going." I should go. I need to go if I want a life.

"What do you mean, you guess?"

"Well… I was sort of considering not attending. I'm not sure it's the right path for me."

"Are you insane?" His voice ends on a high pitch. "You're joking, right?"

What the hell? Eric never cared about my plans. Not until he broke up with me and indicated our different futures was part of the reason.

"I was considering deferring or maybe trying something else." I have no idea what that something else would be, but with Eric acting judgmental, I don't want to sound like an even bigger loser and admit I don't have a plan. "In all likelihood, I'll end up going to law school."

"Yeah—well, good luck with that," he says insincerely. "I gotta go. I need to wrap up finals and search for a place on the peninsula. Me and a couple of buddies are living together. It's gonna be rad."

Did he just use the word *rad*?

Eric got his shit together, so I have to give props for that. My ex and I have switched places. How awesome. Just— fantastic. "Okay, well, congratulations on your new job."

"Thanks. I'll see you around."

Will he? I doubt it. I end the call and toss the phone on the bed, planting my face in the mattress.

Payback is a *biiitch*.

JAEGER STUFFS THE sandwiches and drinks he bought at the marina convenience store into his backpack. He called shortly after Eric did and surprised me with a hike at Fallen Leaf Lake.

We climb down the steps to the beach and walk along the shore to the trailhead. "My ex called today," I blurt.

His gaze slides to me, his pace slowing to a stroll.

"He called to tell me how great his life is." I sink onto the craggy surface of a large rock. What I have to say isn't directly related to Eric, but it needs to be said before things go further.

I stare out at the water. "I don't want to go to law school, Jaeger. Not even to one I can afford. I don't want to go at all."

He sits on the low stone beside me, which puts his shoulders only a few inches above mine instead of a foot.

I turn and look at him. "I might not end up being who you thought I'd be when we started this." Silence. He's watching me with a calm expression on his face that tells me nothing. "What are you thinking?"

Jaeger slides the backpack from his shoulder and sets it on the ground. "I think you are who I thought you were when I saw you again, and that you should do what makes you happy. You're a talented, smart girl. You can do anything you want."

I choke. "Talented? I'm not talented. I'm good at school. Smart, yes, although that's questionable at the moment. A smart person wouldn't give up a top law program."

He looks out at the water. "You're an artist too. Don't put yourself in a box, Cali. And your ex…" He shakes his head. "Dumbass. Better for me." He grins.

Jaeger spreads his feet wider, resting his forearms on his knees. "I never cared that you got into Harvard. I didn't know that's what you were doing before… well, anyway. That's not what impressed me about you, though your intelligence is hot."

The corner of his mouth kicks up, light stubble along his jaw flickering blond in the light.

I grin. His words are like a warm blanket; they soothe and comfort. He sees me better than I see myself. "What did you mean when you said I'm an artist?"

"Your sketches."

"My *doodles*?"

He nods slowly. "They're amazing."

Is he crazy? No one has ever told me my doodles are good, not that I flash them around or anything. Gen likes them, but she also thinks vampire romances are literature and sings along to "Islands in the Stream." Her tastes are dubious. She's not a reliable source.

Jaeger picks up a twig from the ground and twists it between his fingers. "I thought skiing and the Olympics were everything I wanted in life. That skiing was the only thing I could do. When it all fell away, I thought I had nothing left. My knee was jacked from tearing it too many times and my long-term girlfriend broke up with me. The girlfriend thing turned out for the best, but—" He looks up. "I know what it's like to get dumped in life. I understand the doubts that go through your head. Believe me when I say that your ex was an idiot who didn't know what he had."

Those words are easier to believe about someone else. Why any girl would let Jaeger go baffles me. I can't imagine giving him up. I can barely take my eyes off him. "The girl you were with? She broke up with you after your accident?"

"We were together in high school and our first year of college. She broke up with me when I was in the hospital."

My throat tightens. It happened a long time ago, but I'm angry for him. "That's horrible," I finally manage.

He smirks. "Sort of, but she wasn't the person I thought she was. I should have ended it long before that."

Hmm. A curious statement. I want to know more, but I won't push.

"I wish I'd done things differently back then. In fact, after I realized I couldn't ski anymore… You remember me telling you about those years—"

"When you were a man-whore."

He smiles, his eyes crinkling. "When I was a man-whore." Then his face sobers. "It was a stupid, immature reaction to the chaos in my life. In comparison, you've handled what you've been dealt with really well. Better than I did."

I pick at a weed in front of me. "I haven't turned into a slut."

The corner of his mouth quirks. "Maybe, but that's not my point. You're a good friend, Cali. You look out for Gen. I've seen you with your brother and the bond you share. You're a hard worker or you wouldn't have gotten into law school… and I remember you when we were younger. You've always been feisty, with an underlying sweetness." He shifts on the rock, planting his feet more firmly on the ground. "I had a crush on you back then," he says faintly, looking out at the water.

My mouth gapes and I stare at him.

After a moment, he glances over and smiles at what I'm assuming is my stunned expression. "It's not something I admitted to myself back then. I was young and stupid. I thought I was in love with Kate—or at least, that I needed her. I'm not sure now." He shakes his head. "I was busy, training nonstop. I glossed over things with her that I shouldn't have. I didn't trust my instincts. The more I get to know you, the more I realize you're everything I wanted and still want. I know you're going through a hard time, and believe me, I'm trying to give you space, but it's difficult. I want to be with you."

I stop breathing for a moment, my head spinning. I figured he liked me. I wondered to what degree, with all the wooing. I never imagined his interest stemmed from as far back as high school—when I had my own little crush on the younger version of Jaeger. "What are you saying?"

His gaze shifts down, then out at the water. "Just that I'm here. I'm not going anywhere." He looks back. "No matter what direction your life takes. Things feel messed up, but you'll pull through this and you'll have me."

As much as that statement comforts, I can't help but won-der… why? My life's a wreck. I can't handle not knowing where I'm headed. I need to know, or I can't see a future with Jaeger or anyone.

God, I sound like a guy, needing financial security before I can commit. But I was raised differently. My mom taught my brother and me to be independent and to provide for ourselves instead of relying on others. I can't simply wipe that program from my head. I have to figure out what I'm doing before I make promises. But I also don't want to lose Jaeger.

No more serious talks about the future or feelings come up during the rest of our hike, which is a relief. I need time to process everything. Jaeger holds my hand as we check out a small mountain chapel nestled off the trail, but he doesn't kiss me. That doesn't stop me from drooling every time he lunges over a boulder near the cascades, his shorts straining against his perfect ass. The degree to which I lust after him is embarrassing.

He drops me off at my house after the hike and pecks me on the cheek. The gesture is friendly and platonic, and not at all in line with his earlier words. Is he giving me space?

Jaeger said he'd stand by me no matter what I decide, but the only logical course is to plan for Cambridge. There are cheaper and closer programs, but I'd be a dumbass to pass up Harvard. Attending school there is what an independent, intelligent woman would do. I can't stand this fragile, broken thing I've become.

It's the only way I can get back to being myself.

Chapter Nineteen

IT'S BEEN OVER an hour since Jaeger dropped me off and Gen hasn't returned from lunch with Nessa. I check my phone for messages. Finding none, I open a new text, but stop typing at the sound of a car pulling into the driveway.

My eyes bulge. Gen's in the passenger side of a red Jeep in a heated conversation with Lewis from the beach barbecue. Mira's boyfriend.

Where the heck is Gen's car?

I can't believe she's with this guy. He's the A-hole all over again. Is she intentionally trying to ruin her chance for happiness?

I sink onto the couch and twist my hands together. I thought bringing Gen to Lake Tahoe would be a good thing. I can't believe she's putting herself back in the same situation she escaped.

Gen shuts the front door behind her and presses her back to it, her eyes closed. I spring up in full attack mode. "What the hell, Gen? What are you doing with that guy?" I point forcefully at the window and Lewis, his head turned as he reverses out of the driveway.

Gen presses her fingers to her temples. "He's not that bad, Cali. Simmer down." She looks up. "It's not what you think."

"You're doing it all over again!" I'm stressed and taking it out on my BF, but I can't stop. The stress of what I need to do—what I should do to keep my independence—is making me crazy. "Did you learn nothing the first time? Get a clue, Gen, this guy is using you!"

Her hands fist at her sides. "And you know so much about men? Did you know Eric hit on me? He wanted to sleep with me, Cali."

Her words knock my head back. "*What?*"

"I'm sorry. I should have told you sooner."

Gen's phone buzzes. She checks it, then storms into our bedroom while I stand in the doorway, stunned. She takes off her sneakers—*are her clothes wet?*—and pulls a pair of sandals out of the closet, along with a fresh top and bottoms.

"I tried to tell you that day at Eagle Lake," she continues, "but you said things were fine between you two." She sits and puts on her sandals, then pauses, hands on her thighs. "After you and Eric broke up, I told myself I'd be kicking you when you were down. I didn't want to cause you more pain. I panicked and more time passed."

I'm frozen. "What are you talking about?"

Gen whips off her T-shirt and pulls the new top over her head, arms poking through the sleeve holes. She turns to me. "Do you remember when I drove Eric to the store to pick up sunscreen while you were in the shower the first weekend in town?" I nod. "He came up behind me when we were there and wrapped his arms around my waist. He kissed my neck."

My head thrusts forward like a hound's. "What the fuck! Why are you only telling me this now?"

"I was still getting over the A-hole and not thinking clearly. It freaked me out. I worried you'd get the wrong idea and believe I led Eric on. You don't know what it's like."

"Are you kidding me? You're seriously telling me that guys

lusting after you is a hardship that forces you to betray your *best—fucking—friend.*" I can't help the F-bombs. They surface when I'm furious.

She shakes her head, her eyes agonized. "That's not what happened. That's not what I'm saying."

"What are you saying?"

Gen grabs her purse and drapes it across her chest. Her cheeks are attractively flushed from whatever the hell she was doing with her new cheating boyfriend, and her pink blouse, shorts, and sandals fit her tall, lithe body to perfection. I sort of hate her right now.

Her hands twist in the long strap of her purse. "He said he'd always been attracted to me." She looks away, voice light, lips barely moving. "That things were fizzling between you two and that you'd basically become friends."

I sink onto the mattress, my head in my hands. *Bastard.* I can't believe he called me, and I allowed him to make me feel bad. I don't care what kind of job he got or how good his life is. He's a piece of shit.

I look up, pointedly. "What did you say to him?"

"No! I said no! I never wanted that. He made me feel… dirty. I would never…"

That's what was bothering her the day of the hike when we first arrived in Tahoe. Not thoughts of her A-hole ex, but that my shithead boyfriend had made a pass at her.

She walks up and rests her hand lightly on my shoulder. "Cali, we need to talk, but I have to go or I'll be late for work. I'm sorry, okay?"

I don't look up. I don't answer. Gen sighs and walks out of our bedroom. The front door shuts a moment later, punctuating the finality of this moment.

When Gen and I first arrived in Tahoe, she was the broken one and I was her support. Now, we're both broken and there's a gulf between us.

What is happening?

I can't believe I'm questioning Gen's loyalty. She's always been there for me. It wasn't her fault Eric is a jerk. She was put in a bad position. Who knows what I would have done in her place?

THE MORE HOURS that pass, the more I regret my anger toward Gen. I overreacted and took out my pain on her. I was hyped up and agitated before she walked in the door for reasons that had nothing to do with her. She should have told me about Eric, but anyone would be hesitant. Who would be eager to tell a friend that their boyfriend hit on them?

I could wait for Gen to come home to talk, but that doesn't seem good enough. I'm not excited to face the critical looks from my old coworkers at Blue, but I can't let things stand the way they are. I'll try to catch Gen on her break and apologize for the way I reacted.

I go out into the living room and Tyler walks in the door.

He tips his head up in greeting, and toes off his shoes. He drops his keys on the kitchen counter and grabs a beer from the fridge, then slumps on the couch and turns on motocross. He's wearing the same shirt he had on yesterday.

Something seems off, but since I've got many things that appear off in my life, I decide Tyler's issues can wait. "Can I borrow your car for a bit?"

His eyes flick up. "Sure, what's up?"

"Nothing, I just need to talk to Gen about something."

Tyler straightens his leg, pulls his keys from his pocket, and tossing them to me. "When will you be home?"

"In an hour, Grandma."

His mouth twists. "Don't crash my wheels." I roll my eyes. Tyler's Land Cruiser is about thirty years old. If I crash, it's because the steering sucks.

I park in the Blue parking garage and walk in the doors closest to Gen's cocktail lounge, hoping to avoid people. Mason spots me first, smiles, then glances nervously across the room. I follow his gaze—to Jaeger holding Gen in a corner of the lounge.

My feet stop moving and my heart drops into my stomach. Gen's arms are around Jaeger's waist, his hand tucking her head close, comforting her in the same way he's done with me. I try to swallow, but my mouth is dry.

I don't know what's real. I thought I knew—thought I'd jumped all over Gen wrongly. Now nothing makes sense.

The guy I believed cared for me, in a way no other guy has, is embracing my best friend. Right after she told me my ex-boyfriend betrayed me with her. And there's been this distance between me and Gen…

Jaeger said there was nothing going on between him and Gen, but looking at them now, that's hard to believe.

What am I doing here? I have to clear my head, think rationally.

Whipping around, I stumble into a body, my arms tangling with hard limbs. Drake uses my imbalance to haul me off the casino floor by my waist, one arm across the back of my shoulders.

"Let me go, Drake," I growl as he carries me toward an elevator cove.

"We need to have a little talk, pretty girl." His voice is calm, steady, but his grip pinches the skin on my shoulder and he's hurting my ribs with his tight hold.

If he tries to drag me into an elevator, I'll scream my fucking lungs out.

Drake stops in a relatively quiet section beside the elevators, his chest blocking my view of the rest of the casino. "I'm surprised to see you, Cali. Didn't think you'd show your face after you were fired." Vodka vapors waft off his breath.

He crosses his arms and shakes his head. His eyes leave me briefly to glare over his shoulder—at Jaeger hunched protectively over Gen.

Drake's toxic breath and the image of the guy I'm falling for with my best friend bring bile to my throat. I flatten my hands behind me against the wall and swallow the sour taste in my mouth. And realize a moment later how weak that makes me look.

Straightening my shoulders, I say, "What do you want?"

The look Drake levels at me is ruthless. "Your tall friend won't be able to pull the same stunt in here that he did the other night." He taps two fingers to his temples and raises them to the ceiling. "I'm the eyes inside Blue. One move out of line and I'll have him thrown out." He cocks his head. "I could be persuaded to put in a good word for you. Help you get your job back." His gaze trails my body, sending a shiver of repulsion down my back. "With the right motivation."

I pinch my mouth and hold back a gag. "You're horrible. I must have been drunk off my ass to let you take me home. Leave me alone, Drake." I push past him, but he grabs my arm and squeezes until my fingers go numb.

"Remember who's in charge here." He shakes me, wrenching my neck. "Show a little respect."

My eyes open wide at the threat. I'm not an employee. I have no rights. This is Drake's world—his word against mine. What he's doing to me is wrong and looks bad under any circumstances, but how do I know he didn't drag me to the one place no one can see us? Or that he won't tamper with the surveillance footage? "You made your point. Let me go."

Drake releases his hold and plasters a charming smile on his face. "The offer of help stands."

I don't trust myself to respond—afraid that whatever comes out of my mouth will make matters worse. I move toward the exit, glancing over my shoulder to make sure I'm not being followed.

Inside the parking garage, I run to my brother's car and lock the door the second I'm in. The tightening in my chest from holding my breath ebbs, replaced by a sharp pain as images of Gen and Jaeger blind me. It could have been innocent—him holding her—but after what Gen told me this afternoon, I feel like I don't know anything.

My head sinks onto the headrest. I thought returning to Lake Tahoe would help me work through my reservations over grad school. But it's horrible here.

I have to get out. Away from all of this.

THE DOOR TO the cabin slams shut behind me, but my brother's gaze remains fixed on the television. He hasn't moved from his position on the couch. The only difference between when I left and now is that he's watching a surfing flick instead of motocross.

"Tyler, I need to leave."

"Okay," he says without looking up. "I'm not planning on going anywhere. Take the car."

"No. I mean I need to get out of town. I want to visit Mom. She's been asking me to come."

Tyler lifts his gaze. "Uh, okay. When were you thinking?"

I close my eyes briefly and inhale. "Now?"

"Now. As in, right now? This minute?"

I nod.

Tyler clicks off the television and sets the remote on the couch's armrest. "What's up, Cali? What's going on?"

"Everything. Have you ever just needed to get out of town?"

Tyler looks past me. "Yeah."

"Well, this is one of those moments. I can't stay here another minute."

He slaps his knees with his palms and stands. "Okay, then. Pack your stuff. We'll call Mom on our way."

Tears collect behind my eyes. I have an awesome brother. Tyler knows something's up, but he's not pushing for details. He's giving me space.

If I cry, though, he will ask. I blink hard and swallow back the tears. I go into my room to pack.

An hour later, we pull into the drive of Mom's single-level house in Carson City. It's dark and there's not much to see, but the neighborhood appeared quiet and safe as we drove in.

My mom opens the front door, pushes out a metal screen, and takes the first step onto the cement stoop. She clenches her cotton bathrobe closed. "Nobody's sick or dying?"

"We're fine, Mom," I say as I walk up the driveway.

"All right, then. Tyler, show your sister to the guest bedroom. You can sleep on the couch."

"The couch?" He groans. "Mom, last week I was in the

guest room. Now I'm relegated to the couch?"

"Would you like to sleep on the floor? No? Then quit your bitching and help your little sister with her luggage."

Tyler tosses my bag over his shoulder and disappears inside.

My mom grabs my hand before I pass. "We'll talk tomorrow about what's going on."

She can always tell when something's up. She knows me, and she's intuitive. And I need her right now more than I care to admit.

Chapter Twenty

Do not go where the path may lead, go instead where there is no path and leave a trail.

—Ralph Waldo Emerson

M Y MOM'S LITTLE rancher has blue carpeting and brown tile counters, but it's hers. I can tell by the way she flutters around the kitchen the next morning that she loves it. She's making her famous cheesy eggs while Tyler sleeps in. After Mom and I woke and started banging around in the kitchen, Tyler wobbled into the guest bedroom and, I assume, crashed on the bed I'd abandoned.

My mom sets a cup of coffee and some toast in front of me, sliding the eggs from the pan onto my plate. "Okay, Calista. Talk."

I'm not sure if it's her voice, her use of my full name, or the soothing remnants of her perfume, but large tears gather behind my eyes, creeping down the slope between my nose and cheek.

She rounds the table, scooches my butt over on the seat with her own, and locks me in a hug. "Shhh. It can't be that bad, honey."

"It's bad." There's so much crap that's built up, I'm not sure where to start. I begin with the most obvious. I've gone back and forth, but my instincts haven't veered. I take a deep breath and look up. "I don't want to go to law school."

Mom stills for a moment, then rubs my arm. Up and down. Up and down.

"Do you hate me?"

She pulls back. "Why would I hate you?"

"Because I'm not living up to my potential."

She shakes her head. "Cali, you've always lived up to your potential. You've never failed at anything you put your mind to."

"Eric dumped me." Might as well get all the humiliating shit out there.

She snorts. "Never liked him."

"You didn't?" I study her face. "You never said anything."

"I wanted you to figure it out on your own. A mother doesn't tell her daughter not to date a guy. It's a sure way to push her into his arms." She nudges me and winks. "I speak from experience. At least your father gave me you and Tyler. He also gave you his brilliant brain. Thankfully, you have my common sense."

"Mom, you're smart."

She smiles. "Yes, honey."

I roll my eyes. This is a common argument. I hate it when my mom puts herself down. She's had a rough life. She deserves more than she's been given. She sure as hell doesn't deserve a daughter screwing things up.

She takes the seat next to me, giving my ass cheek back its spot on the chair. "What are you going to do? Do you want to stay here for a while? I spoke to Connie. She told me you lost your job at the casino."

I spit the gulp of coffee I took back into the cup and pinch my nostrils. Some of the liquid went up my nose. "She did?" My voice comes out in a high squeak. "And you didn't call me?"

"I figured I'd hear from you soon."

I can't believe my mom isn't lecturing me right now.

She glares at me. "Didn't I warn you that place is a cesspool? Those people have no morals."

There's the lecture I expected. All is well in the world. I'm only surprised she isn't accusing me of making a poor decision with school. I wish she'd had this lax attitude when I was sixteen. Tommy Parson would have been blamed for sneaking in my window instead of me getting grounded for *allowing* it.

"Mom, I worked at the casino. You worked there. Not everyone who does has low morals."

"Well, there are exceptions." She sweeps a lock of gold-red hair from my eyes. "So, you lost your job, your boyfriend, and you don't want to go to the school you've worked half your life to get into. Have I got it all?"

"Shit, Mom. Do you need to spell it out like that?"

"Language, sister," she scolds, which is as hypocritical as it gets. My mom is where I got my potty mouth.

I frown. "There's one more thing to add to the list. I'm not sure, but… there's something going on with Gen."

She leans back like she's farsighted. "Is she okay?"

"I don't know. She's been keeping things from me. I just found out Eric hit on her while we were dating. Gen was kind of a mess at the time, so I sort of get why she didn't say anything until now. She said she didn't tell me because she was worried I would think she led him on. I'd just gotten done telling her things were great between me and Eric when they really weren't."

Mom takes a bite of the eggs cooling on her plate and I glance at my own. No one makes cheesy eggs like my mom. They're the perfect comfort food. I shovel in a mouthful.

"Cali, it sounds like she was caught in the middle and didn't want to lose your friendship."

I spear another forkful of cheese heaven. "I know, but..." My mom sips her coffee, then sets the mug down, waiting. "...she was with Jaeger and he was holding her, and Mom, it made me sick," I say, all in a rush.

"Jaeger? The boy your brother was frien—"

"Yes, yes." I shovel more eggs into my mouth.

"Uh-huh. Okay. So you're with Jaeg now."

"No, Mom! This is not about my love life."

She pushes her plate across the table toward the sink. "Are you sure? Sounds like there's something going on there."

"This is about *trust*. I don't know who to trust. Gen told me she wasn't seeing Jaeger, even though they went out, and then I found him holding her after I discovered she lied to me about Eric."

"And you don't trust yourself with your future. I think I'm getting the picture." She scrubs the dishes in the sink—no dishwasher in her new digs. She places my toast on a napkin and steals my empty plate. "What about Jaeg. Do you trust him?"

I press a finger to the napkin, picking up toast crumbs and licking them off. "I want to, but I panicked when I saw them together. It's partly why I came here."

It was the main reason—that and because Drake scared the shit out of me—but I'm not saying that to my mom. She'd want to know what's going on with Jaeger. What we have is new and fragile. I'm not ready to talk about it yet. And the bit about Drake would have her calling everyone she knows at the casino to take the man down, which actually doesn't sound half bad. But I don't need my mom fighting my battles for me.

"I should talk to Jaeger about what I saw, but I feel like I need to step away from it. Get my head on straight, you know? Aside from questioning what he and Gen were doing, Jaeger's this accomplished artist with tons of money and I just lost my shitty casino job. If I give in to my reservations about a law career, I can add grad school dropout to the list."

My mom rolls her eyes. "Oh, the drama. You can't be a dropout if you haven't attended. Figure out what you want and don't worry about what anyone thinks. Your brother and I will support your decision. We'd rather see you do something you love than something you hate. Have you any idea how difficult you are to live with when you're not happy?"

"Mom!"

"It's the truth. You're a very passionate person, sweetheart." My face flames. The last thing I want is for my mom to talk about me and passion in the same sentence. "You can either be passionately pissed off, or passionate about something that makes you happy. It's your choice."

One of my biggest worries was that my mom would be disappointed if I didn't attend Harvard or some other brilliant law school, but she's acting surprisingly cool about the whole thing. This should make me feel better. It does. I just don't want to end up nowhere.

I have my own life goals, and job success is one of them. What's the point of not attending graduate school if I don't feel good about where I end up? Because I know with certainty that I don't want to be a dealer for the rest of my life.

THAT AFTERNOON, TYLER and I stretch out on aluminum patio chairs in the backyard while my mom mans the barbecue. This is normal protocol in my family. My mom cooks and Tyler and I eat. Neither of us knows how to boil water (okay, we do, but we don't like to). It's extremely hot that Jaeger cooks, and self-preserving on my part to date him. Perks aside, I care for him and want to believe I misinterpreted what I saw. Given my state of mind over Gen at the time, I probably did, but I'm not ready to look into it. Fear is a fickle bitch.

I dig a scooped chip into the salsa and load as much on top as possible to piss my brother off. He frowns, hastily dumping more salsa from the jar into the bowl. "If we run out, you're making a store run."

Bull's-eye. Point one to Cali.

I study the chip in my hand. "Tyler, do you think I'm artsy?"

He chews a double-decker salsa-chip sandwich. "Sure. You make those sketches."

"Doodles…"

If I don't draw, I get grumpy. The doodles are my therapy, but I never thought about doing it for a living until Jaeger said I was talented. Artists are poor, right? Well, except Jaeger. He seems to be doing well. Even if he wasn't, he loves what he does. And that counts for a lot, I'm coming to realize.

Makes me wonder… if I got into an art program, could I do something with it? I'd have to moonlight in town to take art classes during the day.

It's not the worst idea.

Mom rotates the chicken kebabs on her rusted barbecue. She's wearing a V-neck T-shirt and turquoise shorts. Her pale legs look pretty darn toned for her forty-eight years. She tucks a lock of flame-red hair behind her ear. "Have you thought any more about what you want to do, Cali?"

We've been talking about Tahoe and jobs all day. After Tyler woke, I mentioned the reservations I have regarding school. He shrugged and said I should do what I want, so no help there.

"I enjoy the company and all," Mom says, "but you'll have to make a decision soon. You can stay with me, but I doubt Carson has more to offer than Lake Tahoe. What is it you really want?"

She sets the barbecue tongs on the handle of the grill and plops into the chair beside me. She tugs my shoulders around so that my back faces her, and she begins braiding my hair. It's our silent ritual. Mom says it relaxes her, but it downright puts me to sleep.

"I'm not going to law school, Mom." There, I've said it. I'm making it official. It was probably official the moment I told her I didn't want to go, but this is definitive. I don't know why this big decision now, with a tenuous love life and my livelihood and friendship with Gen in the toilet, but I'm taking a leap of faith it will all work out.

Mom's hands still, and I look over my shoulder. "Are you disappointed? You said you wouldn't be."

She shakes her head and scoots closer. "No, I'm not disappointed. Turn back around." I do as she says, and she starts braiding again. "Tyler isn't the medical doctor I envisioned the day he came home in sixth grade and rattled off the name of every bone in the human body, but he's teaching biology and living somewhere that makes him happy."

Tyler shifts in his chair, and I wonder again what he's not telling us. There's a story behind his long visit.

"I want that for you, sweetheart," Mom continues. "Trust me when I say you won't be happy working at the casinos for the rest of your life." From the corner of my eye, I see her shoulders rise and fall. "Do I feel a sense of panic when you say you'll be staying on at the lake? Yes. It's beautiful, but the lifestyle in that town can be crude. People come looking for utopia and wind up broke with an STD and a drug addiction."

My lip curls. "Gross, Mom."

"It's the truth."

I think about Drake and some of the other people I've worked with. She's totally right. The casinos attract people looking to make quick money, not all of them trustworthy or moral.

"You're capable of so much more, but if you don't want to go to Harvard, then you shouldn't." She swings the end of the braid over my shoulder and stands. "I don't want you to ever feel alone in this life. As long as there is air in my lungs, I'm here for you." She bends and kisses my forehead, her perfume and the soft feel of her lips a balm to my frayed nerves.

Chapter Twenty-One

I SPEND THE next couple of days at my mom's kitchen counter using my laptop to research art and design classes in Lake Tahoe. The more I think about pursuing art, the more right it feels. Jaeger put the bug in my ear during our hike at Fallen Leaf Lake, and if I think back, Gen nudged me a time or two about my drawings as well, but I never took her seriously. I wasn't ready.

I'm ready now.

Once I knocked down the walls of the narrow corridor that was the road to my future, the possibilities opened up. Options I never considered, but that were probably always there, waiting to be explored. What better time to try something new than when you have nothing to lose?

I texted Gen when I first arrived to tell her I'd be away, but I haven't contacted Jaeger, other than to tell him I'm out of town. He's called several times and left three messages. I haven't returned a single one. I need to figure myself out before I confront him. The last thing I want is to lose him, but getting myself in order should come first.

By the time Tyler and I return to the lake, I have pages of information on classes, as well as informational phone interviews lined up with a couple of local artists. I know zilch about what it takes to make a living in this field. I'm hoping that talking to other artists will help, and I wanted to do that outside of Jaeger, even though he's an artist too. This career change isn't about Jaeger. He gave me the idea for it, but this has to come from me, no matter what happens between him and I.

I've been sketching like crazy, and now that I've delved into it I wish I'd considered a creative art career a long time ago. It still scares the crap out of me. Art doesn't require a scholarly predisposition, which is what I've relied on to get ahead. Art is about creativity and imagination. A career in this field is a leap of faith that could make me truly happy—or could land me flat on my face. But considering that my nose has had an up close and personal view of the gutter, thanks to my ex-boyfriend and Blue Casino, what's the worst that can happen?

Since my brother and I have been back these last couple of days, both Gen and I have been busy. We haven't discussed the argument we had before I left, and I haven't asked her why she was in Jaeger's arms at the casino. The fact she kept the Eric thing from me for as long as she did has me hesitating. Which is all the more reason to talk to my best friend, because we've never had trust issues before and we need to get back on track.

But first… it's been nearly a week since I fled the casino and I've finally mustered up the nerve to visit Jaeger.

The location of his house from the one time I went there is a little fuzzy. I make two wrong turns and finally find the correct driveway on the third try. I could have called ahead, but I've avoided him for a week and I really want to see him in person to explain.

I'm in luck, because his truck is in the driveway.

My heart speeds up and my hands shake. I'm usually good with confrontation, but facing Jaeger has me scared. Now that I've had some time away from the whole situation, there's a good chance I misinterpreted what I saw going on between him and Gen at the casino, but there's also a chance I was right. It's that possibility that has my nerves in a bundle. Because I really care about Jaeger and I want to continue what we started.

I ease Tyler's old Land Cruiser beside Jaeger's truck and step out, gulping in the pine and earth scent, grounding myself. It's late afternoon and the sun is low in the sky, casting shadows around the front yard. A beam of light shoots past the swing where Jaeger kissed me, making me even more nervous and hopeful that everything will turn out okay.

My heart thumps hard as I jog up the front steps to his house and knock on the door. I pull my hair back and twist it behind my neck and out of my face.

After a long pause, I knock again, and glance back at his truck in the driveway to confirm I didn't imagine it there.

When still no one answers, I gingerly lean over the porch and peer in the window. The living room is dim and lifeless.

Did he go somewhere without his truck?

When I first exited the Land Cruiser, my ears were ringing from the noise of Tyler's beater, but now I'm picking up the sound of birds and insects—and a soft hum coming from the woodshop. He's working?

I make my way around the side of the house and across the pavers. The sound of a machine stirring the air grows louder.

I'm not surprised when no one answers my knock on his woodshop door, with the machine running so loudly inside. I twist the knob and slowly enter.

Jaeger's back is to me. He's in blue jeans and a plain T-shirt that fits loosely around his waist, hugging the muscles in his back and arms. He's working with something that looks like a giant sewing machine with a saw instead of a needle. Attention focused, his gloved hands carefully maneuver the wood in front of him.

The urge to run to him and wrap my arms around his back overwhelms me. I want to smell and touch him and be close. But I don't know where we stand or what I witnessed at the casino. Plus, I don't want him to cut off a finger. Lunging at him while he's operating a saw probably isn't the best idea.

Jaeger shuts off the machine, squats to adjust something under the table, and brushes wood shavings from his head. They fall like snow, and I wonder if that's the point of keeping his hair short.

The air in the shop smells of burnt wood and a faint hint of Jaeger's aftershave. I breathe in deeply and he stills. He pushes clear protective glasses to the top of his head and turns around.

"Hey," I say.

Expression blank, he doesn't move for a moment, seemingly stunned to see me here. Slowly, he pulls off his gloves and tucks them into his back pocket, his eyes darkening.

I move a few steps toward him. "I'm sorry I didn't call. I—I needed—"

My words cut off as he looks down my body with reverence and appreciation. His gaze stops on my mouth, a look of hunger in his eyes making my belly tighten.

How does he do that? Just one look and I want to spring at him and kiss him all over. Okay, maybe I wanted to do that from the moment I entered, but the look he's giving me intensifies the desire.

Jaeger rubs his forehead and leans against the table.

"I had to figure some things out," I finish, crossing my arms to keep the pounding of my heart from lurching out of my chest.

He follows the motion, his gaze in line with my breasts, taking its leisurely time back up to my face. Naughty, naughty boy—putting dirty thoughts in my mind. Okay—truth—they were already there.

Stay on track! "I wasn't sure I could trust you."

He gives his head a quick shake. "What?"

God, his deep, rumbly voice. *Focus!* "I saw you with Gen," I say in a rush. "At the casino. You were holding her."

Jaeger's brow furrows and he peers down, as if thinking. "When?"

"A week ago. I went to visit her and you were there. Your arms were wrapped around each other."

"Cali, I have no idea—wait, do you mean after that piece of shit touched her?"

Huh? Someone touched Gen? Like, groped her?

I have no idea what Jaeger's talking about, and that's just sad. My next point of business is to sit Gen down and figure out what's been going on. "What are you talking about?"

"Some coworker at the casino groped her—I don't know. You'll have to ask her for specifics. It happened while I was visiting Mason. She was shaken up. I talked to her and gave her a hug."

"That's all?"

Jaeger lets out a long breath. "Is this why you've been avoiding me? You still think there's something going on between me and Gen?"

I blink several times. Why does it sound reactionary and ridiculous when he says it? My logic seemed perfectly sound a week ago. "It's not as bad as it seems. Things happened. Gen and I are having trust issues."

"But you can trust *me*." Anger and frustration fill his voice.

He's right. I had no reason not to trust him. "I'm sorry. It's just, well, it upset me—seeing you with someone else. And with my friend?"

Jaeger stalks across the room and I take a step back. I don't think he'll hurt me, but instinct dictates I move out of the path of a large, determined male. He stops abruptly and grabs my hips, pulling me toward him. My hands fly to his arms for balance, and because he's hot and his biceps call to me. If the timing weren't so inappropriate, I'd nuzzle his chest too.

"The only woman I think about is you." He pushes me back and cradles my head before it slams into the wall. "I've been pretty direct about my intentions toward you." Jaeger skims his hands down and around the backs of my thighs, lifting and wrapping my legs around his waist.

I grasp his shoulders and he presses me to the wall, anchoring us. "I'm beginning to understand," I say in as calm a voice as I can manage. In reality, my heart is rampaging inside my chest like a wild animal, my entire body quivering like some virgin about to be deflowered.

He runs his nose down my neck, tickling my skin. "You sure? Need me to be more clear?" His hand slides up my thigh to my ass and squeezes.

I let out a breathy exhale. "It couldn't hurt," I say, voice thready.

Jaeger kisses my neck, his tongue dipping to the hollow at my throat. The scruff of his stubble brushes my skin as he drags his mouth toward my lips. "I want you," he says before taking my mouth in a deep, searing kiss.

I moan and kiss him with everything I've held back—everything I haven't said that's simmered inside from the moment we met.

His arms tighten around me, chest rising and falling more

quickly. He rocks his hard length right where I want it and a ripple of pleasure shoots through me.

Oh God. That. Again.

Using his shoulders for leverage, I mimic the move, but it's not enough. I can't reach all of him while I'm pressed to the wall, and I want more. "Go—" I say, between kisses, "some-where else." I wiggle to make my point, hormones robbing me of succinct speech.

He gets the gist, because one of his arms snakes behind my back, the other secured under my rear as he carries me away from the wall.

I kiss and lick and distract him as best I can. He's walking blind because of it, but I'm feeling a tad impatient. Clenching the back of his shirt, I tug upward, but the dang thing gets caught on his arms.

He needs his arms to hold me—an obvious problem if more than a tenth of my brain were operating. "Off," I mumble.

Where is he taking me? I hope it's close and not the house. That's like a football field away. One of these nice wooden surfaces would—

Suddenly I'm free-falling, gripping his shirt and not much else. I land on soft cushions.

My hands pat the surface beneath me. The old leather couch. Excellent.

Jaeger follows me down. *Now we are getting somewhere.*

I moan my approval about the new locale and whip his shirt over his head, running my hands down his wide shoulders and thickly muscled chest to the ridges of his abs. My finger traces the waistband of his loose-fitting jeans, slipping between it and his stomach. His hand freezes above the breast he's exploring and he lets out a slow breath, his dark green eyes flashing.

I turn my palm flat—fingers pointed south—and slip beneath his boxer briefs. The back of my hand grazes his long, hard length, and my stomach flutters.

He presses his forehead to mine. "Cali," he says deeply, his tone laced with warning.

I spread my fingers apart along his lower stomach and slide through the hair of his groin, tugging at the skin and tightening places I know are aching, because I'm aching there too.

His arms tense and shake beside my head. He's holding his breath. "This is it," he says. "We're together. Okay? No more trust issues."

I nod and leisurely lick his bottom lip with the tip of my tongue.

My shirt sweeps over my head in nearly the same second my pants are yanked down and off my feet. I'm naked in 2.2 seconds, Jaeger's body between my thighs as he takes my nipple into his mouth. I moan and lock my legs around his back, rubbing against the muscles of his stomach. If I weren't hormone-drunk, some of this might seem a little fast, a little brazen—even for me—but this is Jaeger and I really don't care.

Want him.

He reaches around and palms my ass before slipping a finger inside me. In and out that thick, masculine finger goes; every third dip, curling and slipping over the most sensitive spot.

Want. Now.

I yank beneath his arms to pull him up, but it's like trying to heave a semi truck. He swirls his tongue around my nipple one last time, eases his finger out with a couple of last swishes over the spot that has me panting, and glides his hands up my body, shooting naughty messages to every pore.

Damn it! His pants are still on.

I flip open the snap and push them down with my feet. Jaeger kicks them off and settles between my legs, kissing me.

My knees drop to the side as his fat tip rubs at my entrance. I squeeze his ass. He's huge and silky and I want him inside.

He breaks the kiss. "Pill?" he whispers in my ear.

"On it. Have you been—"

"Tested a year ago. The last time I was with someone."

Screech. Whoa, what?

He nudges in a couple of inches, and I lose that train of thought entirely. Another gentle thrust and he's stretching me.

He lifts his head and looks in my eyes as he rocks slowly, going deeper with every movement. My legs weaken, shaking with pleasure. Our breaths mingle, and I'm clinging to him, my arms like thin brackets around his large body as he moves above me.

I'm panting by the time the first spasm hits. Jaeger's gaze turns hazy and unfocused, as if he feels my orgasm building and it pleasures him too. Another spasm shoots from my core, and then I'm bucking in uncontrolled bliss.

Somewhere in the euphoria fog that keeps rolling, I sense Jaeger's pace pick up. He dips his head to the side and kisses my neck. He groans near my ear, the sound so sexy and deep that another quick spasm rocks me. His hips surge several more times and then slow, his breathing fast, his body jolting every couple of seconds with aftershocks.

Jaeger's hand slides under my shoulders and he cradles my head, tucking it beneath his chin as his breathing calms. He wraps an arm around my back and pulls me close, maneuvering to his side with me plastered to his front.

I lie still, listening to his heart pounding beneath my ear, utter and complete peace sweeping over me.

This wasn't sex, it was… I don't know. Or maybe I do and I don't want to ponder it.

My eyelids close, sleep pulling me under.

Chapter Twenty-Two

I WAKE TO a view of the lake through a window at the foot of the bed. Faded light filters over the mountain ridges. Soft sheets whisper over my palms. *What the…?*

I'm in Jaeger's bedroom? The last thing I remember is the couch in his workshop.

Heat floods my face. That couch will go down in history. At least, it will go down in my history. Wow—just, *wow*. Not that my past experience is extensive, but I'd like to think I was thorough with the few partners I've had. None of them gave me an orgasm through straight sex. But I should consider this very important finding later.

How the hell did I end up here?

I glance around the bedroom. It's cozy, with a Mission-style dresser and plain but expensive sheets based on the feel of them. I don't remember getting dressed and walking over. Technically, I'm not dressed, I acknowledge, as I slide my bare legs over the soft sheets. Did the man knock me out with his lovemaking? What the hell happened?

And Jesus. I sit up and pull the light blue sheet to my chest. Why am I calling our sex *lovemaking*? Eric and I never called it that. I tuck the fabric beneath my legs and around my back, as if to protect myself.

Jaeger walks out of the bathroom, a dark blue towel wrapped around his waist, water beaded on his shoulders. My jaw drops; my breathing speeds up. Steam from the shower and the scent of his aftershave waft toward me. He's like a walking aphrodisiac.

His gaze takes in my clamp on the sheets. "Good morning. Everything okay?"

"Yes, but"—I peer around the room—"how did we end up here? I'm pretty sure I was sober when I visited you this afternoon, so…"

"*Yesterday* afternoon."

Shit, it's morning?

I shake my head. "I couldn't have passed out."

He smiles. "You were tired. I carried you here."

Memories of the most amazing orgasm flutter through my mind. He did that to me. Sapped me of all energy and a little piece of my soul.

"And I didn't wake up?"

He shakes his head, his gaze skimming over me again. Only this time, heat emanates from those eyes. "Are you still tired?" The question is addressed cautiously, as if he's trying to be sensitive to my needs—but the man behind the question appears ready to pounce, evidenced by the massive erection building beneath his towel.

This is dangerous, this attraction. I should be careful.

I shake my head, and he walks over, sliding off the towel to the side of the bed. Muscles and long limbs, heat, and alluring, clean male scents smack my senses silly. He pulls the sheet from my body and eases down beside me.

Goose bumps pepper my flesh. My hands go clammy. I'm eager to touch and be touched. I want to kiss his mouth, the lids of his eyes, his temples—the place over his heart.

I'm in so much trouble.

"WHERE THE HELL have you been?" my brother asks, as I walk in the front door after finally prying myself from Jaeger's bed.

It was not easy. The man persuades. I honestly think he could have kept at it all day. Whatever happened to recovery periods?

Gen looks over from the kitchen. She's actually awake, eyes alert, which is proof of how late in the afternoon it is.

"I stayed the night at a friend's house."

Gen's eyes widen briefly. My brother's frown deepens.

"Cali, if you're going to hook up, answer your damn phone," he says.

"Oh my God. You're staying with me. I don't need to check in with you. And how do you know I stayed with a guy? I could have been with a friend."

"None of your friends are in town—"

"I've made new friends."

"—and you're flushed. *Post coitus* flushed."

Fuck! My lips pinch together. I storm into the bedroom and close the door, taking a deep breath.

Leave it to my biologist brother to notice and technically define afterglow.

A knock sounds a moment later. "Cali? Can I come in?" Gen says.

I pull my hair into a bun, open the window, and fan myself, scraping together the remains of my dignity. "Come in," I say.

She shuts the door behind her and sits on the bed. She looks down at her hands twisted in her lap. "I know we haven't talked much. I've been working and you're going through a hard time. I feel like I haven't been there for you."

Gen has known every guy I've kissed since we met. She's

never learned about something secondhand, and though it seems right to keep what's between me and Jaeger private, the strain in our friendship is obvious.

I sit across from her. "That's how I feel. Like I haven't been there for you."

She smiles bleakly. "You have. You're the strong one. I've pulled away, because I—well, I want to be strong. It's in me…"

"Of course you're strong."

She shakes her head. "No, you say what's on your mind and speak up for yourself. I want to speak up. I don't want to be afraid anymore."

Gen is reserved and less outspoken than me—most people are—but I didn't know she's afraid. "What's going on?"

She cradles her elbows and leans into herself. "You know how I don't talk to my mom?"

I nod. The topic of her mother doesn't come up unless I pry it out of her, and even then, I get nothing substantial.

"I won't blame my mom for the way I am and the choices I've made, but some of the hang-ups I have are because of our relationship. It's… unusual. But that's not the point. The point is, I don't want to be afraid anymore."

She tucks a dark lock behind her ear. "There was an incident a couple of weeks ago at Blue. One of the managers forced his hand under my shorts and touched me. He would have done more if someone hadn't interrupted. I'm afraid to say anything to the casino. I'm worried that what happened to you—with you getting fired and all—will happen to me. There are rumors—"

I wave my hands frantically. "Wait, wait, *what*? Jaeger mentioned something about a jerk touching you. He didn't say it was one of the executives, or what he did." My mind spins, bits and pieces coming together. "Who was it, Gen?"

"Some of the executives hang out in my bar after they get off work. One of them asked me to serve a small group he was hosting. He took advantage—put me in an uncomfortable situation."

"*Who was it?*"

"Drake Peterson."

Shit, shit.

"I knew I shouldn't have gone up there alone, but I wanted the extra money—"

I shake my head. "This is my fault." I could have warned Gen about Drake if I'd told her what he did. "Drake took me home the night we went to the club and came on too strong. Jaeger showed up and convinced him to leave." *Would have beat the crap out of him had he stayed.*

Confusion and concern war on her face. "I didn't know... but this isn't your fault. That's what I'm trying to tell you. I rely on you to fight my battles, when the reality is that sometimes it's my fault I get into situations. Or maybe I make myself a target." Her brow furrows and she clenches her fists. "I used poor judgment with Drake. And God, Cali, so did *you*. What were you thinking, going home with him?"

"I wasn't. And I already heard the parental lecture from Jaeger."

Her eyes narrow, scanning my face and neck—very likely taking in the *post coitus flush*, as my brother so elegantly put it. "Were you with Jaeger last night?" she asks gently. I nod, and she shoves my knee playfully. "Next time, text or something. We were worried."

No animosity fills her expression. I trust what Jaeger said about them, but you never know. Anyone can hide their feelings. I did.

The not-calling thing was bad. I would have called if I hadn't passed out from hot, mind-blowing sex.

"So what are these rumors you mentioned?" I say, forcing my mind off Jaeger, where it's determined to drift, and back to our conversation.

"People have asked me why you got fired."

That makes it sound so awesome. "Go on."

"There's a rumor one of the execs has it in for certain people."

"That's pretty much what they said when they let me go, only subtly. It's done, Gen. I'm not going back."

"Right, but... if this has happened before—"

"From Drake?"

She stills. "Drake got you fired?"

I shrug. "I assumed. It happened after I rejected him. And Jaeger, well, Jaeger made sure he remembered it."

I already suspected Drake had me fired. Hearing what he did to Gen, the way he threatened me when I went in to see her—and saw Jaeger comforting her. That must have been right after Drake touched her.

He's horrible. And he seems to have a firm grip on management. They fired me for no good reason, simply because he told them to. I don't care anymore about my old job, because I'm moving on, but I'm worried about Gen.

"Look, Gen, this is bad. No matter what you do about Drake, there could be repercussions. You have to decide what's best for you. As much as I like to believe differently, I don't have all the answers." I press my fingers to my eyes and sigh. "At the moment, I'm not sure I have any answers."

"You're right."

I look up, because *ouch.*

She sees my expression. "No, not that. You're smart, Cali, and you usually have good ideas, but I need to make my own choices. I can do this. I already decided my pride wasn't worth losing my job."

"You're staying on?"

She nods.

The idea of Gen staying at Blue after what Drake did to each of us makes me leery. What if he touches her again, or worse? She shouldn't have to hide sexual harassment in order to keep her job. That's horrible.

But I'm finished telling Gen what to do. She's stronger than she knows. At least she's doing what's right for her and not what others think she should do. It's more than I can say for the job choices I've made these last few years.

"Hey." She walks around the edge of the bed and sits beside me. "I'm glad we're talking again." My back loosens and I lean into her, resting my head on her shoulder. "No matter what happens, it's always ten times worse if I can't talk to you."

"Ditto."

Chapter Twenty-Three

O UT IN THE backyard, I draw the last shape on my sketch. It's a scene of a rowboat on the shore of the lake with the sun rising in the background. The water is made of squiggly circles and, from the corner of my eye, appears to move.

I'm calling my drawings *sketches* instead of *doodles* after I spoke to a professional artist yesterday. She told me I need to approach my work like a business. Apparently, *doodles* isn't a professional term. The jury is still out on whether or not I believe I'll thrive with an art career.

For the first time in my life, I'm not confident I'll succeed. It's scary, yet surprisingly freeing. I'm not pursuing art because I should, but because I really enjoy it and it makes me happy.

Last night, I went online and signed up for an art class at the community college, as well as a CAD course. I learned during one of my midnight Internet searches that some of the patterned drawings I've made could be used to create textiles— who knew? And CAD is a requirement for fabric art.

Whorls of heat rise from the cement patio in the late morning sun. It's only eleven and already I'm sweating in my pajama bottoms and bikini top.

My phone buzzes. I dig it out from where it migrated beneath my thigh on the lounge chair. My smile grows a mile wide.

Jaeger: Dinner this evening?

Cali: Sure.

Jaeger: I'm taking you to Tao. Plan accordingly. I'll pick you up at 5. I have something I want to show you.

Immediately, my mind wanders into naughty territory. But he wouldn't plan *that* and then expect me to be presentable, would he? Tao is the best restaurant in town.

What to wear? I pick up my sketch and pad barefoot back into the house. It's quiet for once. Both Gen and Tyler left early for various reasons.

Shoving the hangers around in my closet, I find nothing that won't embarrass me in a nice restaurant. I have a couple of hours to spare before my date with Jaeger. I'll swing by the local shops and see if I can find a new top on my limited budget.

My financial reserves are dwindling, but I don't have a fifty-thousand-dollar annual tuition fee to worry about anymore. I'll need a job to pay for living expenses and the classes I signed up for, but I'm optimistic that won't be a problem with my work experience from Blue.

Later that night, I slip on heels, black pants, and a short-sleeved, light blue blouse with a crisscross back that I found on sale at my favorite boutique. The color offsets my hair and highlights my eyes, and the front dips low. It also shows a respectable amount of cleavage, except I'm wearing a push-up bra, so the effect is just shy of obscene. I feel a slight twinge at spending money when I don't have a job, but now that I have a plan, I'll start looking for work straight away.

I walk into the living room, where Gen and Tyler are fighting over the remote.

"You're here rent-free!" Gen says. "You don't get control of the remote too."

"We're not watching *What Would William Pelt Do?* I might as well de-ball myself right here."

Gen lifts a finger, her eyes closed. "A—that's gross. B—William Pelt is a hockey player. He's an *athlete.* You love sports!"

Tyler looks to me in exhaustion.

"Leave me out of this," I say. "Gen, if he doesn't let you watch the show, record that shit. William Pelt is haaawwt." Not as hot as Jaeger, but then again, no one is.

"Tyler," Gen singsongs, "if you let me watch this, I'll make you popcorn."

His hand darts out and he tickles her under the arm. She screams, and he grabs the remote while she's disabled. "Dude, you're gonna have to offer more than popcorn to get this back."

Gen glares at him, rubbing her armpit. Tyler's tickles hurt like hell. He burrows deep. "You have the mental maturity of a sixteen-year-old. How do your students take you seriously?"

"I've got skills to pay the bills," he says, and flips through channels.

"I take that back. You're, like, ten, because I haven't heard that juvenile statement since fifth grade." Gen sighs and checks the time on the wall impatiently. The show must begin soon. "Fine, I'll do a load of laundry." Tyler keeps flipping. "Two loads?" Her face brightens and she crosses her arms. "I'll set you up with one of the cocktail waitresses at Blue."

Tyler stops channel surfing and eyeballs her. I grab my purse and steal a twenty from his wallet when he's not looking. He wouldn't want me stranded without cash. I'm doing him a favor by planning ahead. "Keep talking," he says.

"One of the pretty ones." Her expression is all innocence in a way only Genevieve can pull off, but I know better. She may not have gotten straight A's in school like Tyler and me, but that girl has street smarts.

All the exceptionally pretty waitresses at Blue are as dumb as rocks—not that pretty girls are necessarily mentally hindered. Gen is an example of gorgeous and intelligent mixed in one, but in the case of the other Blue waitresses, the stereotype holds true.

"Done," he says, and hands her the remote. She does a victory dance on the couch, complete with bouncing and fist pumping. Tyler stares at her chest, his rapt expression indicating the victory dance alone was worth the sacrifice. Gross.

A knock sounds at the door. My heart speeds up. "Okay, kids, I'm off." I lunge for the knob. I'm not ashamed of Jaeger or our relationship. I'd just rather not face "the parents" on the couch.

Too late.

"And when will you be home?" Tyler asks, his domestic debate forgotten. I glance back and he's scrutinizing me. He eyes my cleavage and frowns.

"If I'm lucky, not till tomorrow. Toodle-oo!" I pinky-wave and open the door. Stepping out, I bump into a confused Jaeger and yank the door shut. I slump against the surface. "Don't go in there. It's dangerous."

He chuckles. "Okay." He grabs my hand and leans down, kissing me softly on the lips. Tingles flutter in my belly just from that one delicate touch. His gaze dips to my top, catching appreciatively on my chest. He looks at the rest of my outfit and smiles. "You look beautiful."

Mission accomplished with the new top. I knew the expense would be worth it.

Jaeger's wearing a button-down green shirt that brings out

the green in his eyes. He looks edible, and smells it too. I wrap my arms around his waist and hug him tight. "I missed you."

His face dips to the top of my head and he breathes in through my hair. "Same here." After a moment, he loosens his hold. "Come on. I've got something to show you." Excitement and a bit of shyness play on his face. He's often quiet, but I've never seen him nervous.

What is this surprise?

Jaeger drives us to his house and my original suspicions resurface. I quickly reject them. Not that sex with Jaeger won't play a part in the evening if I have a say, but Jaeger's tapping the steering wheel as if he's jumpy. Something else is going on.

We walk around to the workshop. He unlocks the door and steps aside for me to enter. The sun hasn't set, but lies low in the sky, leaving the workshop shadowed without the overheads. He flips on the lights.

"Is this a replay of the other day?" I tease.

He looks at me, heat and desire flaming behind his gaze. "No, and you'd better not put ideas in my head or we won't make it to dinner."

He rests his wide hand on my lower back, scorching the flesh beneath, and guides me across the room to where he keeps his final works.

Only a few remain on the tiered shelves today, about half as many as last time. I'll have to ask him how he sells his stuff. Good for research.

It's strange how we both turned to art after the lives we'd mapped out didn't work. I'd never considered art and design before I returned to Tahoe, but I've been thoughtlessly sketching since fourth grade on napkins, notebooks, and just about any scrap of paper that fell into my hands. Jaeger and I are so different on the surface. He's quiet and I'm outgoing, but underneath, our passions are the same. On many levels.

Jaeger steps away and pulls out a tablet about four by four feet in size and covered with a painter's drop cloth. He sets it on the wall display and removes the cover. For a moment, I think, wow, that black drape really highlights the wood nicely, and then my focus settles on the design.

What the...? *"Jaeger?"*

The carving in front of us is the abstract I drew of the lake.

"Gen happened to show Mason and me the design you made on a napkin during one of your breaks. I asked her if I could borrow it. I also saw the sketch you left on the couch when I came by to pick up Gen. Cali, you have crazy talent."

A naughty glint flashes in his forest-green eyes. "I've shown you how special I think *you* are. But this"—his eyes sober and he points to the piece in front of us—"is my way of showing you how special I think your art is."

Replicated on wood, the sketch has dimension and depth, with the outermost lines advancing as though the center is pulling you in.

The amount of planning and work he must have put in to create this piece blows my mind. I'm speechless, which is rare for me.

He shoves his hands in the pockets of his dark slacks. "Well? What do you think?"

"It's amazing. Your carving, that is."

"Your *drawing* is amazing."

This is more than Jaeger telling me he thinks I'm talented. He's telling me he likes me, elevating the wooing campaign— the one I only recently realized exists—to new heights.

A few things come together for me and I finally understand.

Gen... sneaky, sneaky, wonderful best friend. "Does this have anything to do with your clandestine date with my best friend?"

He smiles, exasperated, and shakes his head. "I wanted Gen to look at the early version. I hadn't gotten your permission to use the sketch. I brought her by to check it out and tell me if she thought you'd be okay with it."

And now I feel like an ass. "I'm sorry I jumped to conclusions about you two. I owe both of you an apology."

He steps closer and links our fingers. "It's fine, Cali. I just want you to feel like you can trust me."

The truth is, I do trust him. Jaeger is sincere and caring in a way I've rarely seen from guys. Crap, or from most women. He's a good person.

"There's something else I wanted to mention. I don't want to pressure you or anything, but I have a client who commissioned my work. She's looking for something special. I'd like to show her your sketches. Gen let me borrow the few you've given her, but I can show this lady whichever ones you feel comfortable with."

"Yeah, sure," I say hesitantly. I can't see anyone wanting to buy a carving of one of my sketches. But then, that's the point. To create designs people will want in their homes and businesses. "Let me at least convert the ones you have on napkins and on the backs of bills onto actual artists' paper before you show her, though."

He laughs. "I don't think she'll care. She's got a discerning eye." He pulls me close until I bump into his hard chest. He wraps his arms around my back, his long limbs flanking my hips. "She knows something good when she sees it."

In heels, my mouth aligns with his jaw. I rise on my toes and kiss his lips. "Thank you for making me feel special. And for the carving."

"Oh, that carving isn't for you." He grins.

My head tilts back in mock incredulity. "What do you mean, it's not for me?"

"It's going above my bed, but you can visit it whenever you want." His hands shift and squeeze my ass at the same time his mouth takes mine.

THIRTY MINUTES LATER, we arrive for our reservation at Tao. I think I've met my match in the bedroom department. We didn't actually go there, though Jaeger was ready and willing. After several deep kisses and much teasing about who would get the carving—I won, of course—I put the brakes on the heated make-out session. Not cool to walk into a fancy restaurant with smeared mascara and bed head. Not when we can continue what we started later.

I'm looking forward to my new art. That puppy is going up right next to the orange and yellow needlepoint of a sunflower in the chalet—Gen's and my new name for the heap we live in. Natural-modern meets horrifically outdated fusion.

"Table for two," Jaeger tells the maître d'.

"Right this way, Mr. Lang. Good to see you this evening." The host, wearing a dark suit, smiles warmly and grabs two leather menus, turning to lead us away.

They know him here? Does Jaeger come often or something?

Before I can ask, Jaeger raises his hand for me to follow the maître d', who's already halfway across the room.

The maître d' escorts us past elegant, white-cloth-covered tables. Mirrors behind a full-length bar make the room appear twice as wide and capture windows that look out onto the lake at the far end. Geometric wooden chandeliers dangle in the center of the high ceiling. Wood panels hang to the left… their style familiar.

I glance suspiciously at Jaeger. He's looking straight ahead, maneuvering around our table to pull out my chair. Our section is private, with the best view of the lake and mountains.

Menu in hand, maître d' gone, I glance at the murals again. They're larger than the ones in Jaeger's shop, but I recognize his stamp. "Jaeger, are those yours?"

His gaze flickers to the wall, then back at the menu, as if his art on display in one of the best restaurants in town is no big deal. "Tao is a client."

Holy shit. My boyfriend is famous. Well, maybe not famous, but he's an important artist to be on center display in a place like this.

I grab his hand and link our fingers while I peruse the menu. I have no right to be, but I'm proud of what he's accomplished. This summer has challenged me with heavy decisions and painfully low moments, but I don't regret the time I've spent with Jaeger. It's been some of the best of my life.

He squeezes my fingers and smiles. "The scallops are excellent and so is the—"

"Jaeger?" A high-pitched female voice violates our perfect bubble.

The woman—about my age, maybe a little older—stands behind Jaeger in jeans and a T-shirt. I didn't see her walk up. Then again, when I'm with Jaeger, I tune out a lot of superficial activities.

The woman glances uncomfortably to the patrons on her right, who are staring.

Jaeger's brow furrows. He shifts in his seat and looks back. The side of his face pales, and he loosens his grip on my hand. "Kate?"

"Can we talk?" she says. She smiles at him as if to disarm, but there's a plaintive desperation beneath.

Alarm bells go off in my head.

No. Don't ruin this. Whoever you are, leave. Don't take away the best thing that's ever happened to me.

Jaeger faces me again, his gaze fixed on the table. He glances up, his expression haunted before his mouth turns up in a semblance of a smile. "I'll be right back, okay?"

I nod stiffly. He grips my hand one last time before letting go. He follows the woman to the entrance of the restaurant— where Jaeger's sister is standing with the maître d'.

Why is Kerstin here?

I pound my water and wait for Jaeger to return. Twenty minutes pass before he walks down the aisle to our table, rubbing his brow. He looks up, his eyes serious. "I'm sorry." He swallows, his gaze distracted. "I've got to take you home. There's a family emergency."

"Is everything okay?" Obviously not, but what do I say without sounding like I'm prying, which is exactly what I'm doing? Who is this woman? And why is he ditching me for her?

I stand and grab my purse.

Jaeger walks me out of the restaurant before answering my question. He opens the passenger door and helps me into his truck, sagging against the frame of the cab as if he needs it to help him stand. "That was Kate. My ex-girlfriend. She showed up at my parents' house and my sister was there. Kerstin knew where I was taking you tonight."

"*Which* ex-girlfriend?" Maybe there were a bunch and this

one is some random, innocuous ex who happened to be at the same restaurant. *Ex-girlfriend* and *innocuous* don't exactly go together, but it could happen. I'm in full denial mode.

"Cali, you're the only girlfriend I've had in five years. Kate's my ex. *The* ex. The one who… Well, anyway, she's the person I broke up with right after my accident."

"Jaeger, what did this girl do to you? You look really upset."

Of course his ex would show up after he's moved on. That's Murphy's Law. But he moved on with *me*, and I'm pretty damn happy with him. I don't want to consider exactly how happy, because it will probably break me if it ends.

"She didn't do anything—well, I take that back. She did a lot back then. And not always to me. It's just that she doesn't always lie."

He's beginning to rattle, which isn't like him at all. "Jaeger, what happened?"

"Kate said—" He pushes off the cab and straightens, though he looks about to topple. "She said she had a kid. That the girl's mine. She wants us to be a family."

Chapter Twenty-Four

M Y MIND GOES utterly blank, and then a riotous array of facts and questions, mixed in with a few expletives, clamor to get out.

How could this happen? She can't have him. I—I… *like* him. A lot. A *real* lot. Why did she wait until now to tell him? It doesn't make sense. She dumped him, and he was in and out of physical rehabilitation for a year. He said he never saw her again… and he wouldn't have known if she was pregnant.

Fuck. Just—*fuck*.

I don't remember the drive to my place. It passes in a flash, and then Jaeger is walking me to the front door. "Don't worry, Cali. Everything's going to be okay. Let me find out what's going on." He breathes in shakily. "What *really* happened. Because I don't trust her. There were rumors after we split that she was unfaithful. And, of course, there's all the shit she pulled while we dated. I'll find out the truth, then I'll call, okay? It's just… I've got to take care of this." I nod, and he pecks me on the cheek and walks to the truck.

This is not how I envisioned our night ending. How could something so right go so terribly wrong? Am I jinxed?

Jaeger looks up from inside the truck, a pained expression on his face, before he turns the ignition and eases out of the driveway.

I swallow the knot forming in my throat and open the door

to the chalet. Gen's banging around in the kitchen while Tyler sprawls on the couch.

He sits up. "What happened? Why are you back so soon?"

I slump on the blue recliner, staring straight ahead, attempting to process what I don't want to believe. "Jaeger's ex interrupted our date." I wave my hand, a crazed sensation rising in my chest. "Just showed up in the middle of the restaurant. Told him she had a kid—and it was his."

Tyler's eyes bug out. "*What?*"

Gen walks into the living room, an oven mitt on her hand. She doesn't cook, so the image is absurd. Just like the rest of this evening.

I drop my face into my hands and squeeze my eyes closed. "Can we *not* talk about this?" After a second, I realize hanging my head allows gravity to pull the tears closer to the surface. I look up and swallow, blinking several times.

Gen looks to Tyler, widening her eyes pointedly.

His mouth is still open. He sees her expression and nods, then pulls out his phone and starts feverishly tapping out a text.

"Leave him alone, Tyler," I say. "He's trying to figure out what's going on. He doesn't know either."

Tyler's fingers continue flying over his iPhone.

I stand and walk to the bathroom. "I'm going to bed." I remove my makeup, then change in the bedroom, hanging up the pretty blue blouse I wasted my money on. I lie on the mattress, but I can't sleep. My chest hurts.

The sounds of Gen and Tyler talking quietly in the living room filter beneath the door. That's when the first tear rolls down my cheek.

I won't do it. I won't cry over another guy this summer. It's pathetic.

More tears roll, landing on the collar of my homely flannel pajamas.

Okay, I'll cry tonight, but that's it. No more after tonight, unless… please don't let there be an *unless*. Please let this be a big, horrible mistake.

JAEGER HASN'T CALLED me for two days after our interrupted date. Two effing days!

I'm dying. I've gone from staring at my phone, to spending hours sketching beneath the trees, to walking aimlessly around the neighborhood until I wind up at the lake. On the plus side, my arms are getting ripped from all the rocks I'm cathartically hurling into the water.

Every time I pick up the phone to call him, I remember he said he'd call when he had things figured out. He's never hesitated to get in touch with me in the past. I can only assume he's still dealing with his ex. Or getting back together with her. But, no, this is the girl who crapped all over him—even Tyler said so.

Logically, I don't think Jaeger is getting back together with Kate, but not hearing from him… It's difficult not to think the worst. A part of me hangs on to the hope that this will all turn out to be some ginormous mistake.

In the meantime, I've scoured online job listings for South Lake Tahoe, and have sent out résumés and online applications. Job-hunting is helping keep me distracted.

My art classes don't start for a few more days. If I work at least thirty hours as a waitress or a dealer at another casino, I can swing living expenses plus costs for community college. The student fees aren't astronomical like they are at Harvard and other programs. With new classes, a new job—basically a new life—I might survive getting my heart crushed.

Maybe.

Okay, I'm not sure. Jaeger snuck up on me and now I have all these feelings I've never experienced before. It's going to break my heart if he ends our relationship. Oddly, running off to a law program far, far away would be easier than sticking around to watch the guy I've fallen in love with torn from my arms.

In love? Okay, that's enough introspection for one morning.

I walk inside the chalet from the patio where I've been sketching for the last hour. The patio has become my office and art sanctuary. "Where's Gen?" I ask my brother, who's sitting at the kitchen table, typing on his computer.

"Said she was going out."

"Did she say where?" Our talk helped heal some of the distance between us, but we haven't had time to catch up on everything. These past few weeks, I figured Gen was hanging out with Nessa, but now I wonder.

Tyler pauses and takes a gulp from his coffee mug, the words World's Best Cat Mom scrawled across the front. Either Tyler is less choosy about his mugs than Gen and me, or he's being ironic.

"Nope. Hey, what do you think of that Nessa girl? She available?"

Okay, that came out of left field.

I walk into the kitchen and pull out ingredients for a sandwich. I have an interview this afternoon with the casino across from Blue. It's a smaller establishment, and at this place, I'm being interviewed by the head of Gaming. I have anxiety over this, considering the last head of Gaming fired me, but this casino doesn't seem to put on the same airs that the management at Blue did. Maybe talking to an upper manager at their casino is a good sign.

"I don't know if Nessa's available. What happened to Gen setting you up with a Blue waitress?"

Tyler's face contorts. "Shit, Cali. That girl was crazy. She got hammered and crawled on my lap. *In the restaurant.* I felt like a virgin preserving my virtue."

"You have virtue?"

"I guess I do," he says proudly.

I chuckle, inadvertently inhaling a piece of bread I had popped in my mouth. I hack until it comes back up.

"Easy there, girl. Don't kill yourself. It wasn't that funny."

"I wish I could have been there."

"No, you don't. She was a damned piranha."

"A man-eater? Are you serious?"

"She tried to unbutton my pants!" Astonishment fills his voice.

"You're such a hot babe, Tyler. How do you manage?"

"Don't mock, Calzone. You can't see it because you're my sister, but I *am* a commodity."

Complaining about that horrific nickname results in increased usage, so I bite my lip. "If that's the case, why did you need to be set up?"

He shrugs. "Gen offered, and I thought I'd give it a try." He wags his head slowly. "Never again, Cali. Never. Again."

I laugh and walk into the bedroom to change and get ready for my first casino interview. Having Tyler around keeps my spirits up. No matter what, I'm lucky to have my friends and family. I just wish Jaeger would call.

Chapter Twenty-Five

PAUL SOMETHING-OR-OTHER, THE head of Gaming at the casino across from Blue, looks at his notes, his mouth pinched. "Ah, yes, Cali." He drums his fingers on the desk and stops when he realizes he's doing it. "My assistant just reached your previous employer. I apologize for having you come all this way, but it seems—well, it seems we can't offer you a position."

What? A fly could land on my tongue and I wouldn't be able to close my mouth. With my experience at Blue, I'm a shoo-in for the dealer position at this smaller casino.

An uncomfortably long pause ensues, while I attempt to process what he said. "I'm sorry. I don't understand." The interview has barely started. I haven't even had a chance to screw up his questions. What's going on?

Paul nods, his hands clasped together. The tic near his eye does not bode well. He doesn't come from the same cold stock as the gaming manager at Blue. This guy can't hide his discomfort.

"Because you came all this way, I'll tell you that Human Resources confirmed your employment at Blue, then transferred the call to a manager. The manager didn't go into specifics, but said he would not hire you again. I apologize for the inconvenience, but that's reason enough for us to eliminate you from consideration."

"But—but—"

I was told before I left Blue that the dissolution of my position wouldn't reflect poorly on me, considering it was an issue of fit, as long as I wrote a letter of resignation. Which I did.

Paul stands and extends his hand. "I wish you the best, Ms. Morgan."

My legs lift me, slowly and hesitantly as if they, too, can't believe this. I shake my interviewer's hand and smooth my navy skirt with trembling fingers. Face burning, I pass the receptionist at the end of the hall and press the elevator button to the bottom floor.

How will I find work if Blue doesn't give me a decent reference? My other experience, working at a florist shop and as a tutor, won't help me find a casino job that pays well. I got the position at Blue through a friend of my mom's. I need the Blue reference as a stepping stone.

The next day, two more casinos call and cancel interviews. The last place asked a couple of questions and told me they'd call after my references had been checked. I haven't heard back.

A restaurant—I'm getting desperate and have put in a call to a friend of a friend—said the same thing the first hiring manager did. That they spoke to someone at Blue who couldn't recommend my work.

I didn't even do anything wrong at Blue. Except piss off Drake.

Is he *blackballing* me? That would be just excellent.

I have no job, I'm running out of money, and my future is tenuous. Add to that the fact I haven't heard from my boyfriend in four days, since his baby momma came back into town, and I'm ready to pitch a tent near the ice cream aisle.

I broke down and called Jaeger this afternoon. I told myself I'd wait until he called, but he hasn't and I couldn't hold out any longer. Jaeger didn't answer, so I left a message, but he hasn't called back.

Am I being dumped? Again?

Four days. Four days since Kate interrupted our date at Tao, and no word from Jaeger. Any normal human being would assume it's over. I should have learned after Eric, but I can't wrap my head around it. Everything with Jaeger is different. I strongly suspected it was over with Eric when he didn't call. With Jaeger, I'm not sure I *can* believe it's over until I hear it from him.

I've signed up for classes, but I have no way to pay for them. I refuse to mooch off my mom after she spent years financing college. I'm not even sure she could afford to help me, now that she has a mortgage.

A crazed desperation drives me these days.

I make it home from my interview and work through my second pint of butter pecan, pondering the fact I might end up attending law school after all. At least at Harvard I have a loan established that will cover living and tuition. And isn't that crazy? All this introspection and reinvention to end up right where I started—miserable, but surviving. There's got to be more to life than this.

The front door bolt scrapes and the door opens. Gen walks in. It's after one in the morning and she's dressed in tight jeans and a slinky tank. Meanwhile, Tyler's still out with one of his buddies.

I raise an eyebrow. Gen doesn't just look beautiful tonight, she looks *hot*. Like, trying to impress a guy hot.

I'm instantly suspicious. How dare she not tell me she's dating someone? "Where've you been? Did you go out on a date?"

For a moment she looks like a teenager slipping in after curfew. She sinks onto the couch, glaring at my ice cream. "How much of that have you eaten this week?"

I study the carton. "*This* week?"

She lets out a nervous laugh. "Cali…"

"Five pints?"

She pokes my belly. It's stuffed with slushy goodness. "I think you need to cool it with that. Time for an intervention."

That's funny. I'm usually giving Gen interventions about the smutty books she's addicted to—trashy TV I fully support—and her poor taste in men.

My, how things have changed.

I glare at her and reload my spoon, but I can't bring it to my mouth. I am stuffed. I've eaten so much ice cream these last few days I've grown immune to the sugar high, like a junkie.

"I don't need an intervention. I need a job. I need a life." My voice catches on that last bit.

"I know, hon." She drapes her arm around my shoulders. "You've had some challenges, but it's time to pick yourself up."

"How?" I sink lower and curl into her. Being a loser sucks. "I don't know what I'm doing."

"Yes you do. You're an artist. You took all those fancy classes back in college because it was easy for you and it's what other people would have done if they had your brains. But now you need to think about how you want to live the rest of your life."

Gen's been dealing with the deep stuff while I've lived a relatively charmed existence. Finances were tight, but I had a smooth home life. Meanwhile, Gen mentioned a few of the trials she grew up with living with her mom, none of them good. It's a wonder she came out so normal. She's stronger and wiser than she knows.

"I have thought about what I want to do, and it's not working out. I should just go to law school," I mumble. "It's not too late. I haven't gotten around to notifying them I'm not attending."

Gen pinches my chin and lifts my head until she's staring me down. "Don't throw your life away because you're scared." She's mentioned her fears before and how they crippled her. She's speaking from experience.

I thought I had everything figured out, but it was artificial, shallow. I should have focused on my own life and left Gen to deal with hers. She's doing just fine without me meddling.

Pity party is over. I squish the top of the carton back on the ice cream and set it on the floor.

Gen watches me approvingly. She shifts and taps her toe, her chin propped on her fist like she's thinking.

She looks pretty and powerful. My BF has changed these last two months. She's still her, just more confident. I thought I was confident, and maybe I am, but it was because others told me what I was doing was fantastic, not because I thought it was. When I get out of this, I'll be stronger and it will be genuine. I'll have confidence because I'm doing what makes me happy, not simply what's expected.

"I'd bet money Drake has something to do with Blue giving you poor references," she says. "You'll have a hard time finding a job."

"I know. I've considered he's probably behind it."

Gen's eyes narrow as she gazes absently across the room. She nods as if she's having a silent conversation with herself. "I already put in a call to Nessa. I'll follow up with her. We'll find something."

I close my eyes and let out a weighty sigh. It's difficult to imagine there's a job out there that doesn't require references and still pays enough to cover my expenses. As much as the job situation upsets me, it's not the thing hurting me the most right now.

Gen squeezes my hand, peering at my face. "I don't know why he hasn't called, Cali. He's dealing with stuff. Big stuff. Have you tried talking to your brother? Has he heard anything?"

"Jaeger's off the grid. He's not taking calls. He never returned Tyler's texts."

"Give him time. A few days isn't long, considering what he's going through. Don't forget, he's one of the good guys."

"I know." My eyes bead up with tears. I shake my head. "This hurts worse."

"Worse than Eric," she says, understanding without me having to say it.

"Losing Eric was nothing compared to this. My pride took a hit with Eric and I was sad, but this... this is like someone took an ice pick to my heart and punched a few thousand holes in it." I buckle and lay my head in her lap.

Gen strokes my head for several seconds. "There's only one thing to do in this situation."

"Apply for a heart transplant?" I mumble.

She reaches over me, smashing my skull on her lap in the process. The television clicks on and I look up. She's running through our DVR list. The chalet is ancient, but it has a modern television system.

Obviously, a man owns the rental.

Gen stops on *What Would William Pelt Do?* "We ogle hot William for twelve to fifteen hours until our minds go numb."

As solutions go, this one isn't bad. Gen and I watch William's abs and his dating mishaps for the next couple of hours. I end up laughing so hard my ice cream gut cramps.

Life could be worse. But I wish a few things would start working out again.

Chapter Twenty-Six

A FTER MY NIGHT with Gen and our *William* TV marathon, Jaeger finally called. I was in the shower and missed it, of course. I haven't called him back, because Gen stealthily lined up a job interview for me while we were watching TV last night. She'd been texting back and forth with Nessa, and this morning I woke with this message on the fridge.

Sallee Construction, Pinecone Chalet Business Center. Interview with John Sallee at 2 p.m. Mention me and Nessa and don't be late!

I can't call Jaeger, because I need to get through this interview without falling apart. It's the best lead I've had, and it's supposedly a friend of Nessa's, so I might actually have a fighting chance at getting the job. Four days is too long to go without calling your girlfriend when you know she's waiting to hear from you. I have no idea what Jaeger will say, but I can't imagine it's anything good.

The irony of how this summer began, with me thinking I had everything figured out, determined to help Gen, and how it's ending up with our positions reversed, has not escaped me.

I would have liked to grill Gen about the interview, but she left early—Gen, the thou-shall-not-rise-before-ten person. Something has gotten into her, but she swiftly dodged my question about whom she'd been with earlier in the night, the bugger.

I managed to squeeze a couple of details out of her about the interview via text before she said she'd be out of range. Nessa knows the owner of Sallee Construction, and Gen said to bring my sketches. She didn't mention what the position was for, but I imagine it has something to do with art.

Who cares if it doesn't? I'm desperate.

Fingers crossed, I pull up to the Pinecone Chalet Business Center at a quarter of two. If this job doesn't work out, I'm not sure what I'll do. I threatened myself with going to Harvard, but I won't. In fact, I notified the university this morning that I won't be attending. If this job doesn't pan out, I'll find another. It might not pay as much, and I'll have to put off art classes for a while, but it'll be the beginning of something that feels right.

I enter the office of Sallee Construction and am immediately optimistic. The receptionist is in a pair of light wash jeans and a purple top, her frizzy blond hair pulled back in a scrunchy. She's no-fuss and friendly looking, and the complete antithesis of the receptionist at Blue who handed me my closing papers. That's got to be a good sign.

"Just a moment, honey." She types on her keyboard with the tips of her stubby fingernails and makes a note in a log to the side of her desk. "Okay." She beams. "What can I do for you?"

"I'm Cali Morgan. I have an appointment with John Sallee. Genevieve Tierney and Nessa Villanueva referred me."

"He's expecting you. Go right on back. First door on your left." She smiles and turns back to her computer.

John Sallee's office door is open when I walk up to it. He's flipping through documents on his desk. I tap on the door.

He looks up, startled for a moment, before a wide smile

sweeps his face. "You must be Cali." He pushes the stack he shuffled to the side, though I'm not sure why. His desk is covered in papers and rolled-up blueprints, as is the rest of his office. Shuffling things around won't create space; he'd need a shredder for that. "Come on in."

I take a seat across from John, keeping my back straight to see over the mountain of crap on his desk. Messy desk or not, he has one of those friendly faces, with dark tanned skin and deep laugh lines that match his smile.

"So, I hear you need a job," he says.

Awesome. I'm like a charity case. "Yes, sir. I do."

"And you're friends with Gen and Nessa?"

"Gen is my best friend. We went to college together at Dawson University. I met Nessa through Gen." I don't mention the casino. John can read about it on my résumé. I'm not hiding the fact that I worked there, but I'm not going to remind him about it either. He'd receive the same poor feedback about my employment every other hiring manager did.

He nods, considering me from across the desk. "Gen said you're passing up an opportunity to attend Harvard Law to pursue art."

I thought John was Nessa's contact? When would Gen have spoken to him?

John whistles. "You sure you want to do that?"

My chin tips up. "I've been considering a different career all year." The truth is, I've been considering how I wasn't looking forward to law school all year. I didn't realize until this summer how much I'd been dreading it. In junior high, the fact that I liked arguing with people seemed a good enough reason to become a lawyer, but not anymore. It only took me forever to figure it out. I'm stubborn that way.

"Mm-hmm. Well…" He looks at a piece of paper in front of him. "It says here you're taking a CAD course."

"It begins tonight."

"And you took upper-division economics at Dawson and are proficient with mathematics."

"Uh, higher mathematics, yes."

If he wants me to perform advanced calculus, we're good. If he asks me which way is left or to do simple addition, my brain might implode. The only way I got away with dealing at the casino was by memorizing the card combinations.

"Okay, well, I've got an in-house architect who's been riding me to hire an assistant with CAD experience. Once you learn CAD, you'll work exclusively with him. Until then, you'll do odd jobs for the architect and engineer. An artist comes in handy more often than you would think in this business." He leans back in his chair. "What do you think, Cali? How does that sound?"

Is he kidding? "It sounds perfect."

He chuckles. "Good. You might be asked to do anything from making coffee runs to sketching a foundation, so be prepared. I'll pay you a base salary with benefits. You'll get a raise with your CAD qualifications."

John goes over some figures, and with a few quick calculations on my iPhone back at the car, I realize I can actually survive on the salary he quoted. It's not as much as I made as a dealer, but once my pay increases with the CAD skills, I'll make enough to live comfortably.

More important, it's a job. With health benefits. And I'll be drawing. I could kiss Gen and Nessa right now.

They need someone right away, so I'll start the day after tomorrow. John said he'd schedule a staff meeting and lay down the law so that his coworkers don't pull me apart assigning me to projects. He's actually eager to have me on board, and he never asked for references. My connection to Gen, the few sketches I brought per Gen's suggestion, and my transcripts from college were enough for him to hire me on the spot.

I'm so excited I'm shaking. I pull up to the chalet and Tyler is sitting on the cement pad that is our front porch. His legs are outstretched in the dirt. He looks up, and the permagrin I drove home with fades.

Something's wrong. His eyes are fixed and tense, his mouth stiff. I get out of the car and cross over to him. "What happened? Are you okay?"

Tyler picks up a brown pine needle and twists it in his fingers. "I spoke to a friend who ran into Jaeger's sister."

My heart thumps heavily inside my chest.

I drop down beside him, dust from the powdery soil smearing my navy interview skirt. "Just say it."

Tyler bends his legs and props an arm on his knee. "Jaeger's ex has moved in with him."

The pain hits me like a bullet, instant and sharp.

I swallow and wobble to my feet, gripping the side of the house.

Tyler looks up. "Cali?"

I open the front door and walk into the bedroom, locking the door behind me.

It's over. I don't need to hear the truth from Jaeger and allow things to drag out the way they did with Eric. That would kill me. Right now, I already feel like I'm dying.

Chapter Twenty-Seven

J AEGER CALLS AND texts several more times after I return home from my interview. I delete his number from my phone.

Why wouldn't he tell me what was going on? Didn't I deserve to know he'd gotten back together with his girlfriend before she moved in? What is wrong with men?

During the next couple of days, I stay busy in classes and at my new job, but it hurts. It hurts so badly. It's like the knowledge of Jaeger and Kate together has charred my heart and left an ugly, thick scar in its place.

My first day of work, I met all the guys at Sallee Construction. That's what my workplace consists of—a bunch of dudes, the middle-aged receptionist, and me. I get lots of attention. And I can't appreciate any of it because my heart doesn't feel anymore.

The older men treat me like I'm their daughter, and the younger ones check me out when they think I'm not looking. The architect and civil engineer are among the older pack, and keep me busy on various projects.

I worried I'd be fetching coffee and donuts until I learned CAD, but that hasn't happened. Bill, the architect, saw my drawings the first day and immediately asked me to produce an artist's rendition of an upscale strip mall for a project south of the casinos, complete with landscape specifications. I've had to look up various regional flora, which has given me ideas for new sketches in my free time.

I'm taking one morning and one evening class and squeezing work in between. I haven't figured out how I'll manage to get to and from either place on a regular basis without a car, but between lifts from Gen and Tyler and the bus, I've managed so far.

Almost everyone in my morning art class is female, while everyone in my evening CAD class is male. I've talked to a couple of people from both courses and find each group vastly different, yet equally nerdy in their own right. I'm the biggest nerd of all, because I'm in both classes. My geekiness spans the spectrum.

The evening CAD course is the most difficult to get to because Gen has to work and Tyler wants a social life. I asked around on the first day, and one of the guys in my class was willing to carpool. He lives fairly close to the chalet and doesn't seem to mind picking me up and dropping me off three nights a week.

It's Wednesday, and Leo, the CAD guy, is driving me home tonight.

"Are you hungry?" he asks on our way to his car after class.

Leo's been really sweet, and I've wondered on more than one occasion if he's looking for more than a carpool buddy. Particularly given that I can offer nothing in the way of reciprocation without a vehicle.

"No, I'd better get home. There's a project I need to put a few hours into." It's really just a sketch of the cascades Jaeger and I hiked to at Fallen Leaf Lake.

Why I'm torturing myself with a drawing that brings only bittersweet memories makes no sense. Despite having deleted his number from my phone, my feelings for Jaeger haven't faded or changed. They are as stubborn as I am.

He glances over with a smile. "Maybe some other time."

Leo's cute, with a week's worth of stubble and shaggy blond hair. His eyes are a warm brown and he's on the tall side, if a bit skinny. When I'm with him, I feel nothing. No zing, no spark. Between my new job and classes, I'm surrounded by available men, and I can't appreciate any of them. It's like Jaeger sapped me of the chemicals needed for attraction.

Leo pulls into my driveway and I reach for my book bag on the floor, shoving in a pencil that's sticking out of the side pocket.

"You expecting someone?" Leo says.

I look up and my heart does this weird throb thing that's so powerful, I feel it in my throat. Because Jaeger is waiting at the front door.

"No," I say shakily.

Leo glances from me to Jaeger, his expression hesitant as he takes in Jaeger's size. "You want me to stick around? I could—"

"It's okay. He's a friend."

For some reason, I feel guilty calling Jaeger a friend, like I'm betraying him with another guy when that's not the case. I can't call Jaeger my boyfriend after his ex-girlfriend has moved in. For all I know, Jaeger is here to downgrade me to friend status in person.

Leo nods. "Okay, well, have a good evening. Pick you up same time Friday?"

"That'd be great. I really appreciate the rides, Leo." He smiles.

I step out and close the car door behind me, waiting for Leo to reverse. He holds up his hand briefly before pulling out onto the street.

I slowly shift, shoulders, then feet, then my eyes from the gravel to the house, and to Jaeger with his hands shoved in his jean pockets. His elbows are bent the way they do to accommodate the length of his arms when he has his hands in his pockets, the muscles below the sleeves of his T-shirt tensed and corded. His mouth is tight and twisted to the side in a concerned, edgy expression.

I make my way over, passing him as I approach the front door.

He grabs my hand, but I slip it out of his grip. "Cali, please. We need to talk."

"Tyler told me you're living with Kate."

Jaeger blinks, surprised, but not upset. He lets out a deep breath. "I wanted to tell you."

"Does it matter how I found out? You've moved on. Obviously." I unlock the front door and he follows me inside. No one's home, and that makes me mad. I don't want to be alone with him.

All those chemical reactions that hibernated around other guys flared up the second I saw Jaeger.

I walk straight to the backyard. At least out in the open I don't smell him, feel him so close to me.

"I'm sorry it took me so long to call. I had a commission that was late, and then I went out of town for a couple of days."

He went on vacation? With his ex? He thinks that's an acceptable explanation for why he waited days to call me? "Whatever, Jaeger. Why are you here?"

He flexes his jaw. "I'm trying to tell you, Cali, but you're making it difficult."

"Difficult? *I'm* making it difficult? Do you want to know what sucks? Finding out your boyfriend has a child. Want to know what else blows? Having him leave you for his ex-girlfriend. Get out of my house, Jaeger!"

I'm hysterical. All that pent-up pain unleashing itself on him. At least it's aimed in the right direction.

"I'm not leaving," he says calmly. "We need to talk. You don't underst—"

"What?" I hold up my hands. "That we're over? Oh, I got that when Tyler told me you're shacking up with your ex. Not much to misinterpret there."

"Cali"—his eyes are warm and soft—"if I wasn't so frustrated, I'd kiss you. I missed you, feisty."

I squint. "Have you lost your mind?"

He lets out a loud sigh, walks over, and scoops me up. "Maybe. I feel a little crazed at the moment."

I glance at the dirt I'm no longer standing on. "Put me the eff down, you giant lumberjack!"

"Done." He swings around and stalks into the house.

"Wait, wait," I say in a panic. *Not the house!* What asshole didn't lock the back door? I wiggle to get loose. "Outside, Jaeger. Put me down outside."

He looks back with a concerned expression. "You're not really mad, are you?"

"I'm going to hoist your balls in a—"

"Okay, good. Just making sure."

He shifts me over his shoulder, cups my ass with one hand, and opens the bedroom door.

"Not there! We need to stay in the living room. I'm not going near a bed with—"

I land on my back cockeyed, my breath rushing out in whoosh. "What. Are. You. Doing!"

"Trying to get my girlfriend to listen for a minute." Jaeger leaps on top of me, bracing his weight on his arms on either side of my head.

He completely ignores my frown and pecks my lips before his gaze goes distracted, hovering above me like he's going to camp out there for a while. "Kate's up to something," he says. "I can't prove it yet. I drove up to North Shore, where she supposedly lived for a couple of years."

He's speaking as if we're having a normal couple conversation, not like it's been an entire week since we spoke to or saw each other, and I am incredibly furious with him.

Maybe he *has* lost his mind.

"I tried to track down her friends, an old employer—I found nothing. The woman I spoke to at the Chamber of Commerce said there's never been a business by the name of the last employer she gave me." He leans on his elbow and sweeps a lock of hair off my forehead.

I swat at his fingers.

Just because he explained that his trip wasn't a vacation with his ex, it doesn't justify his absence.

Jaeger's lips quirk briefly, then turn down. He plays with the collar of my shirt. "Kate showed me a picture of the child." He lets out a puff of air. Even his breath smells good and minty. I scowl. "The girl looks like her, but I don't know. I can't tell if she looks like me. Kerstin saw the picture, too, and thinks she could, but I don't see it. I've told Kate I want to take a paternity test. She raged, but finally agreed… as long as we live together." His gaze slides to mine and holds.

And that's why this entire thing is messed up. This chick is *living* with him.

He's not a bad guy, and that makes everything so much worse. It would be easier to hate him if he were selfish and terrible, but he's trying to do the right thing. Plus, he's extremely hot, and if I'm being honest with myself, I'm glad he's here.

"She doesn't have money and says they took her daughter away because she couldn't provide. The little girl lives with Kate's sister and husband in Reno. Kate refuses to give me her sister's number for some reason, but I discovered the address through a mutual friend. I'm driving up there tomorrow to hear her sister's side of the story. I'm positive there's something Kate's not telling me."

As mad as I am, I'm listening, and the one thing that keeps looping is that he called me his *girlfriend* at the start of this discussion. He meant it. In his mind, nothing has changed. "Why does she have to live with you?"

He shakes his head, and suddenly I notice the fine lines at the corners of his eyes. Dark circles mark the tender flesh below them. "She says she has nowhere to go. If this little girl is mine, I can't do it, Cali. I can't turn my back on them. That includes Kate."

I squirm and shove him with all my strength. "Get off me, Jaeger."

He rolls to the side. "Will you please listen?"

I sit up. "You're living with your ex-girlfriend, you jerk!"

"It's not like that! You know I'm not like that. I told you. I'm with you now. I *want* to be with you. I love you, Cali. Being away from you kills me. The only thing that has kept me sane throughout all this is thinking about getting back to you. About making all this right so that we can move on together."

He loves me…?

"If that's true, why did you wait so long to call me?"

"I've called and texted you numerous times." I send him a pointed glare. "I should have called the day after our date. It wasn't intentional," he grumbles. "Have you any idea what a massive pain in the ass my ex is? Trust me when I say I'm ready to move out. I've been sleeping on the couch in the shop. I stay away from the house as much as possible."

He sits up beside me. "As soon as I figure out the girl's paternity, Kate's gone. I'll pay child support, whatever I need to, if the little girl's mine. But Cali"—his eyes are pleading—"if she is mine, I can't abandon her. She didn't have a choice, you know?"

I let out a deep breath. Why does he have to be such a good guy?

He leans over and rubs his nose along my jaw and kisses me below my ear. "Please don't be mad. I mean, you have every right to be upset, but please don't leave me over this. I haven't meant to be an absent boyfriend. I've just had a lot of crazy shit going on that I've never had to deal with before. I love you, Cali. I love you." He kisses and nuzzles me some more.

Oh, Jesus Christ. I want to be mad at him, but I can't! I believe him. "I love you too, but I'm angry with you." He wraps his arms around me and pulls me to him. "Everything's not okay, Jaeger. You waited too long to get in touch."

He sighs. "I did. Not intentionally. My phone ran out of juice on the trip to North Shore. I was in a hurry to get answers and forgot my charger. I didn't bother buying another, just wanted to get back. My parents and sister were ready to wring my neck. I'm sorry, babe." He brushes my lips with his and my mouth softens.

I can't stay mad at him. Not when everything he says makes sense. Jaeger doesn't give me uneasy feelings. He's all heart.

"I missed you." My words come out angry. "And I love you." This time my tone is softer.

He looks in my eyes, searching, and then his mouth is on me before I can get another word out. I'm drowning and burning, a hot-cold fire spreading from my chest to my toes. I clutch him with all my strength and kiss him until we're both gasping. Jaeger wraps my legs around his back and I arch into him.

He moans and kisses me harder. "Love you. Missed you," he says between kisses peppered along my neck and the tops of my breasts.

He leans back and stares at my chest.

I prop up on my elbows, dazed. "What?"

"Are you wearing—a Wonderbra? Your boobs…"

My face heats. "I might have gained a few pounds. Like five," I admit, chagrined. "I sort of ate a pint of ice cream every night this last week."

He lifts his brow.

"Can you really tell my boobs are bigger?"

He gives me a look that says, *Come on, give me some credit.*

"Guys can tell these things?"

He lowers his head, pushes my top and bra down, and mumbles, "Yes," while kissing and licking my breast.

And, wow, that feels amazing… but I'm kind of hung up on this boob thing. If they look bigger… "Do I look fat?"

Jaeger groans. "I hate that question." He reaches around and cups my bottom, pulling me against his erection. I slip off my elbows and land on my back. "You feel incredible," he breathes into my neck. "You smell unbelievable, and you're beautiful and feisty. Have I convinced you how much I want you?"

I circle my hips. "Um, yes. As you were," I say, and place his hand back on my breast.

He grins eagerly and unbuttons my shorts with his other

hand.

We make good use of Gen and Tyler's absence. After an hour of nakedness, I decide I'd better not press my luck. "We should get dressed."

Jaeger looks up from his position at my side, one of his legs with a light dusting of brown hair thrown over both of mine. He groans. "I don't want to go home."

"Then stay here."

"Really?" He props up, head in his hand, looking down at me.

God, did I just ask my boyfriend to move in? I sort of meant for him to stay for the next few hours, but I don't think that's how he took it. I could never let him live here without talking to Gen first. Besides, where would we sleep?

"Maybe not permanently. I have a roommate, and there's not much space with my brother around. But you could crash on the couch for a couple of days if you really don't want to live with Kate."

The offer is purely selfish. The last thing I want is my boyfriend living with his ex.

"Are you sure? Because if you are, I'll take you up on it. I was already thinking of moving back in with my parents until I work things out, but this is much better." He kisses my nipple.

"Jaeger! We can't do this with my brother and Gen around."

"I know, feisty." He grins. "But while they're gone, naked time is in full effect."

Chapter Twenty-Eight

"ARE YOU SURE you don't want me to go with you?" My legs are crossed at the ankle over Jaeger's lap on the couch in the living room. He spent the night, and we were perfect angels while Gen and Tyler were around. Probably because we'd taken care of our pent-up sexual needs before they returned.

"You've got work, and I probably should drive up to Kate's sister's on my own." Jaeger rubs his forehead and runs his fingers through his hair. He lets out a breath, the fine lines around his eyes deeper than ever. He doesn't seem convinced.

"You're worried you might meet your daughter and you want to keep things simple," I say, guessing what he must be thinking.

He sucks in air through his nose and closes his eyes. "If I have one, yes. I'd bet anything, though, she isn't mine. If she is... I'll do what I have to, but Kate's a liar. I haven't figured out why she'd lie about this, but she must be. We were— careful—or I was."

I hate thinking about Jaeger with another woman. "No need to elaborate."

He pulls me to his chest and rubs his lips along my hairline. "I should be back by the time you get off work. See you then?" I nod and he kisses me on the head, then wraps his arms around my waist in a lung-crushing squeeze.

I love his hugs. I could stay in his embrace for the rest of the day without food or water and be perfectly content breathing in his scent for sustenance.

AND THAT'S WHAT I have to hold me over for the rest of the day while I'm at work, the memory of being held by Jaeger and knowing I was so blissfully wrong, thank God. I mean, Kate's still a problem, but she's not as big of a problem as I thought. As long as Jaeger and I are together, everything will be okay.

That doesn't stop me from worrying entirely. If Jaeger has a daughter, what does it mean for him? For us? I like kids, but I've spent next to no time with them.

I didn't expect to need a working knowledge of children until I had my own—a loooong way off. What if Jaeger realizes I'm no good with children? Then what?

"Cali?" Architect Bill jars me from my bout of anxiety. I'm supposed to be working on a new design for the company's business cards, but instead I'm staring off into space. "Do you have time to make an artist's rendition of the Lakeshore property? We think it will help with the planning council."

"Yeah, sure."

"Great, I'll send the principal your way. John's son. Have you two met? Nice kid."

Several of the guys that come through the office are on the younger side, but they spend most of their days on job sites. I'm trying to recall whether any of them work regularly in the office, when a knock sounds at my door.

My office is the copy room with a partition sectioned off for a teeny desk that holds my laptop. Sallee Construction is located in a nice office building, but space is limited. Most employees work on job sites and don't require offices. The existing square footage is taken up by blueprints and a place for client meetings. I consider myself lucky to even have an "office." Plus, this way I get to chat with the receptionist, who's really sweet and always coming in to make copies for John and the others.

I carefully finish the line I'm working on. Some graphic artist will do the actual business card printing, but this is just a mock-up for them to go off.

I turn around to meet John's son, and my head notches back in shock.

"*You?*" The word is out before I can stop it.

Lewis's brow furrows. "Gen's friend," he says as if confirming the obvious. After a pause, he seems to gather himself and takes a step inside. "I've worked offsite the last several days. I didn't realize you were the artist my father hired."

Lewis is Mr. Sallee's son? It makes some sense with the connection to Nessa. Nessa's how Gen met Lewis. After a long hesitation, in which I attempt to process the fact that I now work with Lewis, I gesture to the one chair in my office.

He takes a seat, looking like an adult in a toddler's chair and consuming the room's limited breathing space. He isn't as bulky as Jaeger, but he's athletically built and just as tall.

"How's Genevieve?"

The hair on the back of my neck prickles. Most people don't even know Genevieve is Gen's full name—and it makes me nervous that this guy does. "Good," I answer warily.

Lewis is tall, with dark hair and tanned skin like his father, though his face is free of laugh lines—probably because the guy never smiles. Add high cheekbones and a strong, proud chin, and what's not to like? But no way in hell am I throwing my BF back into the fire with a cheater, and last I checked, Lewis was in some complicated relationship with Mira.

If I've learned anything though this summer, it's that Gen doesn't need me to fight her battles. She's done just fine on her own. I should keep my mouth shut.

I relax my shoulders and tell myself to simmer down.

Lewis pulls two reduced architectural CAD drawings from a file in his hand. He explains the general aesthetic of the Lakeshore building and shows me the landscape plan. The final product will be a multilevel Swiss lodge with a modern bent and eco-friendly plants.

We discuss time lines.

"I'll get started on it right away," I tell him.

Lewis stands and walks toward the door. He glances back while I'm sorting through colored pencils from my stash of art supplies. Sallee Construction could use software for artists' renditions, but the old guys are loath to learn it, and apparently I'm cheaper and leave them time to work on other stuff.

"Tell Gen…" He grips the doorframe. "Tell her I said hello."

I hesitate, then remember he's my boss's son. "Sure," I say stiffly. I trust Gen, but I don't trust this guy. He's uptight and, more important, unavailable as far as I'm concerned.

Lewis walks out, but I hear him talking in the front area, which I can see from my desk. His manner is clipped as he speaks to the receptionist, but she says something and his face softens. She has that effect on people.

While they're talking, the front door opens and Mira walks in wearing a short summer dress and platform sandals. I don't have a good read on Mira. She's super proprietary over Lewis, and that seems to be her main focus. What I can say about the girl is that she's breathtaking, not that Lewis seems to notice.

He looks at her like he does his friends, which is entirely different from how he looks at Gen.

Lewis's body stiffens and he speaks so low to Mira I can't hear what he's saying. She seems to ignore his words and greets our receptionist as if they've known each other for years. They probably have.

After a moment, Lewis pulls Mira aside. They argue, her voice rising, until she smiles without it touching her eyes, and glides calmly out the door, the bells chiming behind her.

Lewis looks over and our gazes meet. I quickly look away, but I catch him storming off out of the corner of my eye.

A door slams down the hall, punctuating my earlier assertion. Lewis is very unavailable.

And maybe this time, I *should* warn Gen.

THAT EVENING WHEN I arrive home from work, Gen's getting ready for her shift.

I walk into the bathroom and sit on the toilet lid. "Lewis works at Sallee Construction. He's the owner's son."

Gen sets the hairbrush in her hand on the counter and stares into the mirror at her reflection.

Not the reaction I was looking for. It answers the question of whether or not she still thinks about him. "You don't actually care for this guy…?"

She sighs and walks out. "Leave it alone, Cali."

"Gen—" I trail after her into the living room. "I was stupid at the start of the summer. I didn't really understand what you were going through, because I'd never been in love. You were more involved with the A-hole than I ever was with Eric. I get that now. And I don't want to tell you what to do, because when it comes to this, I'm not as experienced as I thought, but I'm scared for you."

Gen looks up from rifling in her purse and shakes her head. "Cali, there's nothing to fear."

I lean my hip against the side of the couch and study her. "I'm worried I pushed you to date guys before you were ready and now you're running headfirst into the same situation you escaped."

"You're giving yourself too much credit. I do actually select when and who I want to date, and I told you, the situation with Lewis is not the same as my past relationship. Besides, I'm not actually in a relationship," she adds, and heads into the bedroom while I stand in the doorway.

Gen grabs a shirt from the closet and sinks onto the bed without putting it on. "I can't help who I'm attracted to. That's just nature." She looks up. "But I'm not planning on repeating the past, if that's what you're worried about. Even if I did, it wouldn't be your fault." She tugs the printed T-shirt over her head.

"Okay. But Mira visited Lewis at work today. If you're spending time with him, just—be careful."

Gen pauses. "I will," she says without looking up. She pulls on dark jeans and walks around the bed toward me. "You don't need to protect me, Cali. I'll be okay."

God, right now, I could use protection. Every day with Jaeger is a lesson in what it means to care for someone. I want what's best for him, even if that means not being with me. If I can't be the right person for him and his daughter, he needs someone who can.

Eric spoke to me like I was an idiot when I told him that I'd given up law. He never once asked me what made me happy.

Everything Jaeger does is to make me happy. A profound difference, and something I'd like to be able to return.

Jaeger texts shortly after Gen leaves for work.

Jaeger: *Trip unsuccessful. Kate's sister never showed. Stayed too long waiting around. Have a project to wrap up... could be late before I make it over. Miss you.*

So the wait continues. Not knowing where things stand makes me crazy. I could sit around and twiddle my thumbs, but that's not really my style.

I jump in the shower and then get dressed. Tyler's friend picked him up, so I have the car for the night. I'll visit Jaeger. I won't bother him while he works. I just want to make sure he's okay and give him a quick hug after his shitty day, and I don't want to have to wait until late to do it.

Chapter Twenty-Nine

M Y STOMACH TIGHTENS as I pull into Jaeger's driveway. A black Mercedes sports car is parked near his truck. Kate's car? I thought she didn't have any money and that's why she's living with Jaeger?

I forgot when I decided to come here tonight that I might see Kate. It doesn't matter that Jaeger isn't interested in her. The idea of an ex-girlfriend in his home makes my proprietary instincts flare.

I breathe deeply and smooth the strands that pulled loose from my ponytail into place. I check my teeth for lipstick stains in the visor mirror. I'm not walking in looking shabby. Kate needs to know she isn't going to weasel into Jaeger's heart the way she did his house.

What kind of mother screws up her life so badly she loses her kid? And why didn't Kate tell Jaeger she was pregnant? For as long as I've known him—which is a significant amount of time, given his connection to my brother—he's been a good guy. He would have stood by her if she'd told him. Why come out now?

This chick makes no sense, and when something doesn't make sense there's a reason. But I agree with Jaeger: he has to find out the truth before he tells her to leave. If the little girl really is his daughter, Kate could do anything. Sell the car and leave the country with the girl, who knows? Jaeger's playing it safe, and I don't blame him for it.

The woodshop is silent today. I rap lightly on the front door and look out at the lake through the trees, attempting to remain calm. I'll simply visit with Jaeger, make sure he's okay, then go home. I won't cause problems for him with Kate, though I'd love to give her a piece of my mind.

Nobody answers after several minutes, and the doorbell doesn't seem to work. I'm sure he's here. His truck is in the drive.

I twist the handle, and it's unlocked.

Jaeger's my boyfriend, and he's practically living with me at the moment. I'll just peek inside and let him know I'm here.

I step inside, but it's not Jaeger's presence that fills the house. A hushed female voice floats from the back bedroom. Not Jaeger's room—*thank God*—gotta be his office, the man-cave. I don't see Jaeger anywhere. He's not in the living area, and the door to his bedroom is open, the lights off. The other two bedrooms are located at the other end of the hall.

I should call out, but there's something about the way she's talking on the phone, quiet and professional, like she's conducting a business transaction, that makes me hesitate. I walk toward the back, making no effort to silence my footfalls. It's not my fault that my Keds make no sound.

I stop outside the partly open door to Jaeger's office. And okay, yes, this time I really do eavesdrop, because it sounds like she's—*shopping?* I peek past the door.

"I'll take the twistlock heel in blue and black," Kate says into a cell phone, scrolling with a mouse on Jaeger's computer. "Size seven and a half. And the Jennie stacked platform in red, same size."

Online shopping.

"I want the cutout sundress in a size four, and"—she clicks the mouse and pulls up another screen—"the limited edition skater dress. I want that in pale blue, along with the lightweight biker jacket." A pause. "That's all for now. You can mail it to this address." She bends over to fix a strap on her sandal and rattles something off. Her voice is slightly muffled, and all I catch are the first two digits. Not very helpful. She sits back up. "No, that's not the billing. Hold on a sec." Kate reaches across the desk and lifts an envelope. She reads off Jaeger's street address.

What the hell? If she's using his address for billing…

Kate thumbs a credit card. "Here's my card number." She reads off a series of numbers, the expiration date, and a security code. "The name on the card is Jaeger Lang. My husband and I have different last names."

The bitch!

I've heard enough. I clear my throat loudly.

Kate's gaze darts to me. I cock my head. Her eyes widen a fraction, but her expression remains calm. "Thank you," she says cheerily into the phone, and ends the call. For a moment we stare at each other.

"You must be Cali."

Good, she knows who I am.

Remain calm. I promised myself I wouldn't cause problems for Jaeger. "What do you think you're doing?" Okay, that didn't come out as diplomatic as I had hoped.

Kate lifts her legs, bared to the rump in cut-off shorts, and plants her feet on the corner of Jaeger's desk. Her shorts are so small the curve of her butt cheek hangs out. She's pretty, with light brown hair tumbling over her shoulder in soft waves, but the energy she gives off is cold as that minnow I caught in Lake

Tahoe.

"Jaeger said he had a female friend who might stop by from time to time. I'm Kate, the mother of his child."

My jaw clenches. *Calm, must remain calm.* "Why are you using Jaeger's credit card?"

"Oh, just ordering a few necessities." She smiles prettily. "Jaeger told me to make myself at home."

"That's interesting. I would think you'd be spending less money on *necessities* and more time figuring out how to get your daughter back."

Her brow puckers. "Oh, I am, but there's only so much I can do. I hate this waiting around, but the court hearing isn't for another month."

A month! Freaking hell.

"The most important thing Jaeger and I can do now is create a loving home for our daughter."

No. Way. This has got to end. She's using him. "Where's Jaeger?"

"In his outhouse."

Woodshop, dumbass.

I'm not leaving Kate in Jaeger's office. She might decide to use his credit card to purchase a hot tub or a tropical island. "Do you think you can show me the way?" I ask sweetly. "I always forget which door to use."

Kate smirks. She knows I'm full of shit, but she lowers her slender, mile-long legs and saunters into the living room and out the back door. We pass her fancy sports car, and I do a double take at another luxury vehicle in the drive, this one red. Who's here now?

Kate raps on the woodshop door and walks inside, clearly having no problem barging into his private space. It pisses me off, until I see Jaeger—with another woman.

He's sitting on the couch with a beautiful brunette standing between his legs in nothing but a bra and a short black skirt. The same woman I saw him with at Blue the night I went home with Drake.

"Jaeger!" Kate exclaims in a nasally, high-pitched screech.

Okay, I can be understanding—my boyfriend is living with his ex-girlfriend—but this is taking it too far. "Sweetie, you seem to have one too many women in the house."

Jaeger glances over, his face startled and confused. He didn't budge when Kate yelled, as if he's grown accustomed to tuning her out, but my comment grabs his attention. "Cali?"

The woman in front of him eases back, making no move to cover her chest. She's in a pretty black bra with perfect abs—noticing meaningless details helps keep me from fleeing the scene in a huff of indignation. I've had my fill of shit, but I love Jaeger, and the expression on his face is one of shock. He's as surprised as me, and I don't think it's because I walked in on him.

Jaeger stands and staggers to me. He grabs my hand, angling toward the woman. "Danielle, this is my girlfriend, Cali."

Kate snorts beside us, her face contorted in annoyance. Jaeger doesn't introduce her.

Danielle lifts her purse from the floor beside the couch and casually pulls out a silk tank. She turns and slips on her top as if she dresses in front of an audience every day. "I see I've caught you at a bad time." She walks over and squeezes his thick bicep. I'm tempted to bite her hand like a rabid animal. "Call me later."

I've gotta hand it to the woman—she's got balls.

Jaeger watches Danielle leave, then looks at me. His eyes

widen. "What? She ambushed me. I had no idea what she was up to."

"Jaeger!" Kate screeches. I'd forgotten Kate, and at this point, I'd prefer to tune her out too. "How can you do this? Think about our daughter!"

"Kate," Jaeger says curtly. "Give me a moment with Cali."

Kate leaves and slams the door on her way out. Jaeger marches to one of his worktables. He shoves tools into a drawer and bangs his fist on the table. "What the fuck!"

"Yeah-h-h, my thoughts exactly," I say.

He stalks over, linking our fingers. "Come on. Let's get out of here. We'll go to your place."

"Wait." I tug on his arm to stop him. We will go to my place and talk, because I have a few questions for him about that woman, but first—"You can't leave Kate alone in your house. When I arrived, she was shopping online with your credit card and claiming you as her *husband.*"

"Motherfucker," he mumbles.

Jaeger is judicious with his expletives. He must really be pissed.

After spending his day searching for Kate's sister in Reno, getting ambushed by the lady from Blue, then discovering he's being ripped off by his ex-girlfriend, I guess I can understand.

We walk to the house and Jaeger flings open the back door, catching it a second before it smashes me in the face. He stalks across the living room toward the hallway. Kate moves around the kitchen island with a bag of cookies in her hand, tracking his progress. At the end of the hall, Jaeger pulls out a key, then closes and locks the door to his office.

Kate's mouth drops open. She shuts it and glares at me.

I follow Jaeger into his bedroom. He pulls clothes out of

drawers and a walk-in closet and stuffs them in a canvas duffel he's yanked out from under the bed. He rummages noisily in the bathroom before returning with a leather toiletry bag he tosses in the duffel as well.

Throwing the whole thing over his shoulder, he places his hand on my lower back. "Let's go."

Jaeger stops at the front door and turns toward Kate, who's holding a mug in her hand this time as she watches us leave. "You pull anything like that again, Kate, and I'll file charges, kid or no kid."

He guides me to my car. "I'll follow you to your place," he says.

I have questions, but I get the feeling now isn't the time to bring them up. From the rearview mirror, I notice Jaeger parked and talking on his cell phone as I pull away.

Tyler's still out when I get home. I plop on the couch, and Jaeger walks in a few minutes later. He drops his duffel by the front door and scrubs his face—

The front door swings open and bangs him in the back.

Tyler peeks around the corner. "Sorry, man. Didn't see you there."

Jaeger sinks into the recliner, elbows on his knees, head lowered.

Tyler looks at me. "What's up?"

He knows about Kate's kid extortion. I fill him in on Jaeger's failed attempt to track down Kate's sister and what I walked in on at the woodshop.

I've calmed since seeing the half-naked woman between his legs. If Jaeger were any other boyfriend, I might be suspicious. But he's totally befuddled.

Tyler flips one of the dining chairs around and sits on it

backward. "Older gal, huh?"

Jaeger looks up. "I had no idea," he says stone-faced.

I shake my head in disbelief. "What do you mean? That woman was all over you at the Blue bar."

"But"—he eyes looks around as if mentally searching— "she's my client. I thought she was being friendly."

"Dude," Tyler says, "you're kidding, right? She took her top off in your house."

Jaeger frowns. "I figured it out by then, man. She walked *in* without her top on. Kinda obvious at that point. Still stunned me, though. She managed to back me into the damn couch," he grumbles.

Tyler and I look at each other, and Tyler snickers. If the situation weren't so infuriating it would be funny.

Jaeger glares at Tyler. "Not funny, man. I was attacked un-awares."

"Older women," Tyler says. "Predators, every one of them."

"Tyler!" I exclaim. "What do you know about older wom-en?"

He holds up his hands innocently. "What? I'm in my prime. Older women flock to virile men like me."

I did not just hear that. "I think I just threw up a little in my mouth."

He shrugs. "You asked."

Jaeger groans, leans his head back, and stares at the ceiling.

I walk over and sit on his lap. "It's okay, sweetie. You'll just have to get used to the older ladies not looking at you as a nice young man anymore. They want to get into your pants now."

He glares at me and I smile.

"She seemed like such a nice client," he goes on, as if he hasn't heard anything Tyler or I have said. "She was friendly, but, well, you know." He shrugs.

"Oh, she was nice, all right," Tyler says. "She would have given you a nice, long blow—"

"Tyler!" I yell. "Knock it off, you jackass."

I rub Jaeger's shoulders and his head lolls, his eyes drooping. He's exhausted. Danielle was startling, but not our biggest problem. "What are you going to do about Kate?"

He huffs out a breath. His muscles bunch up again, but his eyes remain closed. "I called my credit card company. Told them the situation and asked them to block those purchases. My father's speaking to a lawyer. We'll need to establish paternity before we move forward with custody arrangements if it turns out... Anyway, Kate acted like we'd live happily ever after. She's nuts." He shakes his head. "Not gonna happen. And she has to have another agenda if she's trying to fleece me now. Gotta get her out of there."

"You think she wants your money?"

I wasn't raised to rely on a man for financial support. My mom taught us to take care of ourselves. It's partly why I'm having issues with the career upheaval. I'm like a guy; I need to know I'm financially capable before I feel complete.

"Oh, I have no doubt she wants my money, my home, whatever she can get. If I was sure the child wasn't mine, I'd kick her out right now, but... I've had Mason and Adam asking around, though Adam's been useless. He's all bent out of shape over his breakup with Breanna."

"They broke up?" I interrupt. "Adam treated her like crap. Why is he so upset?"

Jaeger shrugs. "That's Adam for you. No one knows what goes on inside his head. He's a good guy when it comes down to it, though."

"Let's get back to the part where your friends are asking about Kate," Tyler pipes up. "What did they find?"

"Mason says she ran off with a guy from Reno after my accident. I was in and out of physical therapy and pretty messed up. Didn't keep in touch with friends or hear the news. Supposedly, the guy she's been dating since then deals drugs on the side. Light stuff—pot, acid. He started dabbling with meth over the last year and got caught running a lab out of Sparks. He's serving time for it."

Unbelievable. "How does she go from you to a drug dealer?"

He raises a shoulder. "The guy was loaded. Drove a nice car. Mason heard he bought her a place. I had things going for me back in high school, but once my Olympic career faded, she took off. I guess now that this guy is in prison, her funds have dried up too. She needs someone to leech off and is using our connection—our *kid*... if the little girl's actually mine."

I slide next to him on the chair. I can't stand Kate, but I don't think mentioning it will help the situation. "Kate wants in your life because you're beautiful and wealthy."

He wraps his arm around my shoulders and smashes me to his side. "You think I'm beautiful, babe?"

I frown. "Everyone thinks you're beautiful, including the Danielle's of the world."

"Well, I don't think you're beautiful," Tyler says drolly.

Jaeger ignores him and looks down at me. "You're the beautiful one. I think of myself as a manly sort of guy."

"Fine," Tyler interrupts. "I'm the beauty. And being admired for my looks does not diminish my sense of masculinity."

I swivel my head. "Tyler, why are you still here? I'm trying to have a private moment with my boyfriend."

He stands and shoves the chair back in place, narrowing a

look at Jaeger. "Just don't make it too private." Jaeger glares right back. My man is not having a good day. Tyler had better not push it.

Tyler digs in his jeans pocket and pulls out his keys. "I gotta run another errand anyway. See you in a bit."

He leaves and Jaeger stands, pulling me up with him. "I have something in the back of my truck I want to show you."

Outside, Jaeger grabs two large boxes from his truck bed— one long, the other wide and flat.

I stare at the packaging. "You bought camping gear?"

"If I'm going to stay with you, I need a place to sleep. Your couch is nice, but I'm not looking forward to my knees dangling off the end again tonight." He holds up the king-sized, pillow-top air mattress. "This way, we can sleep together." His grin is highly suggestive.

I like where his head is, but I eye the box skeptically. "Where exactly are we putting it?"

He hoists the boxes on to his shoulder, grabs my hand, and walks to the gate. "Your backyard."

"Uhh, did you learn nothing from our game of catch at the beach? I'm not sporty, remember? That includes camping."

Okay, there's no technique required in camping. I'm just not a fan of cold and rough sleeping arrangements.

He drops the boxes on the cement patio outside the back door. "You go hiking. You can't be that opposed to the outdoors."

Foiled by my own actions. I grumble and he grins at me.

Jaeger rips open the tent box, an act that would have taken me thirty minutes with the help of a large screwdriver and scissors. His muscles and large paws are a huge turn-on. I follow those clever hands as he sorts and puts together the tent.

"I bought one with a skylight." He glances up and smiles. "We can look at the trees and stars at night."

I'm sort of following what he's saying, nodding in agreement. But mostly I'm thinking about that tent and how see-through it is. It's definitely not soundproof. We'll have to be quiet…

This could work.

I grab the mattress box and hand it to Jaeger to open. He tears it apart and I smile happily, admiring the muscles flexing through his jeans as he bends and builds our home with his bare hands.

He glances up and sees me watching. Instead of scolding me for the dirty thoughts that must be evident on my face, his jaw clenches and he works faster.

I love this man.

Chapter Thirty

OUR TENT IS the size of a motor home. Then again, Jaeger is too. Unfortunately for my housemates, the patio has been compromised. Our giant tent-home takes up the length of the cement pad.

I'm lying on the mattress, which is surprisingly comfortable and mattress-like, staring at the stars through the skylight. Jaeger crouches his way in and zips the tent closed. I can stand without having to bend, but that does not apply to overgrown men.

He removes his shirt, and my mind goes blank.

I sit up abruptly. "Wait. We have to talk," I say, but I'm staring at his chest, my gaze trailing to his eight-pack and the waistband of his jeans. I force it up, only to find him smiling knowingly.

I plaster a somber expression on my face. "Don't think it's okay for half-naked women to show up at your place, because it's not." There, *I* told him.

He sits next to me, and I'd like to say the indentation of the air mattress is why I fall into him, but I think it's all me. Damn. Being a hardass girlfriend is more challenging than it looks.

It's a good thing Jaeger's a good guy, but we still need to talk. "Why did Danielle show up?"

He drops onto his back, an arm across his chest. "I had no idea she was interested in *that*. She's bought some commissions from me and introduced me to other clients. We've had a working relationship for a couple of years now, and she's never come on to me."

I hold up my finger. "I beg to differ. She clung to you like a wet blanket in the Blue lounge."

"Really?" He shakes his head. "Okay."

"*Seriously?* You don't know that a woman's coming on to you when she touches you and leans her breasts against your arm?"

"I never thought about it."

"Does this happen often?"

He shrugs, and I can tell the answer is yes, but he's being modest.

"Jaeger, what if a guy had his hands on me that way?"

"I'd tear off his arm," he says without hesitation.

"Okay-y-y, so it wouldn't be all right."

"Hell no."

I stare, and he glances away. "I get it, Cali. I know what you're saying." He sits up. "You understand, though, that I'm not interested in anyone but you? From the moment I saw you in the bar at Harrah's, I did everything I could to make you my girlfriend."

He did? I think back to that night and the days that followed. I suspected he was flirting, but I was still with Eric and trying not to think about my feelings for Jaeger.

He tucks a lock of hair, more red than gold in the moonlight, behind my ear. "No one else existed once I ran into you again. You're all I've thought about. Honestly"—he shakes his head—"I might have picked up on Danielle's intentions sooner if I hadn't been so caught up in thinking about you. And then there's this mess with Kate I've been dealing with."

He rolls me on top of him. "I'm sorry. I'll make it clear to Danielle and anyone else that I'm not interested. I have everything I want."

Whelp, that clears things up for me. I nuzzle his neck and kiss him beneath his jaw, straddling him.

Jaeger needs to push back more when it comes to Kate, but his heart is in the right place. He doesn't want to make the wrong move when it comes to a child's life. Kate weaseling her way into the middle will have to be dealt with—but maybe not right now.

A second later, our clothes are off and we're putting the translucent tent fabric to the test.

THE REST OF the week goes by faster than I can blink. Between my job and school, and Jaeger's commissions and meetings with lawyers, we've only seen each other at night.

Tonight, I'm waiting in our tent, reading one of Gen's smutty books. This one's about a vampire with obsessive-compulsive disorder. I give her a hard time for reading this crap, but now that I've cracked one open, I can't put it down. It's freaking addictive.

The screech of the zipper has me jumping back, tucking the book under my pillow. I roll on my side, head propped on my hand. "Hey," I say, breathlessly, as if I've been caught doing something I shouldn't.

If Jaeger notices, he doesn't show it. His eyes are at half-mast as he slips his wallet from his back pocket, kicks off his shoes, and crawls onto the bed face down. A rumbly sound comes from his chest. I think he said hello, but I can't be sure.

I crawl on his back and dip my head over his shoulder by his ear. "You okay?"

He turns his head to the side. "Now. Don't move. Feels good. I'll be asleep in three seconds."

I'm worried about him. He's wearing himself out. "You're exhausted. What can I do to help? Do you want me to beat Kate up and get her sister's phone number?"

He snorts. "No. My lawyer has people searching birth certificates for information on her daughter. They offered to track Kate's sister Hannah down, but I've got tomorrow off. I'm heading up again. I don't want the lawyer getting involved yet. Don't want to scare Hannah or the girl."

I roll to the side, facing him. "Let me go with you. I'll take the day off too." He studies my face. "It might be nice for them to know there's another woman in the picture. Maybe Hannah doesn't trust Kate. It could help smooth the situation over if she and her husband know you're in a serious relationship. That you're the kind of guy who commits."

His gaze is interested but guarded. "You don't have to."

"I want to."

Jaeger raises his head and kisses my lips. "I'd like that."

THE NEXT DAY we leave at six a.m. to beat traffic and catch Kate's sister before she begins her day. We arrive in Reno at seven thirty, and pull into the Donner Springs neighborhood.

"What's Kate's sister like?" I ask.

"Hannah? No idea. Kate and Hannah didn't get along in high school. I met her a couple of times, but the visits were brief. I'm surprised custody went to her. Kate manipulated her parents, but she had a better relationship with them."

"And the little girl's name?" It could have been intentional on my part, to block what I don't want to believe, but I've rarely asked Jaeger about his daughter. If she's going to be in his life, I need to make a bigger effort to learn about her.

His jaw tightens and he shakes his head. "Kate won't tell me anything, not even that. She's not making sense. Whatever I learn from Hannah, I know it will be different from what Kate's telling me. For all I know, Kate dumped the child on her sister's doorstep and told her to take care of it."

Jaeger checks the address on his truck's GPS and pulls up to a small yellow house with a yard that needs to be mowed. "We're here." A maroon sedan sits in the drive, a car seat in the back.

We walk up the driveway and I grab Jaeger's hand before he knocks on the door. A child's playful screech sounds in the background, along with a thunder of small footsteps.

My heart pounds, my hands cold and clammy. I glance over and Jaeger smiles reassuringly. I think I'm more nervous than he is.

The sound of a chain sliding free scrapes before the door opens. A woman with tawny, shoulder-length hair and dark blue eyes stands on the other side. "Yes?"

"Hannah? I'm Jaeger Lang. I—uh, I dated your sister. Back in high school."

The woman blinks, her quick gaze taking in his size, then settling on his face. "Oh, sure. Hi, Jaeg. Is everything okay? I—uh, I don't really keep in touch with Kate. If that's why you're here?" She glances at me curiously.

Jaeger anchors an arm around my waist. "This is my girl-friend, Cali. I've seen Kate. I'm here because of what she told me. Do you mind if we come in and talk to you for a minute?"

Hannah opens the screen door. "I've got to leave for work

soon and drop off my daughter at school, but we have a little time."

She guides us to a living room with an overworn brown couch, the pillows askew. "Sorry about this." Hannah tucks the cushions back in place. "My daughter's going through a fort phase."

Jaeger smiles and sits on the couch. "Actually, your daughter is why we're here." He takes a deep breath, tension rolling off his stiff posture. "Kate told me we had a child together. She said you've been given temporary custody."

Hannah stares without blinking for a solid minute. "Mark!" she yells without breaking eye contact, her pitch escalating at the end. "Come in here, please."

A man in his early thirties walks into the living room from down the hall, wrapping a tie around his neck in a knot. His gaze goes straight to his wife, then touches on us. "I didn't know we had guests." It's a statement, but there's a question in his voice.

"This is Jaeg," Hannah says. "Kate's ex-boyfriend from high school, and his girlfriend Cali." Her tone is terse, but I don't think it's directed at us. "Please tell my husband Mark what you just told me, Jaeg."

Jaeger clears his throat. "I'm here because Kate returned to town and informed me we have a child together. She said you and your wife are caring for our four-year-old daughter, but she wouldn't give me your number or specifics about the child, and I wanted to find out more information."

"*What?*" Mark's voice is loud like a bark, his tone dark.

A little girl runs into the room and grabs her father's leg. She has straight blond hair pulled back with flower barrettes, and green eyes. She could pass for Jaeger's daughter with her coloring, as long as no one saw her next to Mark. She's the spitting image of her father, right down to the dimple in her chin.

"Sweetheart"—Mark crouches and faces his daughter—"special treat this morning." He smiles, but there's a touch of tension in his voice. "You can play with your dress-up clothes before school."

The little girl frowns briefly, possibly picking up the edge in her father's tone, then seems to realize her coup. Squeals ensue and she runs out of the room back down the hallway.

Mark sinks into a chair next to his wife, his hands gripping the armrests. "What the hell is going on?"

I'm tapping my foot and squeezing Jaeger's hand to death. This is so not right. These people have no idea what we're talking about.

Somehow Jaeger remains calm. Even the contours of his face have softened. "I'm here to find out if I have a daughter."

"Well," Hannah says, "I don't know if *you* have a daughter, Jaeg, but I can tell you that my daughter came from *my* body, not my sister's." She smiles sardonically. "Childbirth is one of those things a woman doesn't forget."

"Okay." Jaeger nods. "Good." He shifts in his seat, his brows bunching in thought. "You said you aren't close to Kate, but do you know if she had a child?"

"I don't keep in touch with her, but my parents do. They would have known if she'd been pregnant. She's close to my mom." Bitterness seeps from her tone. "Mom puts up with Kate's crap."

Jaeger rubs his forehead. "So there's no way that the little girl I just saw or any other girl you've taken care of in your home is my child?"

"There's only one child we've raised," Mark says. "And there is no way she is yours. Kate lied to you."

Jaeger takes a deep breath and leans back. "Okay. Okay—thank you. I'm sorry to have bothered you this morning." He squeezes my hand and stands.

"Jaeg," Hannah says, "before you leave, tell me what's going on with Kate. My mom hasn't spoken to her in weeks. I don't care what Kate's up to, but it sounds like she's getting into trouble again, and my mom should know. We thought her problems were behind her after her boyfriend went to prison two months ago. If she's fabricating lies about having a child…" She looks to her husband. "I'm worried for our daughter, Mark. Maybe we should call the police."

"On it." Mark pulls out his cell phone and walks away.

Jaeger and I exchange a look.

"She's living at my house," Jaeger says. "She said we needed to show a stable environment in order to regain custody of our child. I didn't trust her from the moment she walked back into my life, but I didn't want to tell her to leave just yet in case she was telling the truth. Didn't want anything bad to happen to the little girl."

Hannah nods. "I understand. You did the right thing. You always were too good for my sister. I'm sorry she used you. We'll tell the police what's going on and help you in whatever way we can, but our first priority is to keep our daughter safe." She shakes her head. "What if Kate had kidnapped her to use her? My sister is sick. I don't want her anywhere near my daughter or my family."

Jaeger nods and pulls out his phone. "If you don't mind, I'd like to call my parents. My father hired a lawyer and I want to tell them what we discovered."

Hannah stands. "Of course, go ahead. Can I get you anything to drink? My husband and I will go in to work late today—or maybe I'll stay home." She looks toward the hall. "I don't want to be away from my daughter with my sister making dangerous claims. She's selfish and irresponsible, but I never thought she'd do anything like this."

Jaeger exchanges phone numbers with Hannah and her husband before we leave. He gets a call from them on the drive back to Lake Tahoe. They're filing a restraining order against Kate. Jaeger also spoke to his father and found out the lawyer his dad hired is having a thirty-day legal notice delivered to Kate to vacate Jaeger's home. She's claiming a right to occupancy, which technically she can, since Jaeger allowed her to move in.

We're stuck with her for thirty more effing days. "What if she destroys your house or steals stuff?" I ask as we pull into town.

"My workshop is all I care about, and it's locked tight. We'll swing by, though, and I'll remove important documents and my computer. Mason will hold everything until I get Kate out."

He looks over. "I'm sorry, Cali. For putting you through this."

"I'll be fine. I'm worried about you; you've been kicked out of your house."

"Even if she burned the place down, nothing could be worse than finding out Kate was telling the truth." He stretches his neck. "I'm thanking my lucky stars she lied about the kid. No man should be tied to Kate for a lifetime. Or a child, for that matter. Besides"—he grins, the weight that's been pulling down his features these last few days lifting—"I'm living in the best place in town."

"The tent?" I chuckle.

Jaeger grabs my thigh and rubs it up and down. "Wherever you are is where I want to be."

Chapter Thirty-One

THE NEXT MORNING, Jaeger takes off for a meeting with his father and lawyer. Afterward, he's going to his shop to work. I hate the idea of him near Kate—the woman is ruthless and dangerous, as far as I'm concerned—but he's got commissions due. I understand why he needs to return.

Tyler's sitting at the dining room table typing on his computer when I enter the kitchen.

"What was Jaeger's ex like back in high school?" I've tried less obvious approaches, but Tyler hasn't responded to my subtlety.

"A bitch. I hated that chick."

Okay, that's direct. "Jeez, Tyler, tell me what you really think." I've never heard my brother call a woman a derogatory name. Probably an artifact of growing up with a strong mother.

Tyler's hands still on the keyboard. He picks up the spoon from his bowl of cereal and scoops the last bite. "I barely knew her, but I heard rumors about her being mean to other kids at school. Typical bully. Never understood why Jaeg dated her. She just seemed like a social climber, and then she dumped Jaeg when he was at his lowest."

He stands and walks to the kitchen, dumping his dishes in the sink.

"Hey, this isn't a bed and breakfast. Wash your dishes."

Tyler saunters past me and kisses the top of my head.

"That's what I have you for."

"You've turned into a real ass, you know that?" Something happened to my affable brother back in Boulder. He's always teased me, but he's downright grumpy these days.

"You have no idea. Taking a shower," he says, and locks the bathroom door behind him.

After class that evening, I convince Leo to drive the extra distance to Jaeger's house. Jaeger's been in his shop most of the day and I want to surprise him with the food and drinks I picked up from the on-campus café. It's not much of a dinner, but I don't think he'll care.

Jaeger may not have the stress of wondering if he has a child anymore, but he's still exhausted and not eating enough. He has dark circles under his eyes and his cheeks are growing hollow from working so hard and coordinating with lawyers over the Kate situation. He makes two sandwiches when he gets to my place at night and inhales them both before crashing on our air mattress. Sometimes I wonder if it's the only meal he's had all day.

Leo's car idles in front of Jaeger's house as I grab the bags of food. "Nice location," he says, peering at the moonlit lake beyond the trees.

The front door swings open and Kate steps onto the porch. A motion detector light reveals the scowl on her face. She's got to be in top evil form now that they issued the eviction notice.

I think I'll skip the house and go straight to the workshop.

I swivel my head to say goodbye to Leo, but he's squinting at Kate. I look back to find her looking straight at him as well, recognition crossing her features.

"You two know each other?" I ask.

His mouth twists. "I—yeah, I think. My roommate's into

some stuff. He has these parties. Pretty sure I've seen her at them."

Jaeger walks out of his woodshop, wiping his hands on a towel, his frame bowed. He looks exhausted. His eyes scan from me to Leo and his mouth tightens.

This doesn't look good. "Thanks for the ride, Leo," I say quickly, and hop out of the car.

Jaeger has been pushed to his limit. I've seen the kind of damage he can do to a guy when he isn't trying. I'd rather not give him a reason to take out his frustration on poor Leo.

"Surprise!" I walk over and kiss Jaeger's tense lips. His gaze tracks Leo's small truck as it winds down the lane.

I shove the bag of food at his chest and he looks down and blinks. A sweet smile spreads across his face. "You've been working so hard," I say. "I wanted to check in on you."

"Thanks, babe." Jaeger's eyes flicker angrily toward Kate on the porch. She spins around and slams the front door behind her.

There's the angst.

He holds me close for a moment, his lips skimming over my hairline, the tension in his shoulders releasing. "Give me a minute to clean up and we can get going."

Jaeger puts away tools, wipes down a table, and sweeps the floor of his woodshop. I watch from the couch, enraptured. I could stare at Jaeger all day, moving around in his jeans that fit his butt to perfection, wood shavings speckling his T-shirt and hair, all responsible and hardworking.

He glances around as if checking for remaining cleanup, and his gaze lands on me.

I squirm, suddenly aware of the last time I sat on this couch, or rather, *lay* on it.

Jaeger moves forward and my heart kicks up. He crouches at my feet and runs his palms up my bare legs to the edges of my denim skirt. "What do you want to do?"

Oh, I have ideas, but...

I scowl in the direction of the house. "Let's go to my place."

Outside, Jaeger's face contorts as he looks down the driveway again. He helps me into his truck. "Who's that guy that gives you rides?"

"Leo? He's in my CAD class. We carpool, except it's not really carpooling because I don't give him rides. I usually buy dinner after class to make up for the gas money."

"You buy him dinner," he says in a tone that's not altogether happy.

"I've gotta do something for him, Jaeger. I'd feel like a mooch if I didn't."

He nods stiffly, obviously not liking my answer. "We've gotta get you a car. I don't want you stranded or needing to rely on others to get around."

"Yeah, well, that would be nice, but I can't afford one. Anyway, for now, I'm good. When Gen and Tyler leave in the fall, I'll have to use the bus until I can save up for something."

Jaeger frowns out the front window of his truck as he turns on the ignition. It's damn embarrassing to admit to your highly successful boyfriend that you can't afford a car.

Minutes later, we pull into my gravel driveway, my eyes bugging out at my mom's blue sedan parked on the street.

What the hell? *Shit.*

My mom suspected something between Jaeger and me when I visited, but I haven't talked to her since things became official. She probably knew more about my feelings for him than I did at the time. I was still in denial and dealing with the loss of my job and my graduate school issues.

Crap, crap! I'm not prepared for this confrontation. I love Jaeger, but I'd hoped to have a private conversation with my mom. She might draw conclusions about me jumping into a relationship on the heels of my last. To her, this would look like a rebound, but it's not. My relationship with Jaeger is the first real one I've had.

"So, um, Jaeger?" I say, hesitantly.

He looks over, brow furrowing. My voice is shaky and I realize I'm squeezing the bejesus out of his hand on the seat between us. I loosen my grip. "That's my mom's car. She's here. I didn't know she was coming."

A beat passes. "You need me to leave?" He's trying to hide it, but there's hurt in his eyes.

"No, but it might not go perfectly. I haven't had a chance to tell her about us."

"I'm okay, if you're okay."

I smile. "I'm okay." Or I will be after this confrontation. It's like pulling off a Band-Aid. My mom's a little overprotective. She might react to the suddenness of my relationship with Jaeger, but she'll get over it.

We walk to the front door. And then I remember the tent out back and the fact Jaeger is *staying* with me.

This is going to be awkward as hell.

My mom is washing dishes in the kitchen when we enter, her back to us. She's humming, breaking into the chorus of "Love Bites" by Def Leppard every few bars. It's one of her favorites. If I'm warped, I blame it on the eighties music my mom subjected me to over the years.

"Mom, what are you doing here?"

She spins, gasping, her hand over her heart. "Calista, don't sneak up." She huffs out a breath, and eyes Jaeger. "Can't a mom visit her children?" she says distractedly.

"You usually call first," I point out.

She shakes water off her hands over the sink and walks into the living room, patting them on her jeans. She reaches out a hand to Jaeger, glaring at me. "Hi, Jaeg. Good to see you again. My, how you've grown." Her eyes dart down his body as she grasps his hand.

It's official. Jaeger can't control the effect he has on women. My own mother just checked him out. He's a weakness to the female sex. I should know.

"Mom, Jaeger's my boyfriend."

Despite her obvious admiration, my mom's mouth puckers and twists. She nods.

I hate that look. It's the one that says, *You've got some explaining to do.* I'm a grown woman. Whom I choose to love is my business.

I walk over to the couch and sit down. "What's up, Mom? You don't usually show up out of the blue. Everything okay?"

She slowly drags her suspicious gaze from Jaeger to me. "I'm here to talk to Tyler. Do you know where he is?"

So this isn't about me? It's about Tyler? Excellent.

Now he's done it, though. Mom showed up, so whatever Tyler did, it must be bad.

Come to think of it, I haven't kept close tabs on Tyler and he is acting strange. He comes home reeking of beer and cigarettes, and I haven't figured out why the sudden desire to spend the summer in Tahoe. Getting dumped, fired, and falling in love distracted me. So I've been a shitty friend *and* sister. Wonderful.

Before I tell my mom I have no idea where Tyler is, my

brother walks in the door. He freezes with his hand on the knob. "Hey," he says nervously.

What is going on? I mean, my mom can still put the fear of God into us, though she's tiny and we tower over her, but Tyler looks more nervous than I've ever seen him.

"Your work called," she says. "You've missed the pre-semester meetings and they haven't been able to reach you."

Tyler breaks eye contact and bends down, rustling around in his overnight bag. "I've got it, Mom. Don't worry about it."

"Really? Because it doesn't seem like you've got it, son."

Jaeger sinks on the couch beside me. He's watching my mom and brother with rapt interest. This is the first bit of drama that doesn't involve us. He's probably as giddy as I am.

"What's going on, Tyler?" Mom asks. "Don't lie—you're no good at it."

Tyler straightens and plucks the shoulder of his T-shirt. It's one of his nervous tics. "Well, if you really must know, I'm not going back. I'm staying here."

My mom sits on the edge of the recliner. "What does that mean? Your employers thought you were missing, Tyler. This isn't how you give notice you're leaving a position. The college administration told me they were about to notify the police of a missing person. Imagine their relief when they reached me and I told them you were here."

"I should have called." He knuckles his forehead and sighs.

"Why are you leaving your job?" she asks. "I thought you loved Boulder and your career."

Tyler crosses to the kitchen and pulls a beer from the fridge. Now that I think about it, he's kept the fridge stocked with a steady stream of Sierras. He's been drinking too much.

"I don't. Not anymore," he says.

"Uh-hmm. And how will you support yourself? You planning to sleep on people's couches for the rest of your life?" Mom is pulling out the sarcasm, which means she's about to go ballistic.

"I've been living like a student. I've got money saved to last a few years."

Well, shit, he should be paying me and Gen rent!

Tyler finished his undergrad in three years and a master's shortly after that. He really did get our father's brains. Mom and I could never figure out why he didn't go for his Ph.D.

"Tyler, that money is better put toward a down payment on a house, not"—she waves her hand aimlessly—"freeloading off your sister and drinking all day."

Tyler frowns, and Jaeger and I glance at each other. This is serious stuff going down. I had no idea my brother was so screwed up. Diabolically, it makes me feel better.

"Drop it, Mom. I'll let you know when I have things figured out."

My mom cocks her head. Tyler never talks disrespectfully to our mother—not since he smart-mouthed her at age twelve and had his video games taken away.

She looks at me. "Do you know what's going on?"

My eyes go wide and I shake my head.

"I'm still in the room," Tyler says angrily. "If I wanted you two to know my business, I'd tell you."

He can get away with being an ass to me, but not our mother. "Tyler!"

He ignores me and storms out the front door. I jump up to the window and catch him tossing the now empty beer bottle in the trash can as he stomps across the driveway to his car. I bang on the glass. "Hey! That goes in the recycling!"

Tyler reverses and tears down the street in his Land Cruiser.

"Well," Mom says, "guess we know your brother is in trouble." She stands and pats her back pocket then pulls out her keys. "He won't talk to me. You'll have to help him."

Wait, what? "You're leaving?"

She grabs her purse and looks around the room, her gaze snagging on the enormous tent out back. "Not much I can do. He doesn't want his mother involved in whatever is bothering him. Call me if you need to talk. And don't let your brother drink and drive!"

I spring up. "Mom! What the hell? You can't leave this on me."

"It's not really on you. It's on him. This is his life to screw up. I'm just saying, be there if he needs to talk."

She glances at Jaeger. "And this—" My mom points to the tent and the two of us. "Don't think I don't know what's going on." My face burns. "I expect a visit from the two of you in the next couple of weeks so I can get reacquainted with your boyfriend, Cali."

She squeezes the living hell out of me and smacks a kiss on my lips. "Adios!" she says with a wave.

What kind of parenting is this?

This is what you call the *you're all grown up now, deal with it yourself* approach.

My mom used to ride Tyler and me when she needed to, but she let us fight our own battles when we were younger. It might explain why Tyler and I are so independent. We're capable of lifting ourselves out of the dung when things go wrong, but I get the feeling that whatever is bothering Tyler is big. I just hope it doesn't hold him down forever.

Chapter Thirty-Two

O VER THE NEXT couple of days, I try to probe my brother about what's going on with him, but he's being tight-lipped and giving me nothing. So I don't push it. He'll talk when he's ready. Things are still in limbo with Jaeger's lawyers trying to get Kate out of the house, but the good thing is it's great having Jaeger stay with me, and I'm loving my new classes.

CAD just delved deeper into the structure of 3D design today, and my analytical mind was doing a happy dance over the layering. It's finally getting fun. I'm confident about the progress I've made and hopeful that by the middle of fall I'll have early mastery of AutoCAD for work. A raise would go a long way toward solving my transportation problems.

Leo, however, seems to be struggling. "Damn, that class is killing me," he says as we walk through the parking lot to his car. "You don't find it difficult?"

I'm not going to list the classes I found difficult. Some of the higher math and economics courses I took for a challenge in college, to name a few, the pre-law courses on constitutional and business law for sure—but CAD? No, CAD is not one of them.

"It's okay. I'm happy to help if you get stuck," I tell him.

"Thanks. I'll probably take you up on that…" Leo's voice dies at the end of the sentence.

I follow his gaze to a pale, slender guy with chunky black

hair standing next to Leo's car, his hip propped against the door.

Leo frowns as we approach. "Brad? What are you doing here?"

"Needed a ride home. You mind?" Brad's gaze slides to me, his lips quirking at the corners.

Leo darts an unsteady glance my way. I shrug and Leo unlocks the doors. "Sure."

"Cool," Brad says. "Let's grab a bite first, though."

The café is located on the other side of campus, so Leo drives over and parks in the lot nearby.

I skipped dinner and this gives me a chance to grab some food for Jaeger and me, and maybe pick something up for the morning. Jaeger has to leave early again tomorrow and Leo agreed to give me a ride to work, which is pretty big of him.

Leo works at a restaurant during the day and says giving me a ride is no big deal, but I feel I owe him. He's really helped me get around town these last few weeks, and I hope he does take me up on the offer to help with school.

Gen's still working nights at the casino, and I don't trust her behind a wheel at seven a.m. under normal conditions, let alone after only a couple hours of sleep. And though we've talked, Tyler's been reclusive since my mom's surprise visit. He's been staying with a friend the last couple of nights.

I have *not* mentioned my carpool arrangements for tomorrow to Jaeger. He'll be gone by the time I leave, and I think he assumes Gen's taking me to work. I didn't correct him. I'm worried he'll bring up the car thing, and it still embarrasses me. I'd just as soon not discuss that I can't afford a vehicle. And bumming a ride from Leo is preferable to taking the bus.

Leo, Brad, and I are milling around the campus café, when

Brad holds the cooler door open for me. I've been staring inside at the drinks for the last minute, trying to decide what I want. "What can I get you, Cali?"

It's late and it's been a long day. A little extravagance is in order. "Chocolate milk, please."

"You got it." He grabs the milk, along with a sandwich, bottled water, and a soft drink he hands to Leo, then walks to the counter. He pays for all of it before I can say anything.

Okay—that was nice. He didn't have to do that. I offer him money for the chocolate milk, but he shakes his head.

I grab a muffin and some other items, and set them on the counter to pay. By the time I return home around ten, Jaeger's passed out in his clothes on top of the air mattress, his breathing steady and deep. He managed to remove his shoes, so I don't bother waking him. I wash up, pull on nightclothes, and crawl under the covers next him.

When I wake, Jaeger is gone.

I'm bummed.

The legalities of getting Kate out of his house and keeping up with his workload are taking up all of his time. I pull out my phone and text him.

Cali: Missed you this morning.

He responds almost immediately.

Jaeger: I snuggled you when I woke, but you were passed out. Crushed my ego to have my kisses swatted away like a fly. I expect recompense this evening, and ego-stroking. Other stroking acceptable as payment as well :)

Cali: Stroking to commence this evening. Don't pass out this time before I get home!

An hour later, I'm showered and eating the last bite of my

muffin when Leo's car pulls into the driveway. Brad is in the passenger seat. Did he say he was coming too?

I lock the front door and walk over. Leo holds up his hand in a brief wave, and Brad tracks my progress to the car.

"Morning." I close the door and buckle my seatbelt.

Brad reaches back, holding out a Starbucks cup. "Mocha. I noticed you like chocolate last night."

Not as much as I like lattes in the morning, but I don't kick chocolate out of bed. Ever. "Thanks," I say. "What do I owe you?"

"On me," Brad says.

I glance at Leo, who's watching the exchange through the rearview mirror. He looks away nervously and reverses down the drive.

"Brad, you sure you don't want me to take you straight there?" Leo asks.

"No, I'm good." Brad taps a happy tune on the window with his finger. "It's right by her work. I can walk from there."

So Leo's giving Brad a ride as well. He's way too nice. I've got to at least offer Leo gas money the next time we're alone.

Savoring the chocolatey goodness of my mocha, I glance out the window at the businesses on Stateline Boulevard, taking one sip for every name or title we pass with the word *chalet* in it. By the time Leo drops me off in the parking lot, I've polished off my mocha and have an extra bounce in my step from the sugar/caffeine combo.

A warm sensation runs through me as I enter the front doors. Leftover euphoria from my delightful mocha?

I'm happy. I mean, really happy. It's my job, or Jaeger, I don't know which, but I don't think I've ever been this happy in my life. The world is a wonderful place.

I greet our receptionist, and my smile freezes on my face. Something isn't right. My steps falter after I pass her desk, a mind-numbing pain shooting through my skull.

I pause at the entrance to my office, a spasm of cramps bisecting my midsection, nausea rocking me. I pinch my lips together and grip the doorframe, taking deep breaths. Sweat breaks out over my forehead.

Turning slowly, I look around. *Going to be sick. Bathroom...* Black dots wink in my vision. *Can't think—*

THE SCENT OF vomit singes my nose.

I'm choking and gagging. Choking on my vomit.

Frantic voices clamor above me.

I open my eyes, then shut them. I don't know where I am. Why am I on the ground?

"What has she eaten? Does she take prescription or illegal drugs?" a deep voice asks.

"Is this her purse?"

"Percocet."

"Percocet? What's—" This from a high-pitched voice.

Someone wipes my mouth. A mask goes over my nose and chin. Strong hands lift me.

I open my eyes again, and this time, an image comes into focus—Lewis watching me from the front door, a look of shock on his face.

Men with medical patches hover over me. *Paramedics?* They push me on some moving bed. I'm bumping over the threshold and out the glass doors. *I'm at work?*

My chest rattles with each breath, my heart swooshing slowly in my ears. My head is too heavy. I close my eyes and rest.

Moments later, I hear, "Calista? Calista, can you open your eyes?"

The voice is male, but not one I recognize. I open my eyes and the vision in front of me isn't blurry this time. It's a man in a white coat. A doctor. I move to sit up.

"Please lie still while I ask you a few questions."

The doctor leans over me and flashes a light in my eyes. "They're no longer pinpoint," he dictates to someone over his shoulder, then returns his attention to me.

"Calista," he says loudly, as if I'm hearing impaired. I want to tell him he doesn't need to shout, but my mouth is dry and my chest hurts. I still can't breathe well, and there are popping sounds coming from my chest. "I'm Dr. Gregger. I've just given you Narcan to counteract the opiates in your system. The paramedics said they found Percocet in your purse when they searched for prescription and allergy information. Have you ever used Percocet before?"

I shake my head.

"Were you given a prescription by a physician?"

Another negative head shake. I've never heard of Percocet. I have no idea what he's talking about.

A round of phlegmy, body-rattling coughs steals my breath. I'm gasping. The doctor rattles off orders to someone in the room.

"Calista," he says to me, "the paramedics believe you aspirated when you passed out. We're going to do a chest X-ray."

What seems like only minutes later, but that I suspect is much longer, I'm being admitted into the ICU. My chest X-ray showed pneumonia.

I must have dozed again, because the next time I open my eyes, there's a warm pressure on my hand. Jaeger's beside me, his large fingers wrapped firmly around mine, his head bowed as if he's praying. My mom is at the end of the bed, her hand gripping my foot.

"Mom? Why are you holding on to my foot?" My mouth is sluggish. I sound like a lush.

Mom blinks as if startled. She's been staring silently at me for the past minute. "Calista." She rises and crosses to my side. She kisses my forehead and runs a cool hand down the side of my face, which feels hot in comparison. "You've been in and out with a fever. I wasn't sure if you were really awake this time."

Jaeger watches my face now, his breathing shaky, as if some deep emotion has taken hold.

"What happened?" I swallow, a slightly inflamed sensation in my throat.

Mom glances at Jaeger, then back to me. "You passed out. Your coworkers called nine-one-one, but you got sick and breathed it in."

I glance at Jaeger. I might be embarrassed by some of this if I didn't feel like such a train wreck.

"They've put you on powerful antibiotics, but your lungs…" My mom's lips pinch together, then she bites the top one. "You need rest, honey." She pats my hand. "Lots of rest for your body to heal."

"But Mom, what happened?" I think back to this morning. "I ate a muffin and had a mocha. I felt fine until I walked into work. Then… I don't remember."

"They discovered"—her voice catches—"oxycodone in your system—Percocet. They found more pills in your purse."

I process her words. The doctor mentioned that too. "What's Percocet? I didn't have anything in my purse."

She lets out a choked, quaking breath. "Cali, why are you taking drugs? All the stories I told you about the casinos, how drugs and alcohol ruin lives—" She shakes her head. Tears streak her cheeks. "I just never thought you'd do it. Never thought you'd get caught up in that mess." Her voice cracks the way it does when she's emotional or has just woken up.

God, I hate that croaky voice. It means my mom's seriously upset or seriously tired. Neither makes me feel good.

"Mom, I don't do drugs." Okay, that's a lie. "I smoked pot a couple of times in college," I correct. "That's it. I don't know why they found that stuff in my purse, but it's not mine."

"Honey, the doctors ran blood tests. You had remnants of the drug in your system. And that wasn't the only one. They found ecstasy as well."

"What?" I try to sit up, but think better of it when my arms collapse.

"I don't understand," she says. "Were you experimenting?"

"No." The strangeness of this morning fills my head. I was happy because of Jaeger and our little text exchange, and then really happy after I drank that mocha.

The one Brad gave me.

Why was Brad there, again? He's a strange guy. And he gave me the drink. Leo said his roommate was into stuff—

"Mom, it wasn't me. Look, this morning I got a ride from Leo."

"Yesterday morning."

"Yesterday?"

"You've been in the ICU for twenty-four hours," she says.

I lost an entire day? God, this is crazy. "Mom, check with Leo. Maybe he knows something. His roommate Brad was there and he wasn't supposed to be. He gave me the mocha. I—I think there might have been something in it. Leo's expression this morning—*yesterday morning*—and what Leo said about Kate—"

"What?" The dark voice comes from Jaeger. "How is Kate involved?" On the surface, Jaeger's question sounds concerned, but the edge is threatening, as if he'd like nothing more than to have another reason to wring Kate's neck.

"Leo said he's seen Kate at parties that his roommate has thrown. He said his roommate was into stuff, but he didn't explain. I honestly didn't care at the time. But what if he was referring to drugs? Kate's boyfriend is involved in that stuff. I don't know why Brad would put something in my drink, but he wasn't supposed to be there yesterday. Do you know what I'm saying?" At the moment, I can't tell if anything coming out of my mouth is making sense. My head is not exactly sharp.

The lines around Jaeger's mouth turn white. "What is Leo's number? His full name?"

I direct Jaeger to my purse, which the hospital placed beside my bed. He finds my phone and Leo's number. He seems reluctant to leave, and kisses my forehead. "I'll just go outside for a minute to make the call."

I nod and he walks out the door.

Mom takes his seat. "That boy's been sitting here since I arrived. I was at the end of the bed because there was no room beside you. Didn't have the heart to ask him to move."

She's right. There's a screen and no chairs on my right. Jaeger had the only spot for visitors.

"Don't be fooled by his overgrown size," she says. "He was terrified. We all were. The doctor said he was optimistic. That with your general health you'd recover, but until you woke, I didn't know, honey. I didn't *know*." Her head dips, mouth pressed to our clasped hands. Her shoulders rise and fall on quiet sobs.

This is all so crazy. One minute everything was fine and seemingly working out, the next, all hell has broken loose.

Tyler walks in with paper coffee cups in his hands. Surprise crosses his features, his shoulders dropping as if a great weight has been released.

He comes around the bed and sets the cups on the table beside it. Without a word, he bends over and hugs me, his arm shaking where it rests along my neck.

He pulls away and draws in a breath through his nose. "What's up, Calzone? Glad you're feeling better."

Jaeger returns a second later, followed by a police officer. "Someone notified the police." His voice is stiff, angry. "The police went to your work and traced you to the hospital."

Went to my work? For what? I smile wearily at the officer, and Jaeger looks ready to rip the guy's head off.

The officer asks me some questions, and I tell him everything I know, which is essentially not helpful. No, I didn't take Percocet. I don't do drugs, nor do I keep a stash in my purse—apparently, the paramedics who arrived at the scene found ecstasy and Percocet in a side pocket of my purse when they searched for allergy records and prescriptions. No, I tell him, I don't know why anyone, including Leo and his roommate Brad, would give me drugs without my knowledge.

The officer leaves, saying he'll make inquiries, but his tone is flat, as if he thinks it's a waste of time.

He doesn't believe me.

I'm still processing this and what it means when Gen rushes through the door to my hospital room in her sweat pants, a tank top—probably sans bra, given it's the one she wears to bed—

and a light cropped sweatshirt. Her hair shows signs of bedhead and she's not wearing makeup, meaning lip balm. She has clearly come straight from bed.

"You're awake," she says on a sigh of relief. Lewis follows her into the room, and my mom and brother exit to make space.

What is going on with Gen and Lewis? Why would he come here with her?

Oh, God. I fainted at work. Lewis must have told Gen. The entire office must know what happened. Am I going to lose my job because of the drugs they found? Dammit! I just got that job and I really like working for Sallee Construction.

Why would someone do this to me? I can't believe Leo would hurt me. That leaves Brad, the generous, somewhat creepy roommate. If the mocha is to blame for how the drugs ended up in my system, he was the one who bought it for me. But Brad barely knows me. What did I ever do to him? But Leo said Kate used to go to Brad's parties…

I'm so confused, and my head hurts. The blankets of my bed are stifling. I swat Gen's hands away when she tries to tuck them in.

"Cali," she says. "How did you get mixed up in this?"

Great, apparently everyone believes I'm a druggie. I roll my eyes and defend myself.

I do it several more times before the hospital decides it's safe to release me four days later. My fever is gone and my lungs, though not clear, are improving as long as I take it easy in bed.

But that's not going to happen, because the police are waiting.

Jaeger puts a body-lock arm around my waist and exchanges a few heated words with the lead officer, but it's no use. Aside from the fact that the paramedics found the drugs in my purse, someone called the police anonymously and told them I carried illegal drugs on me. That's why the police showed up at my office, and later at the hospital.

No wonder the officer who questioned me didn't believe me.

Jaeger, Gen, and my family follow me to the police station, but I'm immediately separated from them, arrested, and strip-searched—most humiliating experience ever—and taken to a holding cell. The space I'm in is empty, with the exception of a bench and a stainless steel toilet bowl. I lie on the hard bench in shock and because I'm exhausted. The popcorn sound coming from my chest has gone away, but my lungs wheeze and feel heavy, and I have a nasty cough. Physically I'll recover, but then what?

Aside from reconnecting with Jaeger, I've had some messed-up luck returning to my hometown. This thing with the drugs is like Drake blackballing me all over again. Someone wanted to screw me over, and they did. My own family and best friend didn't initially believe me when I told them I hadn't taken drugs. It didn't take long to convince them of the truth, but they know and trust me. How will I convince the police that the drugs aren't mine when all the evidence points to me?

An officer opens the metal door to my cell several minutes later. "Bail's been posted. You're free to go. For now."

My mom, Tyler, and Jaeger wait at the front of the police station.

Jaeger's the first out of his seat. He pulls me into a tight bear hug and releases me for a moment so I can embrace my family.

He tucks his arm around my waist, holding much of my weight as we leave the building, all of us uncharacteristically quiet. I should tell Jaeger I'm fine, that I don't need a crutch, but his strength is welcome because mine fails me. I've always thought emotional and financial dependency on a guy led to disaster, but I don't mind it so much with Jaeger.

"They've set a court date," my mom says from the front seat of Tyler's SUV. Jaeger and I are in the back. I'm sitting in the middle seat, my body plastered to him, his arm wrapped around me like a bungee cord.

Even with all this love and support, the truth of the matter disturbs me. The police think I'm guilty of drug possession. How will I get out of this? My eyes burn and blur, my raspy chest giving away my emotions as my breaths quicken and sputter.

"Babe." Jaeger lifts my chin. "I'll find out who did this to you."

I nod. Somehow, as scary as everything is, I believe him. Because we chose each other and that makes us right. What we have is real and empowering.

I was the rock in my other relationships, but Jaeger is the boulder *I* cling to in the middle of the deep blue lake.

Chapter Thirty-Three

A lake is the landscape's most beautiful and expressive
feature. It is earth's eye; looking into which the beholder
measures the depth of his own nature.

—Henry David Thoreau

BIG SURPRISE—I'M out of a job for a while. I don't blame
John Sallee; he had no choice. In his defense, he gave me
unpaid leave until my court hearing. John can't ignore the
charges against me, but he's optimistic they'll be dropped.
Which is good of him, considering he's only known me a few
weeks.

Jaeger walks through the gate to our backyard. I'm on the
lounge chair I moved from our patio—now bedroom—to the
dirt. I actually enjoy this vantage point better; it places me
square with nature. I'm thankful for the little things these days,
like beautiful trees, a tasty jar of green olives, and time with my
boyfriend, while everything else flushes down the crapper.

Jaeger lifts me, sketchpad and all, and plants himself in my
spot on the chaise, sprawling me along the length of his body.
My muscles tense at first, bracing for balance, then settle in
comfortably. I pick up my pencil and resume the sketch I'm
working on. The Jaeger lounge is my new favorite furniture.

He plants his hands on my hips, fingers caressing the indent
of my waist. I wiggle as his warm palms send chemical signals to

my girl parts.

A low growl rumbles from his chest. "Easy, or you'll find yourself beneath me, your work tossed across the yard."

I chuckle. That's not a threat, it's something I'm looking forward to, and plan to make happen just as soon as Gen leaves for work.

A week has passed since my prison time—I'm a full ex-con now—and I've regained the bulk of my energy. With heavy antibiotics and bed rest, I recovered fairly quickly once I was home. All things considered, I'm freaking lucky to be alive. In the meantime, Jaeger has hired a private investigator to look into the drugging. It's so police reality show. I've gone from a bad eighties chick-flick parody to reality TV.

Jaeger raises the side of my sketchpad. I'm drawing an abstract of a man pulling a woman from the water, using the million tiny shapes I favor for design. It's possible the expression on the man's face resembles the look Jaeger gave me after I woke in the hospital.

"You're amazing," he says into the hair above my ear.

I lay my pencil in my lap and link our fingers. "I'm a jailbird. You sure you want to keep associating with me?"

His body stiffens, and not the good part.

A shot of panic rattles my nearly healed lungs. "Jaeger?"

"I spoke to the PI this afternoon." His thumb rubs gentle circles along the top of my hand, and I relax a little. "He linked Brad to Kate's drug-dealer boyfriend and notified the police. Brad's got a long prior arrest history—petty theft, a couple of drug charges that had been dropped. He's never served time, but he'll go to prison for this."

I sit up and face him, my sketchpad flapping to the ground. "So Brad is for sure connected to Kate?" The idea seemed the most plausible when I relayed everything I knew about that morning and Leo's connection to her, but somehow it's hard to believe Kate would go this far.

Jaeger picks up my pad and dusts it off. He sets it on my lap and pulls me close. "I'm so sorry, Cali. Brad confessed his history with Kate's boyfriend this morning in exchange for reduced charges. He admitted to planting drugs in your purse. An intermediary ordered him to do it, but Brad guesses the order came from Kate's boyfriend. Brad owes the guy for something. He told the investigators he had no knowledge of why you were targeted, just that he was told to plant narcotics."

"But my drink—"

"That was Brad improvising. He claimed he didn't know you'd have a potentially fatal reaction to the drug." Jaeger's arm tightens around me. "He said he was covering his bases in case the drugs he dropped in your purse weren't enough for an arrest."

Jaeger sits up and I roll on his lap like a buoy, his arms steadying me before I fall. "With Brad's confession, my PI says the charges against you will be dropped. You'll hear from the police soon and you'll be able to return to work, but I'm not letting what happened go. It's my fault Kate did this to you."

He's trying to tell me something here, but all I can think is *it's over.* They believe me. I'm free!

"I told the police about Kate, but the link to her is circumstantial. There's no hard evidence she had anything to do with it."

"It's suspicious, but Brad is going to jail. Pretty soon Kate will be out of your house too," I say. "We can move on."

Jaeger's expression tightens. "She ignored the eviction notice. Says she's not leaving and that I can't force her. She claims

I told her she can live there rent-free and that she has a legal right to be there."

"*What?* How can she do the things she's done and expect to get away with them?"

"She won't. She lied about the pregnancy and she's behind the drugging."

I blink sharply. "We assume there's a link between Brad and her boyfriend, but…"

Jaeger shuts his eyes for a long moment before looking at me intently. "I never told you what she was like in high school." The hand he has on my thigh clenches. "You have no idea how much her being here makes me crazy. I haven't seen her in years and I thought I never would, but after what she's done… I won't let her ruin our relationship or hurt you again."

"You're worried she will?"

"She'll try. She's the same vindictive, selfish person she was when I knew her years ago."

"What did she do, Jaeger? I asked Tyler, but he didn't say much. Just called her a bitch."

"That's apt," he says wryly. "When I first met Kate in my sophomore year of high school, I thought she was this sweet, quiet person, who worked part-time at an ice cream shop with a girl I'd just started dating. The girl was social and outgoing, until a rumor spread she was sleeping with one of the teachers.

"The rumors were graphic, the timing and circumstances difficult to refute. They fired the teacher and I stopped seeing the girl. She tried to defend herself. She told me the rumor was a lie, that she'd never slept with him. She claimed she'd never been with anyone. I didn't believe her. She was pretty. She'd dated a couple of guys I knew by reputation. I just assumed… Anyway, I was stupid and self-involved with my training. I thought if she could lie about being a virgin, what was stopping her from lying about the teacher?

"The school administration believed the rumors too. It was a done deal. Six months later, the girl switched high schools and I never saw her again. I didn't think about her after that. I'd already started dating Kate."

I think I see where this is going, and it makes me sick for Jaeger and the girl he dated. "Kate had something to do with the rumor?" I ask.

"I didn't know it at first. She told me she quit her job at the ice cream shop because her parents didn't want her taking time away from her studies. I discovered a few months later through a mutual friend that she'd been fired for stealing. I confronted her about it, and she said she was embarrassed and that's why she didn't say anything. That not telling me was just a little white lie. That if I loved her I wouldn't make her feel worse. The stealing was one of several lies or omissions I caught her in throughout our relationship."

He looks me in the eye. "I can't explain why I stayed with her, Cali, except to say that I was so focused on training. Being with Kate was easy, but after we broke up, every doubt I ever had about her surfaced.

"During my knee recovery, I had a lot of time on my hands. I looked up that girl I'd been dating when Kate and I met. She told me Kate used her to get the job at the ice cream shop, then pumped her for information. About her. About me. The girl swore she never hooked up with the teacher. That it was all a lie and that the only person who knew her whereabouts that day was Kate. She told me she always thought Kate had been the one to start the rumor, but she couldn't prove it."

Jesus. Kate is evil.

"It wasn't your fault, Jaeger," I say. "You were young. You didn't know."

"I was naïve and selfish, only thinking about my goals. I'm not that person anymore. When I think about what she did to you—" He shakes his head and lets out a hard breath. "She won't get away with it. Even if I can't pin it to her, I'll make sure she pays somehow."

I knew he and Kate had a history. I never imagined this. No wonder Jaeger doesn't like Kate. Though he's never outright disparaged her. He's not the kind of guy to bash someone he's dated, even if she deserves it.

"I remained single for a long time after Kate. Once I stopped drinking and hooking up and actually dated women again, I remembered that good people exist. Kate is not the norm. But even that got old after a while. I stopped having casual flings about a year ago."

The first time we were together he said he hadn't been with anyone in a year. It all makes sense now.

"Then I ran into you and I knew what I'd been missing." The corners of his mouth curve up before a serious look returns. "I won't let her come between us, Cali."

I circle my arms around his waist and rest my head under his chin. "What now? If she won't leave, what do we do?"

"How do you feel about kicking out an unwanted guest?"

Chapter Thirty-Four

"S O, HOW SHOULD we play this?" I ask.

Crazy schemes fill my head. Hauling Kate by the hair, catfight style, and dragging her out of the house kicking and screaming after throwing her likely illegally purchased designer crap in the dirt. Spraying her and her fancy car with a hose until she leaves Jaeger's property. Setting up booby traps inside the house. Or there's the good, old-fashioned "burning all her clothes in the outside fire pit and changing the locks" trick. Jaeger would need a high-tech alarm system in case she tried to climb back in through a window. She's a wily one; I don't put anything past her. Of course, none of my ideas are as vindictive and cruel as what she did to me, but I'm not a crazy bitch.

Jaeger pulls up to his house and I'm bouncing in my seat. This is some serious showdown at the O.K. Corral shit. "Well? What do you think? We need a plan before we go in."

His gaze flicks to Kate's car. "I have a plan. Follow my lead."

Ohhh, a man in charge. So totally hot.

"Check!" I scramble out of his truck and try to match his long strides to the front door. It's like keeping up with walking tree trunks.

Jaeger sweeps into the house, his eyes slowly taking in the room. Crumpled fast food bags lay scattered over tables and the floor. Clothing and trash dangle from the chandelier. Dishes are stacked to toppling in the sink, the counters covered in a rainbow of sticky-looking dried-up spills and leftover food. The place smells like a combination of expensive hair spray and rotting meat.

Jaeger's beautiful home is a disaster. What has Kate been doing?

Music blasts from the back bedroom. Jaeger's office. The one he locked.

He storms back and I follow.

Kate's sitting at his desk, like last time, her feet kicked up at the corner, fingers pounding the keyboard of his computer.

"I thought you took that to Mason's," I whisper.

"I needed it for work, so I left it here. It was password protected," he growls. "Kate!"

Her fingers still, but she doesn't look up right away. She minimizes the window and slowly swivels her head. "Yes?"

"You lied to me about having a kid and you tried to frame Cali. You're lucky she didn't die from the drugs your friend gave her."

I try to not think about the high fatality rate after aspirating vomit. It's kind of frightening.

"I'm sick of your shit. I never want to see your face again. You've been legally ordered to leave my house, and now *I'm* ordering you."

Jaeger is large and imposing, but it's not his size that's so intimidating, it's his voice. The deep rumble directed at Kate could quell a lion.

"Don't act all gruff and intimidating, Jaeger," she says in her nasal whine. "We both know you'd never hurt a female."

He might not, but I have no problem hurting Kate. I step in

front of Jaeger, but he drags me back. I glare at him and he shakes his head.

Kate grabs an aerosol container and pops the cap, oblivious to danger. She sprays nail polish drying formula onto her red toenails—and the surface of Jaeger's oak Mission-style desk.

Jaeger leans his hip against the doorframe and crosses his arms. "Nice car you got out there, Kate."

She leans forward and picks at a hangnail on the corner of her toe. Her eyes flicker in his direction. "What about it?"

"The VIN indicates it's your boyfriend's car. Word around town is the condo you own in Reno was purchased with his drug money as well, and that you played a part in his meth lab."

Her head whips around. "That's a lie!"

"You had your boyfriend order his dealer buddy to drug Cali. You're an accomplice, and I can prove the link between you and Brad. If I want, I can make it so you have a home just like the one your man's in. Nice and compact, living the simple life."

Kate's feet are on the ground in seconds. "What do you want, Jaeger?" Her words are punchy with anger.

Cornered and still a bitch. Impressive.

"I want you out of my house and my life *for good.* Don't go near my girlfriend, my family, or my friends. Matter of fact, might be a good idea if you left California and Nevada and went somewhere far away."

She chuckles bitterly. "You're crazy. I'm not leaving. Besides, I don't have any—"

"Money?" Jaeger's arms drop and he straightens to his full height. "Sell the five grand worth of crap you purchased on my credit card prior to my finding out"—I choke, blinking uncontrollably. *Five grand?*—"and the apartment you own, and move away. You might consider getting a job for once in your life. It's over, Kate. There's no one left to freeload off. Your family filed restraining orders against you."

"What? My mom would never."

"Your mother, your father, and your sister and her family. *Everyone.* I filed one this morning. So technically, it's illegal for you to be this close to me and my property. I could have you arrested."

A stunned moment of silence congeals as Kate takes in Jaeger's words. In her attempt to screw others, she has ultimately screwed herself. She has no one.

Kate looks around the office, as if searching for someone or something to save her. Her jaw hardens and she shoulders past us to the spare bedroom. We hear a zipper unwinding, along with drawers screeching open and closed.

It's music to my ears.

Ten minutes later, Kate is in her car and pulling out of the driveway.

Jaeger and I stand for a few moments in silence, watching her car disappear down the drive, just soaking up the peace that is a Kate-free zone for the first time in weeks. I look back, considering. His beautiful home has been totally contaminated.

Jaeger pulls out his phone, scrolling through his contacts. "Don't worry, I'm having it detoxed. Calling my cleaning lady right now."

"I'll pitch in for new bedding."

He winks. "Already on it, babe. By tomorrow we'll be sleeping on a king-sized mattress inside an actual home, though I did enjoy camping with you. Our tent and air mattress will still get time." He shifts his attention to the phone. "Janice? This is Jaeger. I need you to come over and do a full cleaning and some shopping." He covers the speaker. "What color bedding?"

He's asking me what I like? For his home? I tell him my preferences and he relays them to his housekeeper.

The call ends and it's silent again, except for the sound of the water lapping the rocks below, birds chirping, pine needles rustling lightly on the breeze. I take in these sounds and enjoy them thoroughly. I hadn't realized how much Kate's presence brought the world down. It's like the weight of a mountain has been lifted.

Jaeger grabs my hand. "We have some time while the house gets cleaned. Come on. I have something to show you."

Hmm, everything he's shown me I've enjoyed. I happily climb in his truck, relishing the freedom of going anywhere and doing whatever we want.

Jaeger drives us to a street named Beach Drive in the Keys. It's right along the water, and the homes here are enormous. He pulls into a driveway with a four-car garage. The house itself is about a quarter of a block wide and overlooks the lake. Jaeger's home is on the lake, too, but it's up a rise with more distant views. This place is practically on the lake, and has a façade of decorative shingles and stone. It's impressive.

"Who lives here?" I ask.

"A client I want you to meet. I think you'll like their newest art." He grins mysteriously.

He's taking me to see one of his pieces? Inside someone's home? Isn't that intrusive?

"Wait, this isn't your client Danielle, is it?"

"No way." He shakes his head. "I'm not doing business with Danielle anymore. This is a different client."

"Okay-y-y. You're sure it's all right with the owner that I'm here?"

His smile widens. "Pretty sure. I've told them about you, and they want to meet you."

What in the world? "Your clients want to meet your jailbird, dropout girlfriend?"

"Yup." He leans over and sweetly kisses my lips. His fingers slide a lock of hair behind my ear. The kiss is innocent, but the look in his eyes is naughty and I like it. "None of that was your fault. Besides, adversity makes people stronger. Sometimes it makes them their best self," he adds with a self-mocking grin.

He's right. Where Jaeger is today is infinitely better than if he'd stayed on the Olympic track with Kate by his side. He could have permanently damaged his knees, been crippled. And God knows what would have happened if he'd ended up married to Kate.

I shiver in horror. That is a fate no one should suffer.

It's easier to look at another person's life and know they are better off, not so easy to do it with your own. The only thing I know for sure is that my feelings for Jaeger are the real deal. I never would have known this kind of love had I stayed with Eric or someone like him.

I cup my hand around Jaeger's strong jaw and kiss him softly. I can't believe he is mine.

We walk to the front door, and a man with silver hair and reading glasses answers. He greets Jaeger, and Jaeger introduces me.

"This is Cali?" the man says, as if he's heard of me before. Jaeger said he wanted to shop some of my designs. Maybe he told this guy about my work? "Come on in." The man smiles and waves us inside.

I glance at Jaeger, a big fat question on my face.

He grins and steps forward, following the owner through a large entry, which looks straight back to a wall-high view of the lake. We turn left into a living room about five times the size of the chalet. Wall-to-wall windows overlook mountains and lake, divided in the center by a stone fireplace.

I've never experienced this kind of wealth. I'm star-struck by the view and the elaborate furniture. A minute passes before I realize Jaeger and his client are staring at the wall behind me. It's wide and tall, and blank—with the exception of a single piece of art. One of Jaeger's wood carvings, only this one is on steroids.

The piece is the size of a small car, though the room accommodates it, and it is *a-ma-zing*. I've never seen anything so beautiful.

Another full minute passes before I realize the design is one of my own.

Holy shit. It's my yard—my backyard. The trees I sketch all the time. This is one of the first drawings I did after Gen and I arrived for the summer.

I open my mouth to say something, and nothing comes out. My throat is dry. I cough to clear it, which results in loud hacking, as the cough from my pneumonia hasn't fully gone away. "Excuse me," I choke out.

"I'll get you some water," the man offers, and walks off.

"Well," Jaeger whispers, "what do you think?"

I'm shaking as if I were standing in front of a large audience. I have freaking stage fright, and it's all Jaeger's fault. My wonderful boyfriend sold a piece of my art. Our art. And it's incredible. The way he captured the design elements, the shading from the wood itself to complement the image. There are no words for what I think or how I feel.

It's just a sketch of my simple backyard, but it's stunning— the way I see our yard. And maybe that's art. Seeing the beauty others miss and capturing it.

Chapter Thirty-Five

THE RIDE BACK to Jaeger's is silent, what with the bomb he dropped. It took on nuclear proportions when he handed me a check for my portion of the commission—forty percent. If he shocked me speechless with the carving, I almost passed out when he handed me the check. Jaeger had to get me out of his client's house quickly; my speech had degraded to mumbles and gasps.

Thousands of dollars sit in my sweaty little hand. More than I made in two months working at Blue. One or two commissions a year with Jaeger, plus my job at Sallee Construction, and I'd officially have a new and exciting career in art. Of course, I couldn't do the commissions without Jaeger. His talent brings my drawings to life. Just like he brought my heart to life.

He has a pleased grin as we make our way back to his house, flicking me glances now and then. He knows he's shocked the hell out of me. Seeing my design beautifully displayed on someone's wall is like winning the lottery. There is nothing better, except being with Jaeger.

I've turned into a corny, love-struck girlfriend.

I'm okay with that.

We pull down the long driveway to his house and my heart speeds up as his home comes into view. Near the front door is a brand-new white SUV. It's not a luxury brand, but it's new and my hackles go up. Another one of his female clients? A trick from Kate? Or one of her evil accomplices?

"Don't worry," Jaeger says as he scans my face. "That one's supposed to be there."

"Whose car it?"

I was looking forward to some alone time with Jaeger so I could show him how much I appreciated his efforts with my drawing and helping my art career. He is the best boyfriend in the world and I have plans for how to thank him. Detailed, creative, body-art-type plans. Sort of like Twister, bedroom style.

"It's yours."

Huh? "What's mine?"

"The car. I bought it for you, but really it's an investment in my peace of mind. I might have an aneurysm if I go one more day worrying about you and how you're getting around."

Normally, something like this would go against my whole *I am an independent woman* thing, but all I can do is smile. No one should be dependent on someone else for their happiness, but this is not about coddling. Jaeger loves me, and this is how he's showing his love. He's worried about my safety and wants to take care of me. The sentiment is mutual, because I want to take care of him too. That's a part of the loving business. I don't feel trapped or dependent. I feel loved.

"You bought me a car."

He nods.

I look at my pretty new vehicle. The sports utility aspect will come in handy. Good for Tahoe summers—and winters. "I love it," I say, but I'm looking at him, the emotion he fills me with pouring out.

Jaeger leans over and we kiss, long and slow, merging all manner of feelings into one point of heated contact.

After a moment, I lift my head. "Thank you. For everything. Everything you've given me." And I'm not referring to the car.

"You've given me more."

Epilogue

WHEN I OPEN my eyes, I realize I've been sleeping. I'm at Jaeger's house, out on his tree swing. I was sketching the lake before I passed out.

Hanging out at Jaeger's has become my new favorite place to work now that his home has been detoxed of all things Kate. But his property is also like a drug—I come here and instantly relax. Good for my morale, bad if I'm trying to get much work done.

I sit up and stretch.

"Finally awake?"

I peer over my shoulder to find Jaeger making his way over. "How long was I asleep?" I ask.

He scrunches his face. "Two hours."

"Two hours! Why didn't you wake me?"

He sits beside me and pulls my legs over his lap. "You looked so peaceful. And beautiful. Couldn't do it."

I lean up and wrap my arms around him. "What have you been doing while I slept?"

"Working. Got a new commission. They want to see your designs, too, so it's good you got another sketch finished before you crashed." He picks up the notepad resting on my lap. "This is awesome. It needs to go in the portfolio."

Jaeger and I have become a team with work. I thought it would be great to work on a couple of projects a year with him—was hopeful that maybe one or two of his clients would be interested in our combined art. But so many people have loved the pieces we've done together that it's become a full-on side business for us.

At first we made two sketch/carving combinations and showed them around. Now people simply look at the portfolio I've built and pick the designs they want, purchasing them exclusively for Jaeger to carve. I love working with him, and I love what I'm doing.

"You know," he says, "you could probably quit your job at the construction company."

"No way." I shake my head. "I love Mr. Sallee and working with the guys. As long as they'll have me, I'm staying there."

He smiles and kisses my forehead. "Okay, babe. Whatever makes you happy."

Jaeger stretches his arms above his head and yawns, a sliver of muscled belly flashing me from the bottom of his T-shirt. "I could use a nap myself."

I slide my hand up his shirt before he has a chance to lower his arms. "Or we could do other things." I waggle my eyebrows suggestively.

Jaeger pins me to the swing with his large body, his hands groping and tickling me. "Is that all I am, a piece of meat?"

"Totally!" I screech, giggling and fighting his fingers at the same time.

He smiles down. "I can live with that." He kisses me, and afterward Jaeger takes his nap, wrapped in my arms.

THE END

Acknowledgments

I couldn't have completed a single book without the support of my husband. He entertains the kids when I'm on deadline or need to get an idea down before it drifts into the ether, and places food in front of me when I forget to eat. Thank you, Patrick, for your love and support and for reading my girly manuscripts and finding all the dialogue "a guy would never say." Along those lines, I'd like to thank my children for making me stop and smell the roses—literally, they shove them in my face—no matter how busy life gets.

Heartfelt thanks to my critique partners and beta readers: Lia Riley, Jennifer Ryan, and Marlene Relja. A special thank-you for the expertise and hard work of editors Laura Ownbey, Shelley Bates, and Arran McNicol. No author is complete without her writer's groups, so a collective thank-you to the Rogue ladies and members of the Silicon Valley RWA. Last, but in no way least, a huge thank-you to Louisa of LM Creations for coming up with the *Deep Blue* cover and series design.

In researching Cali's unintentional drug overdose and the subsequent fallout, I received assistance from the South Lake Tahoe Police Department, and my friend and ER doctor, Rob Collins. Any errors on these topics are mine alone.

A final thank-you to the rest of my friends and family who've supported my writing, and to the wonderful readers. Hugs to you all!

Afterword

Please share your love of books and the characters in the Blue Series by leaving a review at the retailer where you purchased *Deep Blue*. Thank you!

The Blue Series
DEEP BLUE (BOOK 1)

BLUE CRUSH (BOOK 2)

TRUE BLUE (BOOK 3)

BLUE STREAK: A BLUE SERIES NOVELLA (BOOK 4)

NEW BLUE (BOOK 5)

The Halven Rising Series
FATES ALTERED: A HALVEN RISING PREQUEL (BOOK 0.5)

FATES DIVIDED (BOOK 1)

FATES ENTWINED (BOOK 2)

FATES FULFILLED (BOOK 3)

Ready for More?

You've just read *Deep Blue*, the first book in the Blue Series. Join Jules's newsletter here: www.julesbarnard.com/newsletter for an email alert when the next Jules Barnard book releases. All newsletter subscribers gain access to FREE Subscriber Extras, including an extra scene that takes place after *Deep Blue*. In the meantime, the Blue Series continues with Gen and Lewis's story in Book 2.

Read on for a sneak peek of *Blue Crush*.

BLUE CRUSH
Blue Series, Book 2

Genevieve Tierney moves to Lake Tahoe after college, determined to go it alone after being betrayed by her boyfriend. Working at a casino and avoiding cheating jerks seems like a good plan, until she meets the one guy tempting enough to drag her back down.

Lewis Sallee is six and a half feet of perfectly sculpted mountain man who threatens her play-it-safe approach and awakens a sex drive she never knew she had. Although Lewis is in a complicated relationship with one of the most beautiful women Gen has ever seen, she can't seem to control her attraction to him.

To boost her confidence, Gen steps out of her comfort zone and signs up for the Alpine Mudder, a gritty endurance race. But as she prepares for the biggest physical challenge of her life, her emotional strength is pushed to its limits after she accepts Lewis's help in training. He tests her willpower and has her fighting her body's response to him—with her mind and heart not far behind.

Preview of *Blue Crush* by Jules Barnard

Chapter One

I YANK UP the bustier that shows more boob than I've ever revealed in my life as my best friend Cali and I make our way into the employee basement. God, this uniform sucks. After graduation, Cali found us summer jobs through her mom's connections at Blue Casino. We plan to save up as much money as possible before graduate school begins in the fall. Cali says she didn't know what the uniforms looked like, but she knew. She grew up near the Lake Tahoe casinos. She could have warned me and I'd have chosen a different position, like, say, dealer. Instead, I became a cocktail waitress, convinced it would be less center-of-attention. Given that my nipples are an inch from greeting the world, I'm thinking, not so incognito.

Cali planned this. I found out before graduation that the safe boyfriend I'd chosen was cheating on me with a girl from his hometown. Cali's been trying to get me back out there since the breakup. I thought she meant emotionally, but Jesus, this is *out there.*

"What?" Cali peers innocently from across the aisle of the Blue locker room. "You look really good in that uniform. You should be thanking me." She jerks her thumb to the left. "You've seen the Harrah's cocktail outfits." Harrah's is to the right of Blue, but Cali's sense of direction is inconceivably terrible.

She's the smartest person I know—borderline genius—but the simple stuff befuddles her. She can, however, break down quantum entanglement like she's describing how to toast bread. It's bizarre, but I accept this about her.

Waitresses and female dealers swarm the lockers, stripping and pulling on freshly laundered uniforms allocated by the seamstress counter around the corner. It's the end of the swing shift, so while some prepare to take to the casino floor, others are finished for the day and dressing for home.

The woman next to me shimmies into a gold lamé skinny dress and stilettos. Clearly, some people have bigger plans than me tonight. I tug on my jeans and slip on black flats.

"Heads up," Cali calls.

Just in time, I see the Milestone Pod that tracks my running distance lobbed into the air. Cali had a two-second hankering for exercise this week. She ran a quarter of a mile and gave up. Apparently, she decided now was a good time to use her non-athletic skills to return my device.

The Milestone Pod veers several feet to the right. I lunge and flatten my stomach to the bench, catching it with my fingertips before it crashes to the ground.

I look up, exasperated. "Jesus, Cali, you're like two feet away. Were you even aiming for me?"

"What? I'm making sure your reflexes are in working order." She shuts her locker and swings a low-slung purse over her shoulder. "How was your night?"

I grab a few more items and close my locker as well. "They started calling me Snow White this evening."

No need to elaborate on who "they" are. While Cali lived the high life of a dealer, training the first several days before her toes even grace the casino floor, I've been slaving away, slinging drinks in three-inch heels and trying to keep up with the veteran waitresses. For some reason, they've picked me, out of the dozen new seasonal waitresses, for hazing.

Cali gazes up, her mouth twisting as if she's actually considering the nickname. I look around and drop my voice as we pass some workers on our way up the basement stairs to the casino floor. "I do *not* look like a Disney princess."

She pinches her thumb and forefinger together, indicating a little bit. "But with a huge rack."

I shift my shoulders in irritation and raise my voice to be heard above the clanging and buzzing of slots as we open the door to the floor. The sound is only slightly below deafening levels at this time of night. "I'm sporty. Athletes can't have big boobs."

She looks at me skeptically. "Girls would kill to have your boobs. You need to be proud. Like me." She grins and sticks out her Victoria's Secret-enhanced breasts.

There's a chance I inherited my rack, as Cali puts it, from my mother, who does in fact have impressive boobs. I might also have inherited her looks, only her hair is a few shades lighter than my nearly black locks and she has true green eyes. Mine are hazel, less obvious. I like my eyes.

I'm sure the nickname has something to do with my dark hair and pale coloring. I'm equally certain the veteran waitresses think I'm young and naïve and not tough enough. I only deliver ten drinks at a time to their twenty, because I can't freakin' find my customers. I lose several a night because they move around the floor like they're pollinating the slot machines. I'm spatially oriented; if people aren't where I left them, I can't find them. So yes, some of the hazing is warranted. But if they think I'm naïve, they don't know me very well.

No one raised by Chantell Dubois could remain innocent—the woman changed her name to something that sounds like a French bordello, for Christ's sake. I'm Genevieve, or Gen as my friends call me, but in spite of my mom's fetish for anything French, I've kept her maiden name of Tierney—a hundred-percent Irish surname. As much as my mom wishes it, there are no Frenchmen in our bloodline.

Technically, I could be French on my father's side, but since I have no idea who he is, the point is moot.

What I haven't mentioned to Cali, because it seems like a shitty thing to say to someone who's struggling with money, is that my mother offered to pay my way through graduate school. I don't technically need this job.

My mom doesn't work, nor do we have rich relatives. I assume she gets by with the help of the wealthy men that have flitted in and out of our lives for as far back as I can remember, which is why I'm determined to earn my way through graduate school and create a healthy distance from it all.

Cali takes in the look on my face. "It's lame they're calling you names, even if you do look like Snow White." I frown, which she ignores. "Tell them to back the eff off. Better yet, I'll do it for you." She cranes her head and glances around. "Which waitress started it?"

Ah, shit, now I've done it.

"Cali, *do not* say anything." She would too; Cali's great like that. But sometimes Cali's eagerness to help me gets me in trouble. "The one who started it is my supervisor. You'll make it worse."

She shrugs. "Suit yourself."

We pass the last bank of slots before the sports bar. A waitress I met yesterday and chitchatted with throughout my shift tonight sees me and smiles this large, wide smile I'm beginning to associate with her. At about five foot three inches—the extra three courtesy of black pumps to match our midnight satin hot pants and electric-blue sequined bustiers—Nessa is petite. Compared to her, I'm like an Amazon at five foot ten—over six feet in my work heels.

I wave as we make our way past.

"Who's that?" Cali asks.

"Nessa. She's really sweet. She's the one who invited us to the dinner party tonight. Tacos. It's casual."

I'm not entirely comfortable around strangers, and meeting guys of any sort after my ex isn't high on my agenda, but it would be nice to have another friend in town.

"Can't go, remember?" Cali says. "Skype date with Eric."

Oh God, I forgot. Even more reason to be out of the house. The cottage we rented for the summer has thin walls. I'd rather not be around for the Sex-Skyping that will ensue. And Cali's boyfriend is on my shit list. He hit on me a couple of weeks ago, which transferred him from absentminded, annoying-boyfriend-of-my-best-friend to a creeper.

If I go to this dinner party with Nessa, it'll kill two birds with one stone. Cali will think I'm recovering from my ex, dubbed the A-hole, and I won't have to plug my ears at the moans vibrating through the walls. Win-win.

I PARK MY dented Camry in the Al Tahoe neighborhood. The houses here sit away from the street with a sprinkling of manicured lawns mixed with yards of pine cones and bristly shrubs. Like most Lake Tahoe homes, many on this street have rounded eaves and shutters with tree-shaped cutouts—the knockoff Swiss Alps look.

The single-level house of Nessa's friend has a V-shaped porch roof that extends to the ground. I lift my hand to knock on the front door, claustrophobically aware of the roof framing inches from my face—

The door swings open while my arm is still suspended to knock. Nessa grins, her straight black hair draped over one shoulder, black, almond-shaped eyes smiling happily at me. "I saw you through the window."

Shouts erupt behind her and I peer over her head, because she's short and I can. My gaze lands on a guy with a baseball hat turned backward who's pounding his fist on a table, a pretty brunette beside him. The scent of chiles and grease smacks me in the face, making my mouth water like Pavlov's dog.

I walk inside and Nessa closes the door, taking my coat and purse and quickly walking down a hall. "What can I get you to drink?" she asks when she returns. "Zach has Coronas in the fridge and I made a batch of margaritas."

"Water would be great." Nessa fills me a glass from the kitchen sink near the food simmering on the stove. We make our way to the others.

The guy with the baseball hat lifts his hands in exasperation at the attractive girl sitting with him. "You call that a drink? *Come ooon*, Mira. That's like a baby bird sip. Quit being a girl and gulp it like a man."

A few coins glimmer on the table; a shallow glass sits in the center.

My heart does a little hop of glee. Quarters is one of my favorite drinking games.

I've been drinking since I was twelve. My mother thought it

would make me worldlier to have wine with dinner—something to do with her French fetish. As a result, my tolerance for alcohol is high. Add good hand-eye coordination that *did not* come from her—her precision is as good as Cali's, which is to say nonexistent—and I pretty much dominate at Quarters.

"Zach," Nessa says. The guy with the baseball hat looks up from the drink he's refilling with a pitcher and smiles at Nessa. Wow, kind of an adoring smile if I'm reading it correctly, though Nessa never mentioned a boyfriend. "This is the friend I told you about. Gen is a cocktail waitress at Blue for the summer."

I recognize Zach as one of the dealers Cali works with in the blackjack pit. "The food smells great."

"Glad you could make it tonight," he says. "This is Mira."

The girl beside him gives me a weak smile.

"Mira is one of Zach's Washoe friends," Nessa adds. "They go way back. Their families have known each other for like a hundred generations."

Zach adjusts his hat and scratches his forehead, his thick brown hair peeking through the hole of his backward ball cap. "Why do you always refer to us as *Washoe friends?*"

"Duh, it's interesting." Nessa shoves him in the shoulder and heads back into the kitchen.

He shakes his head. "Join us, Gen. We're playing Quarters."

"I'm driving; you mind that I'm not drinking?"

"Nope. You can help me get Mira toasted. She isn't nice until she's had a few." His comment receives a scowl from Mira that resembles a runway pout, because the girl's face is stunning.

Zach slides a quarter my way, and I sit in one of his granny-style wooden dining chairs. Grabbing the quarter and holding it between my thumb and forefinger, I angle for best approach. I slam the side of my palm onto the high-gloss wooden surface and let the quarter fly. It sinks into the empty juice glass.

"Nice." Zach smirks in Mira's direction. "We have a ringer."

In college, we used a wide-rimmed cup to catch as many quarters as possible—hence, getting people drunk quickly. The respectable juice glass in the center of the table is so sophisticated. I feel very grown-up.

I glance at Zach and prepare my next shot. "So, Washoe? You're Native American?" I dunk the quarter and gesture to Mira. The look she shoots me burns my corneas. For someone so pretty, she has a hell of an evil eye. I hope Zach is right about her demeanor improving with liquor.

He nods. "We're all part Washoe, the local tribe, including Lewis, who's running late. Mira's the only true blood. Both her parents came from the Dresslerville reservation. Though I'm sure somewhere along the line one of Mira's relatives hooked up with someone on the outside. She just won't admit it."

"Whatever," Mira mumbles. "With your white-ass skin, you wish you were full-blooded."

Zach, who's actually rather tanned, shakes his head my way as if to say, *You see what I'm dealing with?* He frowns at the full margarita on ice that Mira sips. "Mira, if Gen lands the next three shots, you drain your girly drink."

"Make it five," she says with a sneer.

Five? Child's play. If more alcohol is what it takes to get this girl to lighten up, I'm all for helping the team.

Mira has even copper skin and wavy dark-chocolate hair that hits mid-back and tapers around a face that's not quite heart-shaped, not quite oval. It's symmetrical and interesting, and I'm seriously jealous of her defined cheekbones. Mine don't show up unless Cali applies something akin to stage makeup for the effect. Mira's eyes are medium brown, with beige toward the center of her irises, like melted caramel. She's stunningly beautiful.

Guys wouldn't notice other girls with Mira in the room. She'd be the perfect buffer at parties. But crap, she needs to work on her attitude.

Mira huffs out a sigh. "Lewis is such a workaholic."

The first of my five quarters sinks in the glass.

"I can't believe he's not here yet," she continues. *Ping.* Another down, three to go.

"He'll come." Zach glances at the time on his phone. "He doesn't even leave the office until now."

Three. I'm on a roll now. My highest sequential quarter dunking was seventeen—and I was half drunk that night.

"That's not funny. He said he'd be here."

Is she pouting? Lewis must be Mira's boyfriend—and number four goes in the pot.

"His dad's gotta be happy he returned." Zach looks at me, and I pause before tossing in the ringer. "Lewis works for his dad's construction business. Practically runs it for him these days."

The front door creaks open and both Zach and Mira glance up. Mira's lips curl in a satisfied smile as a guy nearly as tall as the lintel steps through the doorway.

For a split second my mind scatters.

With a swift mental shake, I let the last quarter fly. It rims the edge of the juice glass and falls on the table.

Shit. I stare at the quarter as if it betrayed me.

"Speak of the devil," Zach says. "This is Lewis, Gen."

Lewis closes the front door and nods a greeting to Nessa in

the kitchen. He is in a plaid shirt, the sleeves rolled and shoved above his elbows. The shirt hem gapes on one side, as if he tucked in the front in haste, a flat stomach, wide shoulders beneath. Dark jeans hug narrow hips and long legs before bunching atop scruffy work boots. High cheekbones, a square jaw, dark brown hair combed for a tidy appearance—this Lewis guy is mountain rugged meets city sleek, and it somehow goes really well together.

My gaze catches on thick, smooth forearms and ridges of muscles below the sleeves of his shirt.

I blink. Am I seriously checking out his arms?

When I glance up, Lewis is watching me, his brow furrowed infinitesimally. He scans down and my breath catches. I'm sitting and he can't see much, considering I'm wearing a white button-down, open at the throat, but my heartbeat increases.

Which is weird. My normal instinct is to curl my shoulders and hide when I'm being checked out.

Lewis's eyes are dark—black—deep like the lake this area is known for. My face heats and suddenly my rapid heartbeat flutters and bobs in my chest. My Quarters ass-kicking, smooth-as-ice fingers shake.

What the hell? I've avoided guys for weeks. This one is good-looking, but so are a lot of men.

"Hey, Lewis," Zach calls. "Quarters on deck. Gen, here, is kicking our asses. Almost made your girl pound her drink."

Lewis's eyes flicker to Mira, then me.

Mira's face is bright and cheery for the first time since I arrived, and Zach referred to her as Lewis's girl.

Obviously, they're together.

No way am I going near Lewis, even if I were considering it, which I am not.

I roll a fresh quarter between my fingers, thumb a divot on the table, glance at Nessa in the kitchen—distract myself with anything but Lewis's approach. My heart's an irritating pulse in my ears, blocking out sound, cheeks warming to flammable conditions. I cough into my elbow to hide my face, and leap up, sidling toward Nessa.

Hot, edgy; I don't like this sensation, like my skin's about to jump away—or toward something. I should leave. I'm not feeling well. But I can't bail this early; we haven't eaten.

Mira springs from her seat and catches Lewis around the waist before he reaches the table. She hugs him and he returns it with one arm while gazing at me in the kitchen.

What is he doing? That's his girlfriend in his arms. Why is he looking at me?

"Zach, I don't know what to do with this chicken." Nessa shifts a pot on the stove.

"To be continued later." Zach smiles and sweeps the quarters into his hand. He walks into the kitchen and takes over for Nessa.

Zach's grin is friendly. Not hot, or lecherous, just uncomplicated. Kind. Not that Lewis's gaze was lecherous. It was... curious. I don't like curious. Curiosity leads to interest, which leads to things I'm staying away from. Since the A-hole betrayed me, I've stopped noticing men. It's disturbing that my radar pings around this guy. He has a *girlfriend,* and unfortunately, that seems to be the only kind of men I attract.

Being in a relationship back home—which he failed to mention—never stopped my ex from pursuing me, or Cali's boyfriend from making a pass, or any of the men my mom brought home from flirting and letting their hands wander when they hugged me.

"Clear the table, peeps," Nessa calls. "Dinner is on." She delivers homemade tortillas to the dining table, along with a bowl of spiced, shredded chicken.

Zach reaches for a beer from the fridge and Lewis walks up behind him. He slaps Zach on the back and looks at me expectantly.

Zach glances between Lewis and me, then reaches for a bottle opener. "Gen is Nessa's friend from work," I hear him say while popping the top off his Corona.

Lewis studies my face as if he's searching for something. He seems distracted—and interested.

What is his *problem*? His girlfriend is in the room.

So I stared at the guy's arms. They were out there! And kind of hot. *Sue me.* I don't recall checking out a guy's body like that before—apparently, lusty thoughts can come on later in life. Women check out men all the time. Considering Lewis's looks, he should be used to it.

"Sit next to me, Gen." Nessa sets a bowl of Spanish rice on the table and pulls out a chair at her side.

I follow her lead and carry over the salad. My eyes want to stray to Lewis—*is he still watching?*—but I force my gaze down and sit beside Nessa.

"Food looks great," Lewis says.

His voice, like a silky blade, cuts through my better sense, snaring my attention. He's shoveling half a taco in his mouth in praise of the food, or because he eats like a horse. I follow the flex of his square jaw, the thick muscles along his throat, which suddenly still.

I look up. He's watching me stare at him—and he looks intense. More than curious.

What am I doing? I'm making it worse.

Mira glances at Lewis, then glares at me. I take a small bite of rice, willing saliva into my dry mouth. I've never wanted to escape a situation more than I want to escape this dinner party. My heart's jumpy and my face won't drop below a thousand degrees. My fingers, which have never failed me in skill or coordination, can't keep the stupid rice on the fork.

"So you're here for the summer?" Zach says, his muscular leg brushing my calf as he aggressively loads food onto his plate. His narrow grandma table—which matches his thrift-store velvet couch and eighties parquet coffee table—makes dinner unintentionally intimate.

I take a sip of water and clear my throat. "I'm returning to Dawson in the fall for a graduate program in psychology."

Mira's upper lip curls at Zach, as if she's annoyed that he dares draw attention to me. Considering I'd like to hide, I agree. She leans against Lewis as he digs into his second taco, her own food untouched.

I take a huge bite of my taco just to be contrary. Eating like a rabbit to stay ridiculously skinny is lame—and I eat more than the average girl anyway, so she's just making me look bad.

"How's your mom these days?" Mira asks Zach.

Zach's hand pauses above the salad, his chest deflating. "Fine." His tone is flat, devoid of emotion.

I inch forward in my seat. Mira hit some kind of nerve. Zach seems like such a nice guy. What is she doing?

Mira nibbles a piece of lettuce, her caramel eyes cold. "What's she up to?"

Zach's gaze turns cagey. "Not much. She's still in rehab and you know it." He glances at the untouched food on his plate and nudges a taco with his knuckle.

Why would Mira bring that up? Is she trying to hurt him—

because he asked about me?

Nessa squeezes her fork and studies Zach, concern in her eyes.

Lewis peers at Mira with a frown. To Zach he says, "Broken in the new paddleboard?"

"A little." Zach's face relaxes.

"Work's slow. Mind if I join you sometime?"

"Sure, anytime."

Topic changed, tension defused.

To keep things light throughout the rest of the meal, I take the opportunity to pepper Nessa and Zach with questions about hiking and jogging trails. Mira doesn't piss off anyone else at the table, mostly because she's too busy nipping at Lewis in a heated conversation the rest of us pretend to ignore. I'm catching most of it and imagine the others do too. Things like *what are you doing* and *private* and *that girl* rise above our Tahoe trails discussion.

After the meal, I help Nessa clean up. "I should get going," I tell her when we finish.

"Really? So soon?"

"I'm still adjusting to late work hours."

"Yeah, that takes time. What are you doing tomorrow? We're barbecuing at Zephyr Cove. You and your roommate should totally come."

"That sounds like fun." I get the details from her and thank Zach before making my way to the bedroom down the hall for my purse and coat. Mira and Lewis are speaking in hushed whispers in the corner. I feel like I'm sneaking off, but I really don't want to get in the middle of that.

I collect my things and round the bedroom door, head bent, digging for my keys in the pit that is my purse—and bounce off a wall.

I'm going down, and not in a pretty way. My body falls to the side, head at an odd angle, arms tangled in my purse. I'm going to break my neck.

Strong hands haul me up. I scramble to get my legs vertical, gasping to catch my breath.

Heat and the scents of soap and fresh-cut wood hit me. Lightly tanned skin over a thick, muscular neck with a pulse pounding at the base is the first thing in my line of vision, Lewis's intense, enigmatic gaze the next. My heartbeat shifts from a startled gallop to the throbbing, fluttery mess it was when he first walked into the house.

I try to step away, realizing belatedly he's still holding me up in a semi-embrace. "Sorry, I wasn't looking." I shake my head. This is awkward and klutzy, when I'm not normally. The places where his strong arm cradles me burn, heat spiraling down my spine, wrapping around my hips and thighs and sending shivers to all the wrong places.

His breaths grow shallow. What was perplexing in his expression a second ago becomes clear. When he looks at me, it's not with curiosity—though that could be a part of it—but something else entirely. Something I can't say I've seen to this degree but I recognize—or my body does, because my chest tightens, my heart continues its fluttering dance, and I pretty much want to inhale his scent like oxygen.

His head drops a fraction toward me.

What the...? Is he going to...?

"It was nice to meet you," I say in a panicked rush, and step out of his arms. But for some stupid reason, I can't get my feet to walk away.

The hand that embraced me slides into his front pocket.

Other than that, he doesn't move. His gaze dips to my mouth.

My breath hitches and I lick my lips, which suddenly seems like an invitation.

What am I doing?

Instead of reacting appropriately and looking away, my eyes dart to *his* mouth as if on autopilot, not listening to my thorough instructions for all body parts to *get the hell out of here.*

A diagonal scar mars the corner of his lower, nicely shaped lip, a score in an otherwise perfect landscape. For some reason, I can't look away from that scar, feathering at one end into a slight hook. How did he get it? Did it hurt? Would I feel the scar if I pressed my mouth to his?

His lips part beneath my stare and he shifts his feet, bringing him an inch closer, closing the space I created.

My heart pumps so fast that dots form in my vision. *He has a girlfriend.*

I stumble around Lewis, my shoulder slamming the wall, years of athleticism disappearing with the speed of my heartbeat. I glance back once before opening the front door.

Lewis shuts his eyes and turns away.

My hands shake as I make it to the car. Inside, I grip the steering wheel.

What was that? That's not attraction, that's just crazy. *Crazy attraction.*

Visit Jules on her website, or follow her on social media:

Author website: www.julesbarnard.com
Twitter: @jules_barnard
Facebook: julesbarnardauthor

You can also follow Jules's book inspiration boards at:
Pinterest: www.pinterest.com/JulesAuthor/

Printed in Great Britain
by Amazon.co.uk, Ltd.,
Marston Gate.